ACTUALLY SUPER

ADI ALSAID

ALFRED A. KNOPF
NEW YORK

THIS IS A BORZOI BOOK PUBLISHED BY ALFRED A. KNOPF

This is a work of fiction. Names, characters, places, and incidents either are the product of the author's imagination or are used fictitiously. Any resemblance to actual persons, living or dead, events, or locales is entirely coincidental.

Visit us on the Web! GetUnderlined.com

Educators and librarians, for a variety of teaching tools, visit us at RHTeachersLibrarians.com

Library of Congress Cataloging-in-Publication Data is available upon request.
ISBN 978-0-593-37580-8 (trade) — ISBN 978-0-593-37582-2 (ebook) —
ISBN 978-0-593-70537-7 (intl. pbk.)

The text of this book is set in 10.8-point Adobe Text Pro.
Interior design by Cathy Bobak

Printed in the United States of America
10 9 8 7 6 5 4 3 2 1
First Edition

To those trying to leave the world
a little better than they found it

PROLOGUE

Mazunte, Mexico

Why must there always be a body?

Death: what a trap to fall for. We want to know who and how and why, even if we know nothing else.

Fine, a glimpse.

Respectfully, though. Let us not gawk. Not that there is much to see in these depths. Swirls of blue-tinged dark, occasionally shot through with a beam of light landing on exposed, death-paled skin. A creature approaches to nibble, drawn in by some tiny organism on the flesh. Around the left ankle: some rope-like tendril. The cause of death? Hard to tell without an autopsy, without seeing if the water is in the lungs, without seeing what kinds of bacteria are on the skin, in the organs. How life sticks around even after death.

All right, enough for now.

Instead: the Pacific. The waves pounding down, glinting like a huge steel drum in the late-afternoon sun. Tourists bobbing in the water, English- and French-speaking. A nearly nude Argentine couple walk along the beach, selling bracelets and necklaces and home-baked cannabis muffins, all of which they leave, carefree, on the sand to take a dip and make out in the strengthening tide.

Mexican families play reggaeton from tinny Bluetooth speakers near coolers overflowing with beer. Other tourists order margaritas and guacamole; they read books and watch their children dig holes in the sand, connected by finger-width tunnels.

And then a couple of friends, Sam and Chío, awaiting a third: Isabel.

They're sitting on the sand, just beyond the reach of the waves, atop damp and stained hostel towels Sam has taken in direct defiance of a sign posted over the mirror in the shared bathroom, and also in the hall, and by reception. Isabel is late, but that is nothing new. It's almost comforting that she hasn't changed, at least not in this one way. It would have been jarring to watch her stroll up the beach toward them at the agreed-upon time.

They're on the verge of their future lives, these two. They've made decisions for which colleges to go to, what the first few years of their independent lives will look like. Only a few weeks left of senior year to get through, and then those metaphorical open doors. Isabel is not joining them, because she took a side exit a year early. None of that is on their minds, though. They sit and wait, silence between them, even though there's plenty of noise around.

The minutes pass and they do not worry. Sam runs back in the water for another bodysurfing session, getting beat up by the waves and loving it. His light brown skin has already darkened a shade or two. Chío pulls out her book—a murder mystery—and lies back, but fails to read past the same paragraph, instead going over in her mind the speech she's been wanting to give Isabel since she left. So, she closes her eyes and tries to draw pleasure from the sun, tries to soak up her senior-year spring break.

She feels a twinge of panic, but she hides it beneath assurances that it's normal. That Isabel is always running late. There are reasonable explanations for most events, Chío lectures herself, though part of that lecture is intended for Isabel, is part of the speech she's been practicing.

Sam and Chío maintain their quiet insistence that everything is okay even as they have to push back from the encroaching tide. Even as they grow antsy and restless, forget to play with the sand, get up to walk the entirety of the beach to make sure they're sitting in front of the right hotel. They brush their elbows off and the sand falls like delicate Michigan snow. But Isabel herself pinned the spot on their phones a year ago, and they confirmed it just a few days earlier in their group chat, so of course they have the right spot. Sam makes a joke about Isabel running off to fight crime, but neither of them laughs.

This is fine, they maintain, even as the sun starts to dip beneath the ocean and Chío's parents call to ask her where she is. Even as the beach empties out, the only other group a trio of older

Americans floating beyond where the waves break. Chío wonders about the wisdom of being so far out. Chío's parents insist that they come over for dinner at their hotel. Still, they convince themselves that this is fine. On the walk to the resort, the last of the daylight reflecting on the vast, unknowable ocean and whatever it hides, they believe that Isabel will come. She will appear at any moment, at long last, and she will be okay.

1

Dearborn, Michigan

No one believes Isabel when she says she's going to travel the world to hunt superheroes. For perhaps obvious reasons.

She has been forming her plan for months now, but its seeds have been there much longer. Late at night, in front of her computer, the conviction strengthening the way convictions do best: alone in the dark, unchallenged. There are no questions in her mind that she's going to do it. That she is right to do it. Her friends, however, have a lot of questions.

Mainly: Say that again?

Mainly: What?

She has gathered them at Roys's, the frozen custard shop that is full even now, during spring break in Michigan, the temperatures still flirting with the twenties. The others have nowhere else to be, but even if it weren't break, they'd meet at this table most afternoons. She's kept this plan to herself for long enough, and now that she's officially booked her flight, she wants to share it with the two people closest to her.

"But superheroes aren't real," Sam says, as if it needed to be made clear. Isabel says nothing.

"And even if they were," Chío jumps in, brushing light brown hair out of her eyes, "how are you qualified to hunt them? And, like, why?"

"I said hunt them *down*. Of course I wouldn't be qualified to *hunt* them. Also, I don't like hunting." Isabel is undeterred by her friends' so far unsupportive reactions. They will come around, they always do.

"I don't get it," Sam says.

"I'll take follow-up questions."

There is a silence at Roys's, or at least at their particular picnic table. The wind pushes Chío's empty custard cup to the ground. She stands to chase it and toss it into the nearby bin, then rejoins the table, biting her lip.

"No questions, then?" Isabel spoons another key-lime-pie bite, shuddering at both the cold and the explosion of flavor. She isn't sure what she was expecting from telling them. The confusion isn't entirely surprising, but she thought there might be more excitement.

"Too many, is the thing," Chío mutters. Isabel sits, waiting for them to come. Especially from Chío, who questions everything, who uses the scientific method to decide which pizza place in Dearborn is best, who will not allow a statement to pass as a fact unless it can be measured as such.

"And you're not messing with us?" Sam asks.

"No. I know how it sounds, okay? I get it. But it's what I'm going to do. So, let's just move past the whole 'Is she high?' phase and ask any logistical questions you may have. Where I'm going, how I plan to find them, that sort of thing."

Sam laughs and hunches his shoulders against the cold. "I think we need another minute to chew this over, Izzy."

Then Chío, who everybody could tell was working herself up to this, says, "I mean, seriously. What? You can't expect us to just accept what you're saying. It's decidedly bonkers."

Isabel rolls her eyes and blows a raspberry. "You guys are so boring."

Another silence follows, during which Sam pulls his phone out and starts googling superheroes. Little does he know it was this exact move that led Isabel to where she is now. For different reasons, sure.

Sam picks at his ice cream as pages load, and Chío studies Isabel's face. Isabel decides to grant her friends the time they need to process. Meanwhile, she daydreams about the journey to come, the adventures she'll have. She pictures the first time she will meet a superhero, and her heart swells at the thought. It is almost too much to take, so she eats some more ice cream instead.

This is what she's been doing with every spare moment since she stumbled upon that very specific corner of the internet, since she came up with the plan. A weird corner, yes, but the only thing that eased the despair that had been growing in her chest since she was thirteen or so, and her awareness of the wider world increased.

"Maybe you can clarify what you mean by 'superheroes,'"

Chío says, her brow furrowed hard enough to form three deep wrinkles.

"Finally, a good question!" Isabel raises her hands up to the heavens. "I mean people with superhuman abilities. Not necessarily crime fighters, Batman or whatever. Though there's evidence that some of them do become crime fighters."

"Batman doesn't have any superhuman abilities," Sam cuts in, unable to help himself. "He's just a fit dude with lots of resources. So, either way, you wouldn't be going after Batman?" he asks, hopeful, as if ruling out Batman makes this all easier to swallow.

"Correct," Isabel says.

At the same time, Chío shakes her head and mutters, "What the hell are we talking about? You're not even into superheroes."

Oh, right. There's a lot her friends do not know.

"I'm not looking for actual comic book characters or anything. I know that's fiction." Isabel cracks a smile, as if now they'll all fall in line as she expects. As if this clarification is the only one they'll need.

"Just people with comic book powers," Sam deadpans.

"Yup!"

"And what makes you believe they exist?" Chío is trying to keep her voice nonjudgmental, but even she can tell she's failing. She shoves her hands into her coat pockets, looks around at the other tables. There are a few kids from school she recognizes, plus a few she doesn't. She wonders if this could be a prank Isabel is organizing with someone else, but Isabel doesn't have friends outside of this group.

Isabel knew the question was coming, but that doesn't mean it's easy to answer.

Her first instinct is to lie. The problem is that the ridiculous part has already been said out loud, and she can't take it back. No amount of reasoning will make them feel better about it if they can't handle what's already been said.

Telling the truth would only make her friends worry more, try harder to talk her out of it. "I found evidence on the internet" is often a wild thing to say, but when it comes to believing in superheroes, the statement compounds in its ridiculousness. Nothing can justify believing in superheroes. Even the scientifically plausible theories of genetic mutation, or of a subtle variation in evolution, sound more like science fiction than science. All her friends on the forum warned her as much. Not even religion can excuse believing in them (and Isabel, in her late-night internet scouring, has tried to find one that would).

"I just have a feeling," Isabel says.

"That superheroes exist and you have to find them," Chío says, the inflection in her voice aiming to shake Isabel into realizing how delusional she sounds.

"It was a dream," Isabel pivots, improvising.

But no. That doesn't feel right. She cannot lie to her friends. Well, she has been lying. But only by omission. She's hidden this plan for months, but it really goes back years. Not just about the superheroes but about the whole reason she stumbled onto them in the first place. The growing, gnawing sense that the world was more evil than good. The desperation whenever that thought entered her mind, and the urgent need to do something to counteract it. Not just turning the TV on for a light distraction the way people do after too much doomscrolling, but an actual antidote.

She used to spend her time on her phone seeking out evidence that people were good. Videos of strangers coming together to rescue dogs in rushing water. Cheesy stories about people paying for each other's coffee. Heartwarming articles about post-disaster helpers.

And those had worked, for a while anyway. The problem was they weren't big enough in their kindness. When it came down to it, it was just that: kindness. Isabel needed evidence that humanity could counteract evil. Because there was no doubt that evil people existed, or that at the very least people did unthinkably evil things. And it seemed like evil was often winning its war against good.

The despair in Isabel's chest would not go away unless she found evidence that there was balance to the world. That something existed that was unthinkably *good.* Random acts of kindness were great, but they did not cancel out evil.

Now that Chío's prying, that Isabel's truth is starting to come out, lying—outright or by omission—feels wrong. It is tempting to open the faucet fully and let it all pour out onto the table, into the world. Or at least into these two people who love her.

Her friends can tell that the thing about a dream is bullshit, and they stare, waiting for more. What will it be?

Isabel takes another spoonful of custard, begging the tart

dessert to imbue her with the strength to withstand judgment. To just say the rest out loud. It would be freeing.

But she's been so safe in her secret all this time. Safe from ridicule, from others telling her that her idea is flawed, which would simply land her back at despair. As exciting as it is to think of her plan in action, to share it with others, it is hard to step outside the secret's comforting embrace. She swallows, thinking that feeling free can wait until summer.

Chío's hand lands on top of Isabel's. They meet eyes, and Isabel feels the faucet turning a little more. "I had this theory," Isabel says. "Well, it's one that other people have had on this forum I found. I'll tell you more about that later, but the important part is that this theory, that there are people with superpowers out there, it helped me feel . . ." She reaches for the right word, but can only land on "okay."

"Okay with what?" Sam asks.

"The world."

"Why do you need to feel okay with the world?" Chío asks. She says it not judgmentally, but with her scientist brain, digging for information, wanting to connect the dots. But she needs more dots than Isabel can provide. It'll never make sense to Chío.

Isabel takes too big a bite of ice cream, causing not a brain freeze per se, but a cold that digs in too deep. She shivers and stands to throw the rest away. When she comes back, they are still looking at her so expectantly, and she realizes how much she has to explain. Not just the despair, but what led the despair to turn into a plan. Her dad, her grandmother, the stuff at school, the pandemic, so much more. It feels daunting. "I just do," she says.

Isabel finds that the new tone of the conversation is pressing down on her, and she looks away from her friends, hoping to return to the half-joking mood from just a minute ago.

"Speaking of which, guess where I'm going first," she says once she's overcome the tightness in her chest. "You'll never believe how much I found the ticket for."

They stare at the itinerary on Isabel's phone, dumbfounded as she passes it around, the delusion now made real. Detroit to Shanghai, Shanghai to Tokyo. Isabel Madeline Wolfe, seat not yet assigned. August 30.

"I can't believe that's the price," Sam says. He's marveling at the distance represented by the plane ticket, at how much of the world his friend will be traversing. It no longer feels like a joke, no longer feels as if summer will arrive and the only talk of superheroes will be those relentlessly attacking the silver screen. Senior year will arrive and Isabel will not be here.

Chío has been staring daggers into Isabel, and the silence only makes them sharper. "I've been really exploring the world of cheap travel, and the money I've saved is gonna go so much further than I would have ever imagined. There's a rumored Super in Tokyo, and I found that one-way ticket, so it made sense to go there first. I don't even need a visa for Japan."

"Izzy. Please. What the hell are you doing?"

Isabel pretends she didn't hear. "We think his name is Hatori, and he goes around different train stations in Tokyo saving people who need him. He doesn't dress up or have, like, a persona or an alias or anything like that. Most of the real ones don't."

"Right." Sam has more follow-up questions, but Chío is so sullen that he starts looking stuff up on his phone instead.

"Why are you guys acting like I'm dumping you?" Isabel says, joking.

"Oh man, that *is* what it feels like," Sam chuckles.

Chío shakes her head. "Dumping us would be more understandable," she says. "You're leaving us for a delusion." When Isabel says nothing, Chío feels herself soften. She's in shock, but attacking Isabel won't change anything. "Can't you do this after high school? Why go now?"

"I'm taking my GED over the summer," Isabel says. The hurt of being called delusional dulls quickly, smoothed by the relief that she doesn't have to delve into Actually Super quite yet, doesn't have to reveal everything behind the trip. She can't believe she thought this would go well. "I wanted to go right away. I only waited because it'd be too hard traveling underage without my parents' permission."

"Do you even know when you're coming back?" Chío hurls the question as if it's a right jab, as if she wants it to bruise Isabel's eye. So much for not attacking.

A minivan parks nearby, and half a dozen nine-year-olds come pouring out, all uncontainable excitement and shrieking. It is Friday afternoon, and it seems everyone in Dearborn is craving custard despite the cold. There are working professionals and soccer moms, college kids home for spring break, children everywhere. Not a single superhero in sight.

"You're not coming back, are you?" Sam says, his voice taut with both wonder and heartache.

Another silence. Isabel wishes she could tell her friends something that would make them more okay with all of this.

"We still have the rest of the school year," she says. "Summer too."

That makes neither of them feel better, and the air between the friends grows heavier and heavier, despite the laughter from other customers, and the few leaves in the trees rustling gently in the breeze. Isabel wishes she could make them understand how it feels to know she's chasing this dream, wishes she could convey the excitement she's been feeling since she booked the flight and made it real for herself. How it's already helped ease her despair.

Isabel picks at a crusty patch of mint green on the table, wondering how to get the silence to stop. She is going to miss her family, sure, mostly, and definitely these two people sitting next to her. She wishes she could pack them up into her bag and bring her friends on this quest; it is the one trepidation she has about leaving.

Isabel smacks the table with her palm, pulling them from whatever rumination they were having. "You guys should come meet me! A year from now, your last spring break before you go off to college."

Chío perks up the slightest bit at this. “Do you know where you’ll be?”

“Well, no. But we can just pick a place now and I’ll make my way there.” Her phone is out already, and she’s zooming out on Google Maps to see the world in its entirety. *Look at that,* she thinks, *the whole world in my hands.*

There is some discussion about whether Sam can afford to travel, whether their parents will allow them to join Isabel, even if it’s just for a week. They make a few superhero jokes, including one about what they would each do if they had a power, but that topic feels fraught and it wears itself out quickly. Now what Chío and Sam feel most of all is the fact that they’re going to miss the hell out of their friend. So they start studying the map, and looking up articles on places to go, and checking flight prices. It almost feels like they’re simply discussing what movie to watch.

After an hour or so, they all put their hands at the center of the picnic table to agree to the plan. It is a symbolic gesture that feels weird because they’ve never done it before, but appropriate because they’ve seen it done so many times on TV. And though there are still six whole months of normalcy to live through before Isabel leaves them and takes it all with her, they look each other in the eyes, their hands touching, and they promise to meet up in a year in a small beach town in Mexico.

Word gets out that Isabel is leaving. When she goes to bed at night, she is thankful to be away from the looks people give her, thankful to be back in the company of herself, and her bed, where she is allowed to dream of her trip without interruptions. She retreats to the internet, to the forum, where people don't raise their eyebrows or wait for the punch line. Instead, they profess their jealousy, bid her a good trip, offer advice. They debate whether she should share evidence she finds with the world or not, which, as usual, derails into a conversation about why they believe superheroes are kept secret.

Mathilde, a twenty-seven-year-old teacher at an international school who fell into the Actually Super community after what she calls a prophetic dream, right away says that Izzy should come visit her in Jakarta. The thought of spending time in person with someone who believes what she believes is almost more joy than she can bear, and she looks at the calendar to count down the days (though of course she already knows how many are left until she's free to go).

Her parents focus more on the part of her plan that involves dropping out of school than on the superhero part, at least for a little while. She reminds them how much student debt she'll be avoiding. They say that's not the point, but then have trouble articulating what their point is. Once they realize her plan begins on her eighteenth birthday and they will be legally powerless to stop her, their attention switches over to the more peculiar particular of her plan.

"Can't you find superheroes in America?" her dad asks, a whine in his voice.

Isabel sighs. This is the part that's hardest to explain, because the theories floated on the forum feel conspiratorial and a little kooky, even to her. "There's no hard evidence they exist *here,*" she says, making sure to stress the last word so they don't jump at the phrasing.

The truth is, there's a few rumored in the U.S. But who wants to go to Cleveland and Fort Lauderdale? Those two have the least backing evidence anyway, and the general consensus on the forum is that any American superheroes have been kidnapped by the government or have exiled themselves to avoid exploitation.

Plus, getting away from the U.S. is part of the draw of the whole plan. She doesn't make eye contact with her dad, as if he might read her mind and start another fight.

"Honey, why?" her mom asks, trying to add more inflection, somehow, into the sentence than she has managed to convey in the previous eight hundred or so times she has asked.

"Because I think it's important for people to follow their dreams," Isabel says. And for a second, just one glorious, shining, hopeful second, Dorah Wolfe believes she has finally understood. Not fully, perhaps. She has not grasped on with an entirely closed fist, but enough. Her fingertips have brushed up against understanding. Her daughter is making a point. About life, and the way people live it. About what is Truly Important.

Isabel feels for her mom. If it were possible to leave behind a little piece of herself just to provide her mom some comfort, she would.

Then Isabel adds, "And my dream is to meet superheroes." Mrs. Wolfe's epiphany is extinguished like a blown-out birthday candle.

Not knowing what else to do, they sit her down for a talk. Her dad, of course, leading the way, loudly, getting up to pace as he makes his points and then going back to the couch. Her mom sits quietly beside him, fussing with things on the coffee table that do not need to be fussed with. There is a world where Isabel offers her mom to come along on the trip, at least for a while. But that is a world in which Isabel knows where Dorah stands in this argument, other than as an uncomfortable peacemaker, not wanting anyone to be upset but not caring to solve any disputes either. Over the years, as Isabel has woken up to who her dad is, her mom has remained an inscrutable puzzle. Sweet, but sticking by Abel through the worst of his rants.

It is perhaps what makes leaving easy. Knowing exactly how the last fight will go. Her father raising his voice, trying to put his foot down, despite not having any ground to stand on. Her mother not picking sides, not weak, rather displaying an impressive stronghold on the fence. Not flinching at the things her husband says.

Isabel sits there quietly, not pushing back like she has in the past, knowing she will soon be free.

2

Dearborn, Michigan

The day Isabel leaves, she oversleeps. No one is surprised.

Isabel is supposed to meet up with Sam and Chío for coffee before her flight, and when she is ten minutes late, fifteen minutes late, they roll their eyes at each other and go over to her house to wake her up.

"I was sure, somehow," Chío says, "that today would break the mold."

"I bet she is trying to find a way to pack the bed in her bag," Sam says.

A lore has built up around Isabel's bed, its legendary comfort. People assume she will miss her bed, perhaps more than any person in her life, or at least more regularly, more consistently, every, every night.

Isabel has allowed the myth of her bed to build because she cannot admit to everyone that she sleeps in because she's up too late every night on the internet, researching superheroes, talking with other people like her, believers.

It has been like this for all of high school, and it's easier to go along with some notion of her bed being unreasonably comfortable than it is to admit what she's been doing. Even if she wanted to stop the night before leaving, her sleep schedule has been out of whack too long. The routine is set in her bones. She goes to bed, her laptop tucked casually beneath some books on her nightstand. She reads for twenty or so minutes, then turns the lights off and reaches for her computer. She ends the day on the internet, searching for a dose of solace.

The only difference the night before she leaves is that it feels like the solace is finally going to exist beyond her screen. It'll be her entire day-to-day. The search for superheroes will be her main purpose.

Some of the people on the Actually Super forum are eager to give advice about her trip. They've known about it longer than her friends have, and they know her habit of logging on at a certain time. They are waiting for her, offering a sort of digital surprise party to send her off. They go over the list of all the Supers she could track down, sharing in the excitement with her late into the night. It is a relief, as always, to find this acceptance. To exchange messages with Mathilde and feel like they are speaking about something commonplace.

Chío and Sam find her literally rolling out of bed, which they assume is the only way she can manage to escape its pull for this final time. It's as if the bed knows she is going and is trying to convince her to stay. They wish it were better at it.

She hits the floor just as her friends walk in, one leg still tangled in the coral sheets.

"What time is it?" she asks, her voice at once groggy and eager. They tell her. Her forehead hits the carpet softly. "Thank god. Sorry I missed coffee." She looks up at them. "Did you bring me some?"

Sam takes a few more steps, puts the iced coffee next to her. He notices her general lack of clothing and goes over to the window, as if he is looking out at something specific instead of avoiding awkwardness. He plays with the basketball in his hands. Chío sips at her own coffee, uncharacteristically quiet. Her mouth is stretched into the slightest of smiles, forced against the slack muscles of her true feelings. But there in the eyes, it's easy to see: Chío is not happy. She wanted a long, tearful goodbye. She wanted emotions on display at the coffee shop, wanted to laugh through her crying and to hug Isabel over and over again. She wanted one last chance to give her an impassioned speech about reason and science.

Downstairs, her parents open and close kitchen cupboards and drink too much coffee as they eye the microwave's digital clock. They are pragmatists, Dorah and Abel Wolfe, and they can't help but think, despite what their hearts might feel about the departure itself, that Isabel is going to miss her flight and should hurry. They eat Isabel's leftover birthday cake for breakfast in silence, listening to their daughter's furtive movements upstairs. Her dad grips the fork so hard his knuckles are sore the rest of the day. He never imagined having a child he could not comprehend.

Everyone insists on coming to the airport, and since Isabel is green-minded and strong-willed, they all pile into the Wolfes' SUV. It's a quiet ride with way too few words exchanged and the radio playing jazz no one wants to listen to. At the airport, Isabel wants to do a curbside goodbye, but no one else is ready and they're all grateful when Dorah insists on parking in the short-term lot.

They walk her straight toward the security line, since she's carrying her bag on and her boarding pass is loaded onto her phone. *I can't believe she's doing this,* they all think, but no one says it out loud because they *can* believe it, they just don't want it to be true.

Isabel's excitement is palpable when they reach the line. Her mom gets stone-faced. Chío wipes at the first few tears that escape. Her dad crosses his arms, looks everywhere around the international terminal except at Isabel. Sam dribbles his ball a couple of times, forgetting where he is until he feels half the airport's eyes on him and he tucks it back into the crook of his arm.

Isabel doesn't let it become a thing. She hugs her dad first, briefly, just because not doing it feels weirder, just because it will make her mom happy. Then her mom, even planting a kiss on her cheek, though she can't remember the last time she's done that. Dorah Wolfe will steal away for more naps on Isabel's bed and dream about the sensation of that kiss. "I'll call you when I get there," she says, a concession she will provide throughout her travels. Not meaningful updates, but many of them. *I am here. I am here.*

Then Isabel wraps Chío and Sam in a group hug. "I'll see you guys in Mexico," she says. They nod and chuckle, though there's nothing they find funny about the goodbye. Chío's tears run against Isabel's neck. Sam's eyelashes flutter against her cheek.

And then she's shuffling through the line, only turning back to look at them and wave once as the TSA agent checks her ID. She disappears into the terminal as if that's all it will take to make her feel at peace in the world.

The four people she's leaving behind are left standing quietly, knowing they'll have to endure the awkward ride back home together.

Alone in the terminal, Isabel feels her brain starting to do what it does, so she puts on her earphones, listens to music that she hopes will instill a sense of catharsis. This is it! Her months of planning! She is eighteen and unleashing herself upon the world with a dream!

She will prove there is a balance. She will prove that extreme good exists alongside the evils of violence, greed, injustice. She is going to find the superheroes that are somewhere out there, living quiet, unassuming lives trying to counteract those evils. No matter how much questioning she's faced since she announced her plan—from others and from herself—nothing can convince her that her plan is wrong. No amount of scrutiny has undone her conviction that they exist, and that she will meet them. It is, on some level, unreasonable, she knows. But unreasonable excitement is still excitement, and she will take that over despair any day.

Except right now what Isabel feels is alone, and annoyed at the inflated costs of airport snacks. She is playing the right music, but her heart does not soar along with the crescendo of strings and vocals. It feels like just another day. The emotions don't quite reach the highs she had envisioned for this moment. Chío's voice rings in her ears, and all the looks people have given her in the last few months when her plan has come up play in her mind like a montage. Her mission feels wholly unachievable.

She takes a breath, buys a four-dollar dry croissant, tells herself: *No rush.* This is life now. It is not fleeting, it is only the start of what will soon be normal to her. Movement, flinging herself across the globe. Actual superheroes. They are out there.

She waits for that line of thinking to sink in.

On her first flight, she watches movies and sleeps fitfully, her arms crossed over her chest, or tucked into her armpits, to try to combat the plane's poorly regulated temperature. She thinks about starting a conversation with the woman sitting next to her, beginning her search right away. But the woman keeps her headphones on throughout the whole flight, watching bad action movies, and Isabel decides that she doesn't have to start this early. She can wait for Hatori.

She tracks the cartoon plane on the screen in front of her, heading farther and farther away from everyone she knows. It's a scary thought, even if she's known all along that it's the only way to do what she means to do.

She lands in Shanghai, and it's the middle of the day, though it doesn't feel like it. She gets to skip the immigration line because it's a short layover, though she would have welcomed the opportunity to stand.

Isabel is tired and underwhelmed, until she steps out into the open hallway of the terminal and she can connect to the Wi-Fi.

Clicking through her phone out of habit more than anything, Isabel finds herself on the forum, where her fellow Super hunters, as they somewhat embarrassingly dub themselves, have sent dozens of messages of encouragement. Mathilde has sent a short video of herself saying she is proud of Izzy, saying she can't wait to meet her when she makes it to Jakarta.

She remembers: she is eighteen, and has dropped out of school to find people with superpowers. The world holds immeasurable amounts of good in it, and she is going to dedicate a portion of her life—weeks, months, years, who knows—to its pursuit. The thought now, maybe because of where she is, maybe because of exhaustion, brings her to giddiness.

3

Tokyo, Japan

It is on her fourth night sleeping in a pod that Isabel's longing for her bed starts to mellow. It might just be jet lag finally fading, her sleep cycle catching up with her geographic location. Or maybe it's just hard to miss a bed for a significant period of time if you're sleeping well. They've been deep, dreamless sleeps, well earned after exploring the city on foot all day, and running the hostel's front desk from four to nine a.m.

Isabel wakes up feeling instantly ready to face the day, a new sensation after years of lingering in bed, the world beyond feeling too overwhelming to face, her exhaustion from time on the forum making her long for just another hour. Sure, it could be the relative lack of comfort of the thin mattress getting her out of bed as soon as she's had enough sleep, or the claustrophobic enclosure of the pod itself. But part of it, too, is the drive—still persistent despite three days of failure—to find a single superhero in this city of thirty million or so inhabitants. It is not lost on her how quickly she leaves the bed, how she makes it all the way to the bathroom at the end of the hall and turns the shower knob before she thinks of her friends back home. It is more than twenty minutes before she thinks of her dad, of people's secret and not-so-secret lack of care for each other, of her grandmother, who grumbled in Isabel's ears for so long about the sorry state of the world that even now it comes through. Twenty minutes is the longest she's gone in years.

She showers quickly, keeping her hair dry, then gets dressed in the humid shower stall. She drops her clothes and toiletries off at her pod, locks it, and heads to the front desk to relieve Alex, the Swedish girl who never offers more words than exactly enough to answer a question.

"Morning," Isabel says cheerfully, perhaps more cheerful than is appropriate at 3:50 a.m. Alex returns the greeting with the slightest hint of a smile. "How was your night?" Izzy asks. "Anything interesting?"

"Calm and boring," Alex responds, closing the notebook she's often writing in whenever she's at the desk. They sit together for a few minutes in silence, then Alex says goodbye and heads to her pod, leaving Izzy to restlessly await the first guests scheduled to check in.

So far, Isabel's Super count is zero. The forum didn't have a whole lot of information on Hatori, just that he's been spotted in a police uniform, perhaps a security guard outfit, several times around central Tokyo. There was a blurry picture of a man in his forties or so, a little chubby, somewhat handsome, and a hodgepodge of newspaper articles about an anonymous man at a subway station who saved a drunk person from stumbling in front of a train.

As she's been exploring Tokyo, she's been wondering if others around her are hiding superpowers. It's a frequent topic of conversation on the forum, the prevalence of Supers among the population. Plenty of users have posted their theories, guesses, data. The prevailing consensus is somewhere around .01 percent of the world population.

Isabel wasn't expecting the endeavor to be an immediate success. At least, not in regard to definitively finding a Super. It has been successful in other ways. Namely, financially. Her bank account, consisting of bat mitzvah money, her going-away garage sale, and two years' worth of part-time jobs, has not taken as much of a hit as she thought it might.

Her pod is free for three weeks while she helps with the hostel, thanks to a website called Workaway, which lets her exchange her time for a place to sleep. She's spent an average of ten dollars on two meals a day, which is not cheap, but not bad for one of the most expensive cities in the world. Add in just a few vending-machine coffees and 7-Eleven snacks, and she's practically spending less than if she were still in Dearborn.

It hasn't been the most successful journey when it comes to meeting people in general, save for the others at the hostel. There's Alex and Hiroo, the manager, who ran her through her duties and confirmed her hours and dates, and whom she hasn't seen again.

There are a couple of Belgian girls, and they said hi very warmly when they met Isabel, but that seemed to be enough for them.

An hour passes and she only reads ten pages, too antsy, eager for someone to talk to. Three British guys a little older than her arrive at 5:15, abuzz with jet lag and the train journey in from the airport. Isabel can already recognize it, the way the city's immensity, efficiency, and cleanliness invigorate those who've just arrived after hours on a plane. Isabel greets them with her most earnest smile, and the shortest of the three, Gareth, offers a sweet one in return, sleepy-eyed and dopey.

Isabel manages to gather that they're starting a gap year, but before the small talk can elevate into satisfying chitchat, the boys discover that the hostel only has capsules, not rooms with bunk beds. The other two start berating Gareth, who, it seems, was in charge of accommodations. They all sit in the chairs in the lobby staring at their phones for twenty minutes, stewing in their tired bickering. Then Gareth finds a nearby option, all three of them argue about the increased cost, and they get up to leave.

She watches them go, feeling an instant longing for Gareth's dopey smile, an unexpected sense of loss when they're gone.

⁂

After her shift, Isabel bought an onigiri breakfast at the store, well below her budget for a meal. So now she's treating herself to a cup of overpriced coffee from a shop overlooking the inside of Shinagawa Station, watching the masses head to work. It's enchanting. There are so many people in this world. She draws comfort from the sight. Not only the sheer number of people, how each passing salaryperson makes it likelier that there's someone Super among them (*False,* the Chío voice in Isabel's head says), but that they too are moving through the world alone. They listen to whatever's in their earphones, they hold their laptop bags to their sides to avoid excessive bounce. They move forward, unaccompanied, like Isabel herself, but surrounded.

Soon, though, the sight of so many human beings together sends Isabel toward familiar stomping grounds for her brain, well worn thanks to her dad, and her grandmother. Isabel has wondered if it's genetics, if she was always going to go down this path, if they created the path for her or if it was already there.

When she was thirteen, Isabel used her dad's computer to look something up online since she'd left hers at school. And that was her first glance at her dad's secret brain. He'd kept a tab open, and even the name of the website had made Isabel's stomach drop. She hadn't known exactly what it was, but she knew it was associated with the worst of the internet. The headline of the article had been about overpopulation, which had seemed innocent enough at first. But a few scrolls revealed it to be deeply racist and even casually calling for people in poor nations to be allowed to die.

Isabel had wanted to give her dad the benefit of the doubt that he had accidentally found his way to the article and shut the computer in disgust. Or that he was reading it for some sort of research, to try to understand wildly hateful perspectives in order to combat them somehow.

But the truth was that she didn't know her dad all that well. At the time, she was just starting to get a glimpse of her mom and dad as whole human beings outside of their roles as parents. Their annoying habits and traits. Their political leanings, their worldviews, their actual personalities. And so far, Isabel had noticed her dad was a closed book. He wasn't much for small talk, didn't make inane jokes with servers at restaurants, didn't mutter his opinions at the news he watched, like Isabel's grandmother did. He was a serious and quiet man who, if he wasn't at work, spent his time the way, it seemed, so many American men did: with a beer and a television screen showing sports or movies. Which hadn't bothered Isabel as much as it piqued her interest.

But suddenly she was getting a look at what went on in his quiet thoughts. She had been sitting at the kitchen island, and after shooting a quick glance into the living room to confirm he was still on the couch, she had looked through his search history.

And now, looking at the Tokyo crowds, she wonders how many people marching through the station also have secret brains. How many have a fuse lit within them by hurt or anger or fear, and how will they pass that on to others. How many of these people would stomp on one another if given the chance?

She pushes away from her stool, angry at herself for not being able to go even a week without falling into old mental habits. Angry, too, that she expected not to have any bouts of despair on her travels, that she expected to be magically cured. Angriest, though, at humans, at the world.

4

Tokyo, Japan

Isabel jerks awake beneath the shade of a tree in Yoyogi Park—sticky with sweat and deeply disoriented—to the feeling of her phone buzzing in her backpack. She had spent the day searching for Hatori near where he'd reportedly been sighted, but to no avail. She shoves her hand inside, rummaging around for longer than should be necessary, considering the size of her bag.

Her waking brain barely recognizes Chío's name on her screen as she answers. "Hey."

There's a pause on the other end, and Isabel wonders briefly if she's dreaming the whole exchange. Then Chío's voice comes through. "Hey. What time is it over there?"

Isabel pulls the phone away from her face to check, starting to remember where she is and how she got there. "It's four. How come you're awake?"

Another pause, one that feels heavy with Chío's unique, if loving, brand of judgment. "I'd called and texted, but you didn't answer. So, I couldn't sleep."

"Funny. I was just napping." They rarely talked on the phone in Michigan, but this is their second time since Isabel arrived in Tokyo. It feels more appropriate, somehow, although it is shaping up to be awkward now too. At least Chío made the call through an app, so it won't run up her bill or eat up Isabel's minutes. Isabel peels away her T-shirt from her lower back, her skin tingling from the grass.

"You're okay?" Chío finally says.

"I'm okay," Isabel responds quickly. Then: "Of course I'm okay. Why wouldn't I be?"

Chío takes a pass on that opening, and Isabel is grateful for it. "Any luck with Hatori?"

"Was just taking a little breather from looking now. But no. Turns out Hatori's a pretty common name, so I haven't been able to google him. I'm going off some pictures and some sightings on the forum." Isabel reaches into her bag for her water bottle and takes a long pull, thankful that the water is still cool.

"Well, at least you're having fun, right?" Chío says.

Isabel doesn't quite understand. "What do you mean?"

Chío laughs quietly. "Izzy. You're allowed to have fun." Isabel can picture her lying in bed in the dark, trying to keep her voice down so as not to wake anyone up. Despite the image, which is probably accurate, Chío feels very far away. "While you look, I mean," Chío adds. She's being considerate, conceding to the basic premise of Isabel's trip, even though Isabel knows it still pisses her friend off.

"Right, yeah. I'm having fun," Isabel says, but until now she hadn't even considered the thought.

“You better be. Higher purpose or not, you’re in a privileged-as-fuck position traveling the world, and if you’re not enjoying yourself while you’re doing it, I will track you down and bring your ass back to Michigan myself.”

Now Isabel laughs. “I believe it.”

When the conversation ends, Isabel feels renewed. Not just physically, thanks to the nap, but spiritually. Chío is right. There is no reason she has to hang about with a heavy heart while searching for Hatori. Supers do not need her gloom and seriousness to exist; she can seek them out while still enjoying what the world has to offer.

Isabel decides to return to the subway with a new plan: meet someone new. Super or not. The more people she meets, the better her chances that eventually one will be a Super.

The problem there: How the hell does one make friends, or even acquaintances? Especially in a place where you don’t speak the language. Isabel has had Sam and Chío since she was thirteen, and does not remember how to meet anyone new without them or at least the benefit of a classroom setting.

The trains are deathly quiet. Even the groups of obvious other tourists who board don’t say a word, falling in line with the local customs. Isabel can’t tell if she can approach them in English (nor would she dare disturb the silence, which feels hallowed). So, she keeps an eye out for Hatori amid the many, many faces around her.

She arrives back at the hostel two hours later so defeated she wants to cry, wants to climb into her bed and let it coax her into a good mood.

Then, hope. The sound of people chattering in the lobby. Alex and the Belgian girls are drinking vending-machine beers and talking with two other girls. Isabel stands there, waiting for an in, afraid that they'll just look at her and then glance away again, forcing her back into her little pod to scroll through her phone all night.

Alex rescues her. "Hey. We're going to get some dinner. Want to come with us?"

Is it Tokyo at night, or is it the company of people?

The six of them—Izzy and Alex, the Belgian girls Sienne and Annalise, and the Korean girls Daisy and Ha Yoon—are squeezed into a booth at a loud and lively izakaya. Isabel is abuzz with energy, so much so that she feels like confessing, like blurting out her true intentions to this table of strangers. Maybe they will want to help her.

She swallows it, though, looking around the restaurant at all there is to take in: the cooks at work at the griddle behind the bar, the group of already-drunk college boys singing in the corner, customers picking at dozens of dishes she's unfamiliar with.

"How long are you in Tokyo?" Ha Yoon asks the table, opening it up for all to answer. She and Daisy are there for a week, to meet a guy that Daisy has been talking to online. Alex and the Belgian girls are sticking around only a few more days before continuing on to China and Vietnam, respectively. All of their answers sound impressive to Isabel, but then they turn to look at her expectantly.

"I don't know," she says. "We'll see." The last few months have taught her that people hate this answer. They can't process it, prodding her to change her words. Surely, she can't mean that.

This isn't Dearborn, though, so the comment isn't met with raised eyebrows. They ask how long she's traveling for in general, and when she has the same response, they laugh warmly and say that it's cool. What a wonder it is to have her choices validated. Isabel smiles down at the table, embarrassed at how good she feels.

The others transition into discussing food, and then the peppy server returns with a round of beers for them. From there, it feels almost too easy. It is not the kind of deep friendship she is used to; it has nothing to do with superheroes, but it's fun. It's welcoming.

Alex still responds with only two or three words at a time, but Daisy, Annalise, and Sienne more than make up for it with chatter. Isabel feels comfortable just listening in, laughing at the appropriate times, picking up the Korean girls' habit of pouring beer for the others from the large bottles into the glasses they all drink from, never pouring for themselves. What a lovely gesture it is to think of others in this small way.

An elaborate birthday celebration breaks out for another group, every izakaya employee bursting into song and dance, and the birthday woman is presented with a plate with her image drawn on in chocolate syrup. By the time they leave to go to a nearby karaoke bar, Isabel feels a little tipsy, and she has not thought of the ills of the world in hours.

Isabel had this preconceived notion of Japanese people being completely prim and proper, always calm. This was cemented in her mind by the salarypeople she's been seeing at subway stations since she arrived, the quiet on the trains, the cleanliness everywhere. Now they feel completely loosened, drunk and joyous, gleeful bouts of laughter echoing through the music emanating from bars and restaurants. It occurs to her that she has only the slightest understanding of the culture, its similarities and differences to the specific way of life she's familiar with. It makes her hungry for more. Hungry to chip away at her ignorance. She's only brushed up against understanding, tasted it with the tip of her tongue.

She resolves to learn as much as she can while she's here, to interact more meaningfully with the places she will visit on her journeys. She will do what Chío might: take notes, read books, talk to locals, study the languages. She won't ever learn it all, but something feels right about attempting.

They make their way into a private karaoke room for the six of them, not much bigger than the booth at the izakaya. Daisy and Ha Yoon start off with a K-pop song that everyone in the room knows. Isabel is reminded of Sam, his little stint as a B-boy (he was terrible and he blamed his elbows for being sticky, whatever that meant), choreographing moves after school with the K-pop club.

Isabel is by no means a singer, barely even allowed herself to belt in the car with Chío sitting beside her, but the booze and the mood of the evening have built up her confidence, and she joins in with the rest of them. They pay for another hour at the karaoke room, though Alex has to leave to work the desk. Thankfully, Hiroo gave Isabel an evening shift at the hostel the following day, so she doesn't have to pull herself away to sleep quite yet. Right now it feels like she will never want to leave. She picks a song no one knows, but they all try to sing along for her sake anyway, and the world feels bred for joy.

But eventually the moment comes to leave. Their energy is sapped by beer and lack of water and hours of singing and dancing. They emerge back into a still-lively Tokyo dawn, which seems to match Isabel's drunkenness. A man is throwing up into a trash can. A group of boys laugh at him, though they look seconds away from joining him. There are signs of the coming day ahead: salarypeople in freshly pressed white shirts, a jogger in brightly colored shorts.

Isabel opens up her bag to get her water bottle, but finds it completely empty. Eyeing the 7-Eleven at the corner, she looks to the other girls and says, "Anyone need some water?"

Annalise checks the time on her phone, then gestures over her shoulder. "There's a train arriving in nine minutes. We can catch it if we hurry."

Isabel makes a quick calculation over what she prefers: the continued company, or some immediate hydration. She knows the risks of being a young woman alone in a city, but the daylight breaking through makes her feel safer. She'd looked up crime rates for Tokyo before coming, and she has a pleasant vision of herself walking back while listening to a podcast or some music, the sky brightening as she makes her way to her pod. The night of companionship has her feeling uncharacteristically unpessimistic about the world.

Plus, this way she'll be able to keep an eye out for Hatori without having to explain herself. The hostel's address is saved into her phone, which has plenty of battery. Maybe Chío will be awake for the video call. The guy by the trash can retches again, and her body starts to almost ache for water.

"You go ahead," she tells the others.

"You're sure?"

"Yeah, it's okay. I didn't walk enough today."

Sienne grabs Isabel's phone and saves her number in it. "I won't fall asleep until you text me that you're back at the hostel."

They each give her a quick hug, and then they're gone. Isabel watches them retreat into the crowd, which continues to morph from late night to early morning, and a swell of pride builds up within her, though she's not sure she can say why she feels it.

A bottle of water and another onigiri later (perhaps the best meal of her life so far), Isabel walks back to Shibuya Station, feeling in love with the world. She tries calling Chío, but it goes straight to voice mail. Isabel feels a stab of hurt, but it's replaced by the deepest affection she's ever felt for her friend.

Instead of leaving a message, she sends an audio recording through her chat app like a normal person. "I wish you were tiny so I could have folded you into my backpack and brought you with me. This trip is helping me so much, you have no idea. Already. If only I didn't miss you so much." She ends it with a hiccup.

A moment later, Chío sends a text. *In class, can't listen, what's up? You okay?*

Just wanted to tell you I took your advice and I'm having fun. Love you!

Love you too, but hate you for not being in class.

I'm attending the school of life!

Chío responds with a candid selfie taken from under her desk, sticking her tongue out, giving Isabel the finger. Isabel laughs, then feels a rush of dizziness hit her. She leans against the wall, cringing at the feeling, and also her decision to walk back alone when she's this drunk. The station is just a minute away, though, and she has faith that she can keep it together. Fortunately, she's not alone on the streets.

At the station, it takes her an embarrassing amount of time to figure out how to swipe her card and get the little plastic gate to open for her. But there's a group of loud tourists out for an early morning likewise struggling with the card reader nearby, and so the attention is off her.

She chugs the rest of her water and finds the right platform. It's sparsely occupied, quiet, but at least not creepily so. There's a man in a bright yellow vest reading a newspaper on one bench. A young couple sit on another, six inches apart, legs angled toward each other but not touching. Overhead, a sign shows that the next train will arrive in three minutes, and all of a sudden exhaustion hits her, along with another dizzy spell. The loud tourists who came in through the turnstiles at the same time arrive on the platform, not mindful of the societal agreement for silence.

Isabel walks over to a pillar near the tracks, leans against it, and closes her eyes for a second. She breathes in through her nose and out through her mouth, wanting to laugh at the night she's had, at the fact that she's not in school, she's out in the world. Then her head starts spinning. She pictures the man retching outside the karaoke bar and takes another deep breath.

At last, she can hear the sound of the train approaching, that far-off whoosh coming in from the tunnel. She'll have to hold out a little longer.

But her head is still spinning and she opens her eyes to try to fight the nausea.

When she does, she realizes she's swaying, and has stepped away from the pillar. She leans back toward it, thinking it'll steady her. But she's misjudged it, somehow. She stumbles.

The platform fills with the sound of the train approaching, a slight rumble beneath Isabel's feet as she feels herself losing her balance. It occurs to her that this would be an incredibly stupid way to die, even as she notices just how close she is to the edge of the platform. The lights of the approaching train fill up her vision.

Before she succumbs to gravity, though, someone grabs her by the shoulder and yanks her backward, changing her momentum. She slams against the pillar, the force of it knocking the wind out of her.

She turns over her shoulder to see who's helped her avoid death or injury or even just an embarrassing tumble onto the floor. But there is no one standing close enough to have pulled her to safety.

Her heartbeat quickens. She studies the platform. The loud tourists are looking over at her, laughing. The couple from the bench are rising to their feet, preparing to board the train. The man reading a newspaper is still doing just that. She has no clue who has helped her, or how. She's far enough away from the others that they would have had to have unrealistic speed, or the ability to move things from a distance.

She gets a strange feeling in her gut, immediately sobering her enough to stop her from swaying. For a second, she thinks she might throw up, but then it passes and she feels clearheaded, the rolling in her stomach transforming from nausea into butterflies. Has she imagined what just happened? Or is she simply too drunk to make sense of it?

She wants to approach the couple, or the man with the newspaper, wants to run around the station to see if anyone at all might have seen. But the train doors ding open, and she clearly needs to get to bed. Heart still pounding, wondering what the hell just happened to her, Isabel boards the train.

For some reason, she keeps her eye on the newspaper reader,

wanting to get a good look at his face. Her phone is in her hand, and acting on some instinct she can't name, she goes to the camera function.

The doors whir closed, and after an automated voice says something in Japanese, the train rumbles to life. Isabel keeps her eyes on the platform. Right before the train disappears into the tunnel, the man sets down his newspaper and looks almost straight at Isabel.

It's a face she's seen before.

5

Mazunte, Mexico

One more glance.

The rope-like tendril around the ankle has unraveled in the constant ebb and flow of the tide. Now the invisible forces of the ocean tug at the body, and it is dislodged. A moment of suspense to see what will happen next. If there's air in the lungs, the body will rise. If not, it'll take days or weeks from death for gases to form and send it bubbling back to the surface. Hair and clothing dance in the current, lively in the dark. The arms follow, as if controlled by some puppeteer way above.

Above is not a puppeteer, but Isabel's friends, walking toward the resort where Chío and her family are staying.

Chío's mind is conjuring up images she'd rather not focus on, all the things that might have gone wrong since she last spoke to her best friend. A plane crash, a kidnapping, some rare flesh-eating disease.

The truth is, she is also thinking about Isabel's bed. She is remembering—as she steps into the still-warm, soft sand, watching her footprints appear and disappear in the tide—how it felt to lie on that bed as a bad movie played on the laptop set up between them, and they either chatted over it or smoked some weed and made jokes at the movie's expense.

Chío has managed to get her family to enjoy bad movies too, but their hearts don't seem to be in it, and obviously she can't ask them if they'd like to be high to watch. In the past year, Chío, always close to her family, has discovered the fulfillment of spending time with them. They have become her closest companions; she's even been eschewing time with Sam to hang out with them.

Still, she can't help but miss Izzy, miss those nights of stoned giggles and snacks. For months she's been reexamining her memories, wondering if the seed for Izzy's odd adventure was planted there, if Chío is somehow at fault for encouraging weird, marijuana-induced thoughts.

"Yo," Sam says as they arrive at the resort, "this place is dope."

"The perks of traveling with parents," Chío says. "The downside is that it doesn't really feel like Mexico at all."

From the beach, where employees are stacking up daybeds, cleaning up abandoned margarita glasses, Sam and Chío have found their way onto a winding path lit with soft orange lights. Around them, older couples and families, many of them white, thrust their English into the pleasant evening air, enjoying beers or glasses of wine. Two men in Hawaiian shirts puff on cigars that suffuse the ocean air with musk. The pool is a dream, and when she first arrived that afternoon, Chío had momentarily forgotten why she was in Mexico, focusing instead on the joy a place like that can bring.

There is only one group left in the water and it is Chío's family. Her brother, Fran, and her father, Santi, twins separated by three decades. They have the same wavy chestnut hair as Chío, but cropped shorter. Like Chío, they're tall and lanky, though Chío inherited her mom's lighter skin and eyes.

They're throwing a ring-shaped Frisbee back and forth, trying to catch it with their feet by diving down and doing handstands. Chío's mom, Aída, is reading a book despite the lack of light, and her little sister, Liz, who looks like none of them and all of them at the same time, is scrolling through her phone. They both look up simultaneously when they sense the duo approach.

There are hugs and kisses and genuine warmth (shy eye contact toward Sam from Liz, awkward, earnest waving from Fran), the kind that had always felt so strange to Sam and Isabel, so bizarrely wonderful, this open affection from family. They used to joke with Chío that they were going to take her place, live as her and soak up the familial love.

"But my parents would gladly adopt both of you."

"Nope, we have to assume your identity," Isabel had said. "It's the only way."

"We are all now Chío Guzmán-Stein," Sam agreed.

Chío used to feel self-conscious about it, for some reason. Like their ribbing was a way to criticize her. But over the past few months, she's come to embrace it. She doubts Isabel would have left if she felt the same way about her parents. Sam had dropped the joke eventually, but Isabel kept it going, occasionally writing Guzmán-Stein as her last name on school assignments, in her notebook, giving the full name at coffee shops.

Chío's mom releases Sam from a hug only to smack him on the back of the head. "I have to come to Mexico to see you? Where have you been?" Then another hug without waiting for an answer.

"Ma," Chío says, an indictment, a plea.

From the pool, Santi, not pausing the game: "You're having dinner with us, right?"

Chío and Sam check their phones, as if now is the moment that Isabel will choose to show up. Across the pool, a family of four returns from the beach, towels slung over their forearms like waiters at a fancy restaurant.

"There's also this communal dinner thing at my hostel," Sam says, scratching his neck.

Chío imagined they'd be having tacos right now, being themselves again, like magic, the year undone by the reunion. She figured that right around now is when Isabel would admit that the superhero thing was bullshit, that she hasn't found any, hasn't looked for any, only wanted a quirky thing to say to excuse herself for leaving. A gap year, and normalcy would resume.

Santi laughs at Sam, tossing the Frisbee too far over Fran's head, ignoring his son's complaint when he has to climb out of the water to go chase it down. "You don't want to eat some hostel's volunteering Dutch dude's unseasoned pasta dish. You'll eat with us. The food here is superb."

No question, then.

Sam accompanies the Guzmán-Steins to their suite. He sits on the balcony, alternately watching the waves and scrolling through his phone as they get dressed. Chío joins him until the bathroom is free.

She checks her phone again in the bathroom before she steps into the fancy hotel shower, but Isabel hasn't texted or called, hasn't been online.

For the next twenty minutes, as she bathes and gets dressed, Chío can't help but imagine ridiculous scenarios that might be responsible for Isabel's absence. Isabel's become a sidekick to some superhero, and they've been called away on an important mission. A villain (if there are people with superpowers, it tracks that some would misuse those powers) has kidnapped Isabel in order to accomplish some nefarious plan. Isabel has fallen into a toxic vat or been struck by an alien artifact and is now Super herself.

She shakes away these thoughts, scolding herself for having them, and steps into a dress, feeling self-conscious about her slightly sunburnt cheeks and forehead. As soon as she joins Sam on the balcony, though, she wishes she could continue thinking about superheroes. Because the more realistic reasons for Isabel's absence are not in the least bit reassuring.

"I hope she's okay," she says.

"She's okay," Sam says, sounding sure of it. "She's got superheroes for friends now, remember?"

Dinner goes better than she would have expected. Chío's parents are warm as ever, funny, moving the conversation along with questions and segues in that way some adults have figured out. It helps Chío and Sam resemble, more or less, their former selves. They don't mention broken routines, or Roys's, or the deterioration of their friendship.

They laugh about the time they tried to make pizza from scratch but forgot to add yeast, then tried to sprinkle some on top while it was in the oven, despite Chío explaining it didn't work that way. Isabel had still eaten three slices, trying to convince them that it was delicious.

It had been a great night, during the pandemic, shortly after they'd all been vaccinated (Isabel in secret), and the relief and joy were palpable. Their laughter had been loud—eager, almost. Isabel's especially. None of them had thrived during those times, of course, but Isabel had been more down than most people she knew, her sleep schedule wild, her humor leading quickly to darkness.

Chío doesn't think about that now; she thinks about that joy that had been waiting so long to be unleashed. That's what tonight was supposed to be.

Then: sirens.

The clamor of cops on the beach, just beyond the dining room, which faces the water. The surf had barely been visible in the toenail moon's weak light a second ago, but now that a pickup truck is pulling up on the beach, the flashing blue and red lights show how the waves have not taken a break. They're still out there, crashing relentlessly against the sand, as if angry at it.

The diners rubberneck, but the Guzmán-Steins try to ignore the commotion. An Isabel-shaped hole forms in the conversation.

Chío's mom calms her down, slightly, with a hand resting gently atop hers. Sam's brow furrows in concern, but his mole enchiladas command most of his attention. He washes them down with a beer that the Guzmán-Steins have allowed him to order. Dessert comes and goes. Chío barely touches the tarts and sorbets in the middle of the table, her eyes constantly flitting toward the lights outside.

Sam tries to convince Chío to go to a party at his hostel, but she is in no mood. Her mind is too busy churning up reasons for Isabel's absence, for the sirens. It wants to link the two together and is begging for more evidence to prove or refute her hypotheses.

Santi insists on paying for an unnecessary taxi ride for Sam, despite how close the hostel is. Chío hugs him goodbye, even though they make plans to meet the next morning at the beach and spend the whole day together. "Izzy will show," he says, and the words provide not an iota of comfort, though his familiar smell does, the softness of his embrace despite the muscles she can feel beneath her arms.

Chío watches TV with Fran and Liz late into the night, pretending to have fallen asleep on the couch when her parents stumble into the suite, giddy-drunk from margaritas at the hotel bar. She lets them drape a blanket over her, feels the joy of their tender forehead kisses. When they retreat behind the door, she continues watching sitcoms on her phone, and falls asleep at almost four in the morning.

When she wakes up, Sam is calling her, apparently for the fourth time that morning. She picks up, groggy.

Sam's voice comes through, steady but somber. He does not sound like he just woke up. "There's a body," he says.

6

Tokyo, Japan

When Isabel wakes up later that day, it's past noon. For a moment, she doesn't remember. Her sleep was the deep, dreamless sleep of the drunk, her mind a blank slate through it all. She comes to in a haze, with the need to pee, but no real trace of a hangover. She smiles into the pillow, knowing it was a good idea to get that extra water to end the night.

Then it comes back to her, and her mind snaps into clarity. She reaches for her phone. There's a slew of notifications on the screen, but she swipes past them and goes to her photos. Part of her doesn't trust what she remembers, is sure that she's confusing dreams with reality. It could not have happened the way she thought it did.

There is at least this piece of evidence: the photo of the man on the bench. It's just as blurry as all the other ones on the internet, but coupled with her memory, it feels undeniable. It's a picture of Hatori.

She jolts up in her capsule. "Holy shit," she says.

What to do with this feeling?

At first, Isabel can't wrap her mind around it. There's too much excitement in the realization to stay in bed. The implications are invigorating, but also paralyzing. *Holy shit. Holy shit.*

Not knowing what else to do, she checks her notifications. Sienne sent a good-night text after Isabel had told her she was back at the hostel. A smiley emoji from Chío once she'd listened to the voice message Isabel had sent. There are a couple of emails updating her on activity on the forum. They're going to lose their minds when she tells them. Isabel plops down onto the bed, then laughs into her pillow again.

A quick shower later, she's back on foot, headed to the nearby Ikebukuro Station. She waves to Alex at the front desk and skips the elevator to bound down the stairs. As she steps out into the muggy Tokyo afternoon, she dials Chío.

"I hope you're calling me from a classroom of some sort," Chío says as she answers on the third ring.

Isabel laughs. "Yeah, that was a bit of a dick move. Sorry. I promise no more fun gloating when I know you're in school."

"It's okay. But not really. Tell me about last night. I'll let you know when I'm starting to bubble over with rage and/or jealousy."

Isabel crosses the street, following the path she's taken to the subway station every day since she checked into the hostel. It's a point of pride for her that she knows the way by heart. In Michigan she was constantly getting lost—she needed the help of a GPS to get almost anywhere. "I have big news."

"You miss me and you're coming back."

"Well, yes, but no."

"Yes to which part?"

"Yes I miss you, no that's not my news. I saw him." She laughs, hardly believing it herself. She slows her gait, wanting to appreciate the words coming out of her mouth, the feeling swelling in her chest. "I saw Hatori."

There's a long pause on the other end. "Tell me about last night," Chío repeats, measured.

Isabel sighs, but even Chío's lack of excitement won't temper her own. So, she tells her everything that happened since they last spoke, from feeling like making friends was impossible to the sudden ease with the girls. Dinner to karaoke, the smart decision to go get more water for herself.

"I wouldn't quite call it smart."

"It was day out already. Tokyo's safe, it was fine. More than fine, because—"

"Are there men in Tokyo?"

Isabel laughs, conceding the point. "Okay, fair enough. No more doing that alone." Then she describes the end of the night, the stumble (downplaying the drunkenness that caused it), the mysterious yank backward. "I'm telling you, there is no way something normal saved me. No one was close enough. I had this feeling like someone was looking out for me. And then I looked at my phone when I woke up and I had taken a picture. It was him. It was Hatori."

When Chío is skeptical—Isabel can feel it in her silence—she sends her the photo, insisting she look at it for at least ten seconds, and compare it to another photo she sends through of Hatori posted to the forum.

"Hard to tell."

"It was him, trust me."

"No offense, Izzy, but that seems highly improbable. In a city of thirty million, going off nothing but a few pictures posted to a forum of"—they both sense the tenuousness of her word choice—"fans, or whatever, you happen to find the one guy you're looking for? What are the odds of that?"

Chío has a point, Isabel knows. But she also knows her friend too well to have approached this conversation without a rebuttal. "Maybe he found the forum too. He could have known I was there to find him, and he either wanted to talk to me, or he didn't want to be found, and was making sure I didn't get too close. That's one of the theories about why people don't know about them. They stay hidden on purpose. Avoid the public eye, the media frenzy that goes with it, government involvement, scientific experimentation, whatever."

"Why would he follow you if he didn't want to be found?"

Okay, she just had the one rebuttal. "Shit, I don't know. But either way, it's amazing, isn't it? I'm gonna go back to that station and try to find him again."

She's at the entrance to Ikebukuro Station near a circular structure called the Global Ring. It's relatively quiet, only a few dozen people walking into and out of the station, the manic lunch rush over. Above her, storm clouds are rolling in. Which is fine by her; she intends to spend the day at Shibuya Station.

"Isn't it a lot more likely that you're wrong? Or even if you're right, if he wants to stay hidden, why would he return to the same station?" The words go straight to Isabel's stomach. She chews her lip, stares at the ground, and Chío speaks again after a beat. "Just don't go falling onto train tracks looking for him. And no more walking home drunk alone at night."

"Don't worry, I used up a week's worth of my budget last night. No more booze for a while." There's another pregnant pause, and Isabel can just feel Chío's worry coming through the phone. "This is helping me, Chío. You know that, right? It's less than a week in and it's already helping."

"I'm glad to hear that," Chío says. "I just wish you would tell me what it's helping you with."

Four hours later, Isabel has taken fifteen thousand steps inside Shibuya Station and has looked at so many faces she's not even sure she can process people's features anymore. She feels Chío's words echoing in her head, but she does what she can to escape them. Podcasts, music, a download of a book of essays by Japanese students she finds through her Dearborn Public Library app.

She posts her picture of Hatori to Actually Super, along with a lengthy description of what she calls her "close encounter." She tries to write about it as honestly as possible, without exaggerating the events. Though when discussing how it all happened, it's hard not to up the emotions she felt. Just the act of writing them down brings her excitement back.

Then Sienne texts her to see if she wants to meet up for some food. So, Isabel searches online for cheap restaurants in the area, not wanting to stray far from the station, and now the two are sitting at the bar of a popular soba noodle spot.

"How was your day?" Sienne asks, her English barely accented with the clipped vowels of Dutch.

"Pretty good. Just walked around. Yours?"

"Really good. A bit hungover from yesterday, so it was a perfect day for museums. I went to the Borderless place. You know it?" Isabel shakes her head. "Oh, it's so cool. It's interactive. I'm sure you've seen it on Instagram. Lots of bright colors."

Their noodles arrive. Isabel picks up her chopsticks, looking around to see how everyone else is eating. Isabel would like to think she's well read and well informed enough to have been prepared somewhat for the cultural differences between Japan and the U.S. But reading a couple of Murakami books and watching Netflix food travel shows in the months before her trip didn't exactly bring about deep-seated knowledge. Even talking to people online who have traveled to Japan or lived there didn't come close to filling in all the gaps. There's something wholly different between knowing about a custom and seeing it performed before her in all its normalcy. She's an outsider here, and even if she felt like an outsider in Michigan, there was a wider culture she could still more deeply understand.

"Are you used to slurping yet?" Sienne asks.

"Oh, I love it."

Sienne laughs. "I try! But all I can hear is my mom's voice in my head yelling at me. I can't do it." As if to prove it, she clumsily picks up some of the grayish noodles from her tray and dips them into the accompanying broth. She starts slurping, then shakes her head and chews, cutting off the noodles hanging out from her mouth and dropping them back onto the wooden tray.

"You almost had it," Isabel says.

They laugh again, then fall quiet as they eat. Though Hatori is still on her mind, Isabel marvels that it was just yesterday that she felt it was impossible to make friends. Now here she is, with a near stranger, one whom she might only know for another day or two, sharing a meal, laughing.

Isabel takes a sip of water, thinking. "When do you leave the hostel?" she asks.

"Day after next. You?"

Before she can answer, Isabel's struck by an urge. "Can I tell you something?" she says instead, setting her chopsticks down and half turning in her seat to look at Sienne. She wasn't planning on a confession at all, but now that it's on the tip of her tongue, her excitement is immediate. "It's kind of weird. But since we're only going to know each other for a little time, it feels . . . safe."

Sienne doesn't run, so that's something. She raises her eyebrows. "Okay, sure."

Isabel takes a breath, and then lets loose. She opens the faucet fully, liberated by the knowledge that if she's met with judgment, she won't have to live with it for long. She tells her everything about Supers, about what happened last night. And because she doesn't need Sienne to believe her, because she's simply unloading, she tells her the reason she needs to believe in superheroes so badly. She tells her how she's had a dark view of the world since she was little. For the first time ever, Isabel tells someone about her grandmother, how she would always say that, deep down, people are evil. They will cause harm to anyone else just to not be inconvenienced, just to make themselves feel better.

Isabel's great-grandparents survived a concentration camp, and once Isabel learned that, she understood her grandmother's mentality, even if she managed to resist it. Old people had lived through bad times, and so were grumpy. But that was in the past, and did not have to be how Isabel saw the world.

Then growing up did its thing. She started to notice headlines, to read history books, to focus on how people could let others die and suffer and brush it off if the tragedy did not land on their doorstep. Isabel told Sienne about her dad's secret brain, too, about learning that the people closest to her might not be what she thought at all.

When she had stumbled onto the part of the internet that believed in superheroes, she had felt her first glimmer of hope. An idea started forming. And when other events happened that made the world feel irrefutably dark, the idea became a flotation device she could hang on to.

By the time she's done speaking, their plates are empty and the rain outside has finally let up to a drizzle. They stand outside the restaurant, Sienne with an umbrella over both of them, though Isabel is comfortable in her rain jacket.

"You probably think I'm crazy," Isabel says. She doesn't like that word, but it's the only one that comes to mind.

Sienne starts digging around her backpack and comes up holding a pack of cigarettes. She offers them to Isabel, then lights one for herself when Isabel waves her away. "I think everyone is crazy. Working your whole life for companies making other people rich is crazy. Having children before you're ready for them just because it's what's expected of you is crazy. Superheroes are a little crazier, yes. But looking for good in the world?" She exhales and shrugs, as if that's all there is to say about the subject. Isabel wonders if that's a skill smokers practice, how to punctuate their statements with a well-timed exhale. That's even before it sinks in: she's told someone the whole story, and instead of meeting her with ridicule, Sienne has given her a sort of blessing.

Despite the long day at the station, the exhaustion, Chío's doubts, and her own misgivings about what she saw or experienced the day before, Isabel feels her convictions renew. She walks back to the subway with Sienne, then, happily riding in the quiet car toward the hostel, thinks of all the encounters yet to come.

7

Mazunte, Mexico

Sam wants to call it a hangover. He wants the feeling in his stomach to be because of the beer and tequila he consumed the night before at the hostel.

He was able to ignore his thoughts for much of the night, psyched as he'd been to be in Mexico, to be at a beach with his best friends. Even if he'd seen only Chío, it still felt like he was there with both her and Izzy. Then he'd gone to his hostel, where a party was raging. There'd been people from all over the world, and it had felt like he was getting a taste of Izzy's life.

Plus, there was the fact that he didn't have to worry about the legality of his drinking, and there were all those attractive people at the hostel. He had no idea how people went about hooking up with strangers at a place like this—or anywhere, for that matter. Sam needed the benefit of at least three months' worth of conversation, a couple of those possibly spent pining hopelessly, thinking there was no way the other person shared his feelings. Only then could he imagine a make-out taking place. But at a hostel party, it seemed like it was always a possibility. Like that girl at the bar, or the guy floating on the inflatable donut in the pool. It felt like just being nearby could lead to an adventure, make-out or otherwise. He wondered if that was how Izzy had felt for the past eight months, and despite himself, he kept looking for her at the party, convincing himself by the third or fourth beer that she would show up here at any moment.

Now, though, as he drinks bad coffee on his walk to Chío's hotel, there is nothing that can keep him from feeling a little sick. Even if last night's booze is adding to it, there is no way Isabel's absence and the rumor he'd woken up to aren't the root cause. A body has been found on the beach, and it belongs to a young woman.

Sam expected the beach to still be awash with cops and caution tape. But the only evidence that there may have been something wrong is a set of tire tracks in the sand, and a red-flag warning of a strong tide. There are a couple of joggers running along the shore, and a group of women doing yoga on the sand, unaware. Otherwise, it is quiet and calm. Sam tries to take this as a good sign.

Chío is in a lounge chair, a colorful shawl around her shoulders. She barely notices his arrival, her gaze fixated on the horizon, her phone teetering on the edge of her thigh. He wants to sit on the chair with her, try to provide some comfort. Instead, he takes the adjacent one.

"Hey."

Her eyes flit toward him. "Have you heard anything else?"

Sam shakes his head. "Couldn't really confirm. Anything from Izzy?"

"Still hasn't been online."

"She could have lost her phone."

"Yeah," Chío says, unconvinced. "I can't sit and wait for her, though. I think we should go talk to the authorities or whatever." Just like that, Chío starts crying. Sam doesn't know what else to do, so he joins her on the chair and holds her.

Where else can his mind go but to that night in Isabel's room?

It was just a few months before Isabel announced her plan, a Friday night like so many others they'd had. After basketball practice, Sam met Isabel and Chío at the mall for some aimless wandering, followed by Zo's Good Burger. They toyed with the idea of watching a movie, but nothing interesting enough was playing, and so they went back to Isabel's to play board games.

Chío had an SAT prep class the next morning, so she left on the early side. Then Sam and Isabel had shared a joint while walking around the block, the giggles almost instantaneous. After that they barreled into Isabel's kitchen, rooting around for the ideal snack. Thankfully, her parents had gone to a dinner party of some sort, leaving them free to be a loud, giggly tornado. After making some grilled cheese sandwiches with apple butter and kimchi, they went up to her room and put on a movie.

They'd hoped for something laughably bad, but the one they'd landed on was a little boring and a little darker than they'd expected, and their giggles died out shortly after they'd devoured their sandwiches, a strange mood taking over the room. Sam couldn't tell exactly why, and so he looked over at Isabel.

She hadn't been crying, but there was something in her eyes that made him sober up, at least a little bit. It was always hard to know while high how much he was imagining, all the narratives that the brain can invent based on nothing, so he didn't say anything for a while. But he kept looking over at her, and when she finally caught him looking, she gave him a slight smile that didn't reach her eyes.

"Everything okay?"

She nodded and looked back at the movie, but a few moments later she slid over closer to him, resting her head on his shoulder. "Do you mind?"

He shook his head, not sure what any of it meant, thinking of Chío for some reason, but sensing somehow that Isabel needed the comfort of touch. At one point, Sam fell asleep, and when he woke up, their hands were clasped and his shirt was damp where Isabel's head was resting. He pulled his hand away quickly and fled, telling himself he was doing it just so Isabel wouldn't get in trouble for having him sleep over.

On the beach, Chío catches her breath, and Sam feels a pang of guilt because he's feeling some joy. Joy to be there with Chío, joy to be able to provide her some comfort, especially when he's been missing Isabel for eight months. But what kind of an asshole can feel joy under the circumstances?

Chío sniffles, then sits up straight, wrapping the shawl tighter around her. Sam removes his arm from her shoulder. "I'm not sure I can eat," she says. "But my parents were headed down for breakfast in a bit. We can catch up with them first."

An hour later, they are at a tiny municipal police station, waiting to speak to someone. Sam sits at the end of a row of chairs against a wall, Chío next to him. She's holding her mom's hand, her eyes closed. Her dad is standing at the window at the front of the waiting room, talking to a cop in his Argentine Spanish.

There are two women on the chairs across the room from Sam, and he keeps his eyes on them just because it keeps his mind off everything else. They're speaking in English, but in hushed tones that he can't catch. They seem stressed, but he supposes few people arrive at a police station while on vacation without being stressed. He finds himself hoping that there's some other missing girl, that they're here because they heard about the body too. Then he admonishes himself for wishing harm on someone else, even if it's a hypothetical person. But isn't that better than the alternative? People die every day. He'd rather it's not Izzy.

A few minutes later, Santi returns. "They can't give us a description of the person found because they're still investigating. The autopsy is scheduled for later today, and we might be able to go see . . ." He strains to find a tactful way to phrase what he wants to say. "But he couldn't guarantee it. They'll call us."

"So, what, we just wait?" Chío asks, an edge to her voice.

Sam tries to come up with something helpful to say, maybe repeating the advice to check around town. But he knows it won't work. Nothing will provide comfort except for Isabel walking in through the door.

8

Hualien, Taiwan

Three weeks after her run-in with Hatori, Isabel has not seen him again. She has spent countless hours at train stations, staring at passersby, at mothers picking up their toddlers as they hurry to catch a train, at men with laptop-bag straps cutting across white button-up shirts, at bright-vested station guards patrolling the platforms.

She even started reenacting the night of the encounter. Or, at least, pretending to. She'd fake-stumble down the stairs to the station at night and lean against the same pillar, swaying like a strong breeze could send her into the tunnel at any moment. A few Good Samaritans came by and asked if she was okay, but no invisible forces pulled her back, no impossibly quick person ran by nudging her to safety. She didn't experience a single inexplicable thing.

The longer she went without an encounter, the more she found herself looking at her phone at the train station, exposed to more and more news of a terrible world. She couldn't help but read newsletters, click on links, get lost in the endless feeds on social media. It felt like she was right back in her living room during childhood, when her grandmother would pick her up after school and watch her until her parents were home.

Grandma's favorite thing was to turn on the twenty-four-hour news networks and click her tongue at whatever violent act had been most recently perpetrated. The blinds would be drawn, and Isabel would sit at the kitchen table doing her homework with the help of a lamp so that Grandma wouldn't have to deal with the glare from the sunlight. It would be hard to focus, sometimes, over Grandma's muttered curses at the screen, each headline confirming what Grandma knew to be true: people were monsters awaiting the chance to do harm.

Now it was Isabel's brain offering muttered curses, and Hatori was nowhere to be found. It might have all been a hallucination, a drunken dream, imperfect human perception, never knowing how things really are, just guessing, always guessing.

Both Chío and Mathilde had asked her how long she was going to stay in Japan, and she hadn't known how to respond. Yes, she had a long list of Supers elsewhere she'd planned on tracking down, some of whom had been recently sighted, according to other people on the forum. But it felt strange to leave when she'd come so close. How likely was it that she'd have another run-in? It felt easier to stay and keep exploring rather than start anew in a place she didn't know at all.

But then the days stretched on with no Hatori, and just as

Isabel was feeling like Tokyo was too big to ever run into him again, Mathilde sent her an article. There had been an earthquake in Taiwan, and a woman helped pull six people to safety from a collapsed building. A quote from a witness at a coffee shop across the street said the woman lifted a piece of concrete she should not have been able to, and Isabel immediately felt a tingle of hope. A new lead.

What do you think? Isabel texted Mathilde, since she was in a close enough time zone to respond quickly. They'd been talking more and more because of that, and because Isabel felt she needed someone when it came to Supers.

Mathilde thinks it's nice that there's a witness, there's a path beyond just exploring one of the biggest cities in the world and hoping to run into Hatori again.

Coupled with the fact that her free stay at the hostel is ending soon, Isabel began looking for flights that night. She also searched for Workaway opportunities in Hualien, where the building collapsed.

Now she is on the first leg of a long day of travels: the train to the airport. She had meant to see more of Japan, had meant to meet more people and do more, and if she spends too long thinking about it, she is sent into a tailspin of regret, a sort of FOMO for more things than she could ever do in one lifetime.

Thankfully, Chío and Sam are awake and available as distractions.

Describe what's around you, Chío texts.

Leave out the most fun parts though, Sam chimes in.

Isabel smiles, instantly on board for the silly game. It makes her feel like they're there with her, and she remembers to be grateful for the parts of technology that temper loneliness.

I'm on the train to the airport, she starts, then thinks of what to describe. *Mostly empty, though there's a few others. White backpacker dude, late twenties, maybe. Earphones in, head resting against the glass, maybe sleeping. A Japanese family of four all wearing matching outfits.*

She hits send, but keeps typing away, feeling no detail is too small, no tether to the present is too weak.

There are posters here about being a considerate person: No talking on the phone on the train. Don't stand or leave your bags in the walkways.

The sun's up already, but there's still some bright orange clouds on the horizon.

It's quiet, no surprise. Just the occasional announcement from the speakers in Japanese and English.

Leaving the city now, reaching the countryside between Tokyo and the airport. Rice fields, I think. Amazing how it feels like it never ends when you're inside. But it does. There's an edge to everything.

She puts her phone down, the act making her really take note of where she is, what she's doing. She is eighteen and has unleashed herself upon the world.

With a new stamp in her passport, Isabel takes the subway into Taipei, just to take another three-hour train ride, to Hualien. She decides to save money and not buy a Taiwanese SIM card for now. Anyway, Chío and Sam are fast asleep.

She watches another city disappear into countryside and reads a book about the Japanese occupation of Taiwan. Not exactly the best choice to convince her that the world is good.

How is it, her brain wants to know at this particular moment, that human beings can still find it within themselves to oppress one another? To fall into the trap of thinking that a whole group of people is worthy of ill will.

At least she's chosen wisely, sitting on the left side of the train, which faces the ocean. It's a brighter blue than she would have guessed, at times almost Caribbean. To her right are cliffs covered in vegetation. She puts her tablet down and switches to listening to music, wondering what the next few weeks of her life will be like—because it's better than wondering how many times she came close to Hatori and didn't know it. It's better than thinking she imagined the whole thing, that this trip is a pipe dream.

This time Isabel will be working at a guesthouse in exchange for room and board. There's no front desk to operate, and she's not even sure what her duties will be.

At the Hualien train station, she connects to the Wi-Fi and plugs the guesthouse's address into Google Maps. The city does not look like what she'd expected; it's a collection of squat gray buildings and roads busy with cars and motorbikes. She walks past a strip of clothing shops with discount signs and the kind of electronics store she associates with Canal Street in New York, from when she went with Chío and her family a couple of years ago.

There are a few signs of the earthquake—the odd broken window, diagonal cracks along the column of one cordoned-off building, bits of concrete on the sidewalk—but the city seems to have moved on quickly. Isabel thinks about trying to find the fallen building but decides that's best left to another day.

Thirty minutes later, sticky with sweat, Isabel peels her backpack off and fans herself before ringing the doorbell outside the gate of a rather cute house. It's outside the main part of the city, almost rural. There are green mountains to the west, and to the east the hint of the ocean.

The gate buzzes open, so Isabel walks up the driveway toward the house. There's a beautiful yard with flowers and a dry fountain on the left. There's an SUV in the driveway, along with a motorbike and two dusty bicycles that look like they haven't been ridden in years.

The door opens and a Taiwanese woman in her thirties or forties steps out. "Isabel?" she asks, her face already breaking into a warm smile. Without even waiting for Isabel to confirm or deny, she points to the shoe rack near the entrance.

"Always slippers inside, okay?" she says, her English accented but easily understood.

Isabel does as she's told, sliding her shoes off and stepping inside, where there's an identical shoe rack lined with plastic slippers of varying sizes and colors. She chooses a pair almost at random, then follows the woman past some stairs and into the living room, which is adjacent to the kitchen.

"Sit!" the woman says, gesturing toward the couch while she goes into the kitchen. "You want water? Tea? Do you like pomelo? Do you know pomelo?"

Isabel seats herself at the edge of the couch, trying not to get her sweat on the fabric. Almost instantly the woman is in front of her, setting a plate on the coffee table at Isabel's knees. A big green citrus that kind of looks like a grapefruit is on the plate, cut so that Isabel can easily remove the wedges. "Thanks," she says.

The woman takes a seat on an armchair across from the couch, up until then a whirlwind of energy, now completely still and calm, a smile on her face as she regards Isabel. "So, tell me, Isabel, why did you want to come to Taiwan?"

Isabel's taken by surprise by the question and has to improvise. "I just went to the first place that accepted me on Workaway," she says. "I'm traveling for a while, so this is an easy way to decide where to go." It's not a lie, even if it's not the whole truth.

The woman's name—or at least the anglicized name she gives Isabel—is Daphne. She's the owner and operator of the guest-house, and though she seems to be always moving—rising to fetch them tea, chatting with a couple of guests on their way out the door, wiping the kitchen counters clean—she speaks calmly and gently, her voice as soothing as a practiced audiobook narrator's.

At first, Isabel feels an antsiness to be shown to a room, to shower and message her friends and unwind from the day of movement. But Daphne keeps asking her questions about her travels and herself, and she does it with such genuine curiosity and interest that Isabel feels not just at ease, but also cared for.

Over the next hour, Isabel and Daphne talk as if they are old friends. Isabel learns that Daphne has a daughter who's four years old, that she spent some time living in Mexico ("I'm going there in March!" Isabel can't help but say), that she'd been running the guesthouse for three years on her own before someone told her about Workaway. Now she has a constant flow of people from all over the world helping her, teaching her languages, customs, dishes.

Isabel drinks more cups of tea than she can count, and the pomelo disappears one wedge at a time. Guests come and go throughout, most of them speaking with Daphne in Mandarin. The conversations are cheerful and warm, from what Isabel can tell. The guesthouse feels less like a hotel and more like a large home, host to several familial visitors.

While talking about her desire to travel and see the world—leaving out any mention of superheroes—Isabel finds herself bringing up her grandma. Memories she didn't know she treasured. How her grandma would pick Isabel up from kindergarten and they would swing by a different ice cream spot every time on the way home. How that made Isabel think about the world as a place full of hidden joys to be found, but you had to step outside of routine to find them.

"That's beautiful," Daphne says. "Your grandma was a wise lady."

Isabel considers that, remembering the permanent scowl she seemed to have.

Then, cued by something Isabel isn't privy to, Daphne stands and says, "Okay, you'll be in room one for now." Isabel scrambles to pick up her things and follow Daphne past the kitchen and down a short hallway that leads to a door labeled 1.

Daphne turns away and is back out in the living room before Isabel has the chance to show her the article about the woman who rescued people during the earthquake.

Isabel drops her bag by the bed in the inexplicably nautically themed bedroom. She digs in for her toiletries, then takes her shower, washing off the day's travels. When she's done, she sees a missed call from Sam from just a few minutes before. She calls back, keeping him on speakerphone so she can get dressed.

"You're awake!" Sam says as a response. It is her friends' most common greeting now.

"It's seven p.m. here. I should be saying the same to you."

"I'm about to head to school."

"Gross."

"We talked about this. No gloating about not having school or I'll tell Chío you don't believe in education."

"Fine, fine. What's up?" Isabel sniffs at a tank top to see if it's clean enough to wear. Since she's started having to pay for laundry by weight, she's become convinced that 80 percent of loads are unnecessary.

"Just wanted to see how your flight was. Tell me about Taiwan. What's it like?"

“I don’t really know yet. Walked to my guesthouse and talked to the owner for the last hour or so. Gonna go out exploring now.”

“You should go to a night market. I’m sending you a list of foods you have to try.”

Isabel laughs. “You’re doing research on my behalf now?”

“I gotta do something to make you remember I’m still here and seething in jealousy,” Sam says, adding his own little chuckle at the end. Isabel can’t help but feel chastened by the comment. She knows he means well, and the sentiment is rather sweet, but it feels like it carries an edge. Isabel hangs up her towel in the en suite bathroom, trying to swallow her hurt. Sam seems to pick up on this, because he says, “I move to have my previous comment stricken from the record. Tell me about your plan to find this new maybe-Super.”

Just like that, the weight is lifted from the conversation, and from Isabel’s shoulders. Sam has always been able to do this. If it were physically possible at the moment, she would hug him for his ability to bring lightness to anything.

When she’s talked to Chío about her trip, about Supers, there’s a sense that Chío is placating her, acknowledging what Isabel believes only because she thinks it’s better for Isabel’s mental health. Sam, however, has taken her perhaps unreasonable obsession to heart. He’s even joined the Actually Super forum and seems to be genuinely interested in whether she’ll meet a Super.

“Okay,” she says. “Well, the article about the rescuer quotes a witness. Her name is Shu-ling, and she works at a coffee shop across from the fallen building. So, my plan is to try to find her first, and see if she knows the mystery woman by name, or what else she can tell me."

"Look at you. Such a detective."

She's ready to leave, and starving, but without a SIM card, she can only talk to Sam in the guesthouse. So, she decides to take her time unpacking, thankful that she at least has this way of keeping her friend nearby. "Tell me about home," she says. "What have you and Chío been up to?"

There's a bit of a pause, some background noise that sounds like he's pouring himself cereal or something. "Kind of our own things, actually. Not on purpose or anything. But basketball's started up, and you know how Chío gets super into school the first few weeks."

"Slash years," Isabel adds. "Fitting of you to say 'super' just then. If she had a power, it might be studiousness."

"What would yours be?"

"I don't know," she answers, as if she hasn't thought about it a million times before. "Maybe pessimism? Or maybe optimism about the stupidest things."

"Being so self-deprecating that you make me want to fly across the world to both hug you and smack you is impressive, but not a superpower, I don't think. Try again."

Isabel laughs, swatting at a mosquito on the wall nearby. "Do I get to choose what I want, or am I saying what I think it would be based on personality, et cetera?"

Sam takes a moment, chewing on either the answer or his cereal. "Both."

"Okay, if I'm choosing, give me flight. But, like, I get to sit in the air at five hundred miles an hour reading and watching movies and stuff, but for free and without a carbon footprint."

"Nice. Curious about how you're using the bathroom in the air, but we can leave that for the follow-up portion of the interview. What about if it's the universe that grants you a power based on how well it suits you, if that's how the universe operates?"

"The bathroom thing is easy. Just pull over, use a bathroom wherever. As to what superpower I deserve . . ." She trails off, pretending to think. She tosses her empty backpack into the closet, and though she knows Sam will need to go soon and she's starving, she plops down onto the bed. "I'd like to think that the power I deserve is the ability to see straight through to a person's soul."

"That'd be an interesting one."

Isabel says nothing, and shortly after, they hang up.

9

Hualien, Taiwan

Another new, strange routine develops for Isabel. She wakes up early and helps Daphne prepare a hectic breakfast for the guests. Congee; fresh fruit; mushrooms cooked with garlic, chili, and Shaoxing wine; smashed potatoes. It's Isabel's favorite part of the workday, despite the fact that she's never been a morning person, despite how Daphne gets annoyed by Isabel's slow way of moving, how the miscommunications frustrate them both ("Cut like this, not like that!").

When the guests have eaten and are off to explore Taroko National Park, Isabel gets to savor the food and mentally check out on her phone, seeing what people are up to back in Dearborn. Day after day, though, she feels more disconnected from high school, from the U.S., from the drama of relationships and college acceptances. She spends more time on Actually Super, getting tips from people on how to track down Earthquake Woman, as they've taken to calling her. Despite their enthusiasm, though, they don't have the most practical advice. One person suggests faking a disaster to see if she shows up, which gets the user temporarily suspended for violating community rules.

Isabel does fifteen minutes of Mandarin learning on an app, and then it's off to get annoyed by cleaning rooms.

There is something particularly exhausting about cleaning guest rooms. Isabel can't put her finger on it. She likes menial tasks, likes the freedom to listen to podcasts or music while she does it, likes the mere act of helping Daphne run her guesthouse. But good god, the hair. There is so much hair. Isabel feels justified in her decision to leave school simply because never once did school teach her that human beings are in fact 90 percent hair.

And duvets! Duvets are an invention forged in the fires of hell, or at least in the home of some incredibly rich person who wanted cleanliness and comfort but never had to stuff six fluffy duvets into their covers in a single afternoon. All laws of physics seem to disappear inside that stupid piece of fabric; the duvets twist and turn and flop without ever finding the corners they're meant to be in.

Every now and then she gets caught in one of her mental spirals, but she has to admit that the disgust for human hair and her hatred of duvets have taken over a lot of her anguish since arriving at Daphne's. And annoyance is always preferable to dread.

But invariably when five or so comes around and Daphne reluctantly frees her, Isabel is furious. She considers leaving, considers making stipulations for how long she should be expected to work. She practices long, self-righteous speeches in her head every day, complaining to Daphne that she's sick of hearing that she's slow, saying she deserves some time off. But her bank account is diminishing, and even though there's still enough in there for a few more months of travel, she doesn't want to spend more than she already is. Plus, she has yet to find Earthquake Woman.

Her first free afternoon she went straight to the coffee shop to meet Shu-ling, the witness who was quoted in the article. Isabel sat at the counter and they communicated via a translation app for two hours, Shu-ling telling her everything she could remember, even a description of the rescuer. But the woman was a stranger, and no one got her contact information. It felt like a dead end, even though Shu-ling seemed excited about Isabel's goal to track the woman down.

Sam and Mathilde separately encouraged Isabel to keep going back to the coffee shop. Maybe the woman's daily routine takes her past the coffee shop, Mathilde said. She might even frequent it. Isabel also had the idea to check camera footage from stores nearby. Shu-ling went with her one afternoon, but other businesses either didn't have security cameras or weren't interested in obliging them. Eventually they designed a flyer together to post around.

So Isabel hangs up the flyers wherever she can. She goes to the coffee shop and faces the collapsed building, paying close attention to every passerby. She bikes around the city, getting to know it to the point she no longer needs her phone to make her way to

Dongdamen Night Market, and then back to Daphne's at night. She sends pictures of what she's eating to Sam, who invariably responds with a drooling emoji.

When Isabel returns, Daphne always seems a little disappointed that she has been out for several hours. Whether to be annoyed or touched by that, Isabel isn't too sure. She vacillates between the two. Sometimes Daphne and the other guests chat in Mandarin, and Isabel pretends to read a book while trying to catch words she recognizes. A few times, Isabel walks in on karaoke parties happening in the living room. On those occasions, she remembers the night in Tokyo and feels a swell of hope and longing that keeps her up too late, her brain whirring.

Her favorite nights are when Daphne is watching TV by herself and Isabel can join her on the couch. Sometimes they sit quietly together, saying nothing, as if they are family. It both causes homesickness in her and alleviates it, because that was exactly when she was at her most comfortable with her parents, in easy silences. They never saw eye to eye on many things, and whenever they tried to talk or bond, it inevitably led to her dad saying something infuriating or gross or just generally annoying. Her mom would tell her not to make a big deal of it, and tell her dad to change the topic. But when something innocuous was on TV that they could all laugh at, a world they could all get caught up in together, Isabel felt like she was part of a normal, loving family. It was easy in those story-occupied silences to forget.

Sometimes Daphne watches the news, and Isabel looks away

when there's footage of robberies, of another shooting in the U.S., of some racist politician in Europe firing people up.

Other times, Daphne turns the volume down on Taiwanese talk shows and they chat, Isabel forgetting the frustrations of the day and learning about Daphne's life, her time in Mexico, her daughter, who lives in another city with Daphne's ex. The routine continues. Isabel shakes out the duvets while staring at the green mountains outside the windows. She rides into town, more and more comfortable with the motorbikes zooming around, the unpredictable traffic. She sits at the coffee shop and texts Chío and Sam if they're awake, Mathilde if they're not.

Two weeks into her time in Hualien, Isabel gets a message from Shu-ling. *He's here!*

Isabel stares at the message until her brain can fully process it, then remembers that "he" and "she" are the same word in Mandarin and most translation apps annoyingly default to the male. When she realizes that Shu-ling would only text her about one person in particular, she casts aside any tendencies toward shyness and asks Daphne if she can take the rest of the afternoon off. When Daphne says yes, Isabel practically runs straight to the bike she's come to think of as her own and starts to pedal madly toward the coffee shop.

Please be there, she thinks the whole furious ride into town. *Please be there.* She doesn't wonder whether the woman will want to talk to her, or whether or not she's a Super. It's a funny thing how wanting something so big can make you latch on to the tiniest of hopes, each pebble a stepping stone.

Though she wants to leave the bike in the street and sprint into the coffee shop, Isabel hops off calmly, even taking a long drink of water from her bottle after she locks up the bike. A reflection in a nearby window shows her she's sweaty and flushed, and it would be a shame to finally meet a Super only to scare her off by being Too Much.

Once she's composed herself, she pulls open the door to the coffee shop. Inside, the air is slightly cool from the shaded windows. There isn't that blast of AC common in the States, and though right now it would probably feel really good, she's learned she generally prefers being without it. The coffee shop cat she's come to know so well, who the baristas call Mao, is playing with a customer's dangling shoelaces.

Isabel sees Shu-ling behind the counter, working on a latte. She scans the crowd for Earthquake Woman, even though she doesn't have a strong sense of what to look for. Dark hair, medium build. *Please be here.* There are two middle-aged women in the spot where Isabel usually likes to sit, facing the site of the collapsed building. They're chatting quietly, their voices not carrying at all despite the subdued environment. The guy whose shoelaces Mao's playing with is on his own, scribbling notes as he reads from a thick textbook. A group of three high-school-age girls are in the corner, laughing about something. Isabel feels a pang of longing for her friends, but brushes it aside, more pressing things on her mind.

As she approaches the counter, she takes one last look around the room, her heart sinking. Shu-ling finishes her latte and calls out a customer's name, or perhaps their order, and then spots Isabel. She smiles and says hi, and before Isabel can say anything, she gestures with her head toward the two middle-aged women at the window.

Isabel does a double take, which is not subtle at all and makes Shu-ling laugh and give her a light smack on the arm. She says something to Isabel, then types into her phone. *You do not stare! He speaks English and is okay talking if you are not a journalist.* Isabel's heart starts racing. She wants to leap across the counter and hug Shu-ling. Instead, she just beams a stupid smile at her and stands there bouncing on her feet until Shu-ling says in English, "Coffee?"

Mug unsteadily in hand, Isabel approaches the women. She racks her brain for the right way to say "Excuse me," but before she can, the women notice her awkwardly standing there. The one on the left, wearing glasses and a great peach-colored dress, looks confused. Then the other woman, in slacks and a flowing linen shirt, smiles. "Isabel?" she asks. Isabel nods, and the woman says something in Mandarin to her friend, who rises and leaves.

"Oh, she didn't have to . . . ," Isabel says weakly.

"It's okay," the woman says, her English carrying a hint of a British accent. "My friend needed to go anyway. Please, sit down."

"Thanks." Isabel is sweating again, and she nearly spills her entire mug as she sets it down on the counter and takes a seat on the stool next to Earthquake Woman. She wants to stare at her face, dive right in. But all her excitement notwithstanding, the adherence to societal norms is stubborn, and she does not allow herself to come right out and ask if the woman has superpowers.

"Shu-ling said you wanted to talk to me," the woman prompts.

Isabel takes a breath, nervous and giddy. Over the last few days, she's been messaging Mathilde about how to have this conversation, counting on the fact that Mathilde is older, better at these things. But now that a Super might be in front of her, Isabel can't recall anything they'd talked about. It was hypothetical then, texts on a screen, easy to think of a set of questions as a strategy. This is a real person, flesh and blood, even if there might be more there. "I'd like to know what happened the day of the earthquake," she says. "How did you save those people?"

The woman smiles and turns to her latte, which is nearly gone. She picks up the spoon resting on the saucer, then puts it back down. "Anyone would have done the same thing," the woman says. Now she drinks from her mug, tilting it back so she gets to the dregs.

Isabel, sensing the woman's reticence, afraid that she might scamper away like a frightened cat, tries a new approach. "I feel so rude, I didn't even ask you your name!"

"Yin," she says. For the next ten minutes, Isabel treats the conversation like she's talking to Chío's parents, maybe, not someone who necessarily deserves fascination but an adult who is generally more interesting than most. She asks Yin about how long she's lived in Hualien, what she does for a living, easing them toward the conversation she really wants to have. Yin's originally from

Kenting, in the south, but moved to Hong Kong for university and stayed through her early twenties. She's lived in Hualien for over twenty years now, working as an engineer for the city.

Yin even asks Isabel a few questions, as if they are just old friends catching up. "You are smart to travel when you are young," Yin says. "Many people say they will travel later, they think it will happen in the future, but they never actually make the plans. Then they grow old and they haven't seen the world, and it's too late to go. The money and the time you thought would come and make it all easier never materialized."

Isabel smiles. She's not sure if she's heard an adult compliment her so sincerely yet, without any caveats. That gets her thinking about the whole point of her travels, though, and it seems as if Yin senses that Isabel is about to redirect the conversation again. "I will tell you anything you want about that day," Yin says, "but I want you to promise not to share anything about me. There's a reason I didn't talk to the news. I don't want the attention. I like my privacy. So, I want your word that I will not find this story on a news site, or a blog, or as a viral story on social media. I do not want more people coming to find me."

Isabel hesitates for a moment, thinking of the forum. She shouldn't care about withholding from a bunch of strangers online. But they've been a refuge and a balm for her soul for years now, and she would feel terrible if she has come across an actual Super and cannot confirm it to them. Still, she figures that she can confirm Yin's existence and powers without giving her away.

Mathilde and the rest of the people on the forum already assume that Supers want privacy, and Yin's caveat makes Isabel feel that she is about to confess. "I promise you I won't."

And so Yin tells her what happened that day.

She didn't notice the earthquake right away. She'd just had lunch at a nearby lu rou fan restaurant and was headed back to the office. She'd been preoccupied, focused on a problem she'd had at work with a colleague. She'd been crafting an email in her mind when she finally felt the ground swaying. At first, she'd thought it was a truck passing by, but a moment later she heard glass breaking, and she saw clouds of dust from falling debris. Then she heard the horrifying sound of the building she was next to rocking into the adjacent one. There was a terrible creaking and groaning.

Her first instinct was to run toward the building and help people evacuate, since no one was streaming out. She hoped that this was because it was the middle of the day, and few people were home. Yin wanted to go inside, especially for any elderly people who might need assistance. But the groaning was getting louder and there was more debris falling, so with her arms covering her head she ran toward the middle of the street, to safety.

A few onlookers who'd come out from neighboring stores screamed. Someone yelled "Run!" and everyone in the vicinity did just that. Yin, however, had her eye on the building. Since she had studied structural engineering and had even taken a seminar on earthquakes' effects on tall structures, she had a suspicion that it was about to pancake and that she was a safe enough distance away. None of the other buildings nearby seemed like they were going to fall. So, she stuck around, taking in a sharp gasp of breath when it finally gave out, like a giant crumpling.

Isabel is captivated, unable to fathom what it would have been like to witness something like that. She knew from the article that one person had died in the collapse, but she can't imagine what it would feel like not knowing that at the time, to see all that steel and brick on the ground and envision how many people were trapped inside. In the back of her mind, Isabel waits for the other shoe to drop. For Yin to casually mention she's always had incredible strength. Or maybe that she never knew she had this strength, and it was unlocked by the fear and desire to help.

"By then, the shaking had stopped," Yin continues. "I waited for a few moments, in case there was going to be any more danger. I could hear people crying and screaming, some from the rubble, some I didn't know from where. Other streets. The whole city, it seemed. Though I didn't know at the time that it was the only building in the area that had come down."

"What did you do next?"

Yin picks up her mug again, even though they both know it's empty. Isabel notices her hand is shaking slightly, and she feels bad having her relive the trauma she must have experienced. Super or not. "I ran toward it. The ground floor was completely gone, the lobby destroyed. That happens when buildings have lobbies. A big empty space on the bottom makes a structure lack stability.

"The first person I saw was already trying to crawl through a window. I reached in and pulled him out, thinking that at any moment what was left of the building could crumple even more and kill us both." Yin's voice catches, and she pauses, looking down at the counter. Isabel is surprised by the emotion, though she's not sure why. She has asked this woman to recount that horrible day, and Yin is doing just that in detail. She wants to tell her that it's okay, that she doesn't have to go on. But this is it. This is what she's been wanting to hear for years. What Yin says next could make Isabel feel like the world has always been a little better than it's shown itself to be. It has always contained people like Yin, willing to risk themselves to save others.

After a few moments, Yin looks up and smiles, then goes on. The first man she rescued without much help. She brought him to the opposite side of the street, where Shu-ling met him with the first aid kit from the coffee shop. Yin ran right back to the building after that, calling in through spaces in the rubble. They might have been windows moments before, it was hard to tell. She could hear a woman calling out, "My children! Please, I have my children with me."

Yin managed to locate where the cries were coming from. She had to climb over concrete slabs toward the woman's voice. Somewhere nearby it sounded like there was water running. Yin hoped it wasn't fuel of some sort, hoped there wasn't a gas leak anywhere. After a few endless seconds of searching, she saw a hand poking out between piles of brick and pipe. At first, Yin started lifting broken bricks and tossing them to the side. But those had just been on top of larger slabs, which she had to move on to next.

"How'd you find the strength to lift the slabs?" Isabel asks.

Yin furrows her brow. "No person could do that. I found a metal pipe, a piece of rebar, I think. I slid it into the space and was able to use leverage to raise the slab enough so that the woman could lift her children through. Eventually she was able to climb out too. She hurt herself quite a bit. But she was out."

Isabel blinks, processing what Yin is explaining, trying to picture it. "How about the other people? You rescued more, right?"

"Yes," Yin says, like it's no big deal. The funny thing is, it's feeling to Isabel like it *isn't* a big deal. "It's a very helpful trick, leverage. Luck too. When disasters arrive, nothing is better to have on your side than luck. One man was saved because he was changing his mattress. It created a space between him and the ceiling."

Yin goes through the details of the other rescues, because she assumes that it's what Isabel wants to hear. But there are so many terms that Isabel's missing, and she starts to tune out. She feels cheated somehow. She feels like an idiot.

Just in case, she dares to say the words out loud. "You're saying you were able to save all those people because of . . ."

"Engineering," Yin confirms, with an oblivious smile. "It was just engineering."

10

Mazunte, Mexico

What do you do when you're waiting to see if a dead body is your friend?

Perhaps you sit in denial. Perhaps you are frozen in place, unable to process.

Chío needs to act, and though she tells Sam he's free to go to the beach, he insists on coming with her. She tries to gain comfort from his easygoingness, the way he doesn't seem to worry. Instead, it bugs her, creates a stone of resentment in her stomach.

They go to the business center at Chío's hotel and print out copies of a recent selfie Isabel had sent them. She was in Peru, going on incredible hikes while Chío was waiting anxiously for college acceptance letters. Chío crops the photo so that Isabel's cute hiking guide isn't in it, just her smiling face. In the background there's a glacial lake and the impressive, dramatic peaks of the Andes. As the printer whirs, Chío finds herself thinking that, at least, Izzy saw the world. If she's dead, at least she saw more of the world than most ever get to.

Pissed at herself for the thought, Chío leads her family and Sam around town, dropping pictures at every business possible, Chío's phone number scrawled on the bottom. When they run out of places to go, Santi, sensing his daughter's dissatisfaction, rents a car to make the hour-long drive to Puerto Escondido. Liz and Fran are offered the chance to stay behind and hang out at the pool, but they opt to come, and Chío's heart melts a little when they insist on accompanying them.

Puerto Escondido is a significantly larger city, with more places to hand out copies of Isabel's smiling face and tape them onto lampposts. They park the car and go into businesses, exhaust themselves, get back in the car and do it all again in another part of town.

Chío is keenly aware of her father's phone, its silence meaning the local authorities aren't reaching out. They have a quiet lunch on a hill overlooking the beach. The waves are pounding down on the shore, a steady, echoing drumbeat that underscores the meal. Sam gets a whole fried fish, and Chío can't stomach seeing its slack-jawed smile, the eyes staring vacantly ahead. She takes two bites from her tostada but it turns dry in her mouth before she can swallow.

She looks out at the water, pictures the scene of the body being pulled from the water the night before. Of course, she has no idea what it was like—the imagery is stolen from movies, making it that much worse. Isabel, pale and bloated, dead-eyed.

Forcing the thought away, she remembers the phone call

when Isabel was leaving Taiwan. Chío had expected to give Isabel another pep talk, to have to remind her—subtly—that there was more to gain from her travels than meeting superheroes. But Isabel was in great spirits, to the point that Chío had to wonder if she was faking. Chío worried about Isabel not because she was traveling, but because she'd always had a sense that her best friend often hid her actual mental state.

Chío knew that during the pandemic Isabel had been somewhat depressed. So had everyone else. Chío herself had started seeing her therapist that year. It had never felt like anything but situational, anything but annoyance at the same revelations they were all coming to terms with: that humans cared for each other a lot less than they should. For Chío, it had felt hopeless because she built her life around scientific reasoning, but what use was that if people thought science was something that could or could not be believed in? After things had gotten better, so had Chío, despite what she had learned. Isabel was still moody sometimes, but it had seemed to pass for her the same way.

"Of course I'm a little bummed," Isabel said during that phone call when she was leaving Taiwan. At that point Chío could recognize what Isabel was doing based on the background noise that came through her phone. Loud, echoing voices, the occasional bark of laughter, hip music. A hostel lobby, probably. "But there's a reason I'm doing this as a long-term thing. I'm not going to give up right away. I'm not going to think that just because one person turns out to not be a Super, no one is going to be."

Chío remembers swallowing a scream at that. "That's a good way to look at it. The woman does sound incredible, though. She saved eight people's lives."

"She is. That's why I don't feel so bad." There was a slight pause, and Chío had wanted to dig in, to make Isabel elaborate on that point, not for Chío's sake, but for her own. So she could understand. But Isabel had closed it too quickly. "Did I show you a picture of the dog I'm going to be sitting for?"

"No."

"Oh god, he's adorable. Here, I'll send you one now."

For the next month and a half, Chío's phone was flooded with various pictures from Isabel's dog-sitting ventures in Hanoi and Bangkok and Seoul. She pulls out her phone now and scrolls through to find them, trying to remember the various Supers that Izzy was chasing at the time, but it's hard to focus. They're not in her own photo roll, so she goes to the messaging app to check the history. Then she sees that her last texts to Isabel, which had been growing increasingly frantic and pleading, now have two little check marks next to them. Isabel's phone last logged on to the app forty-five minutes ago.

Chío calls a dozen times, but there's no response. Still, the drive back to Mazunte feels hopeful. Sam cracks a joke about how Isabel is likely to have gone to some great eco-hostel nestled in the

Oaxacan mountains with no signal whatsoever and is still in bed. Chío finds it within herself to laugh, to complain about Isabel's well-established ability to forget time.

Sam seems to sense Chío relaxing, and his voice gets louder as a result. He's eager to laugh too, and finally does when he meets her eyes. There's still an inkling of discomfort in Chío's stomach, but it's easier to ignore it now, to convince herself that tragedy, common though it may be, is not the reason for every silence. There are dozens of other plausible explanations. The speech she wanted to deliver to Izzy is still there in her mind, but muted for now.

They call the police station again and are told to try back at six, that the body is still being examined. So, with a couple of hours to go and her worrying appeased by a day of action and the slight development of the two check marks, Chío wades into the water with Sam.

She floats on her back, appreciating the warmth of the sun on her face for the first time since Isabel failed to show. It was a long winter without Isabel, a long winter spent studying, applying to schools, to scholarships.

She senses Sam's eyes on her before he speaks. "You're really gonna miss your family next year, huh?"

She opens one eye, squinting it against the sun. It's an unexpected question. "Why do you say that?"

"Because I'm gonna miss them, and I'm not even going that far," he laughs. Sam had applied early decision to the University of

Michigan, and will be in Ann Arbor in the fall. Chío does not know yet where she's going, but it'll be at least four hours away, the farthest she'll have ever been from them. "They just seem like they're there for you. And I'm guessing it'll be hard not to have that."

Sam looks away from her as he says this, eyeing the shore. Only now does it occur to Chío how little she's seen him throughout the year. Chío has spent more time with her family, but who has Sam been hanging out with? He has the basketball team, but they're not exactly his favorite people on the planet.

"Really, you're gonna miss my family?"

"Way more than I'll miss you," Sam deadpans. Chío splashes him, and he dives under to avoid it. Chío feels his arms pushing water toward her, a finger grazing her side. She feels herself flush at the contact.

When he resurfaces, the sun hits his eyes and makes them shine golden brown, and she remembers how Isabel would sometimes look at him, not that she ever said anything about it. Chío suddenly gets it, in a way she hadn't before. Their eyes meet, and again Chío flushes. She hopes she's sunburnt enough to hide it. Sam looks ready to splash her back, but stops short when Chío looks away. All of a sudden, she wants him to keep going, longs for stupid silly splashing that might lead to more accidental grazes.

She looks over at the shore, wanting Isabel to be there, reading, looking through her phone. Maybe that will be the case, soon. Maybe she's calling Chío back now.

"I have a question, and I want you to be a hundred percent honest," Chío says.

"Sure."

"You never really believed her, did you?"

He doesn't answer for a moment, just bobs there, though Chío is on her tiptoes—so obviously he can easily stand. "Which part?"

"Any of it. The reason for leaving, the superheroes, the close calls. I know you were *trying* to believe her. That you wanted to. I did too, even though it was really hard to. I know you joined the forum and everything, that you were trying to be there with her as much as you could. Because you're a sweet guy and a great friend. But you never really believed. Right?"

A swell of water lifts them. Chío's stomach roils with the sensation. Then she remembers being a kid, loving that feeling. How it felt like floating. When does that happen? That shift in feeling? When does leaving the ground stop feeling like the ability to fly, and become instead a loss of control?

Then she's back on the ocean floor, watching Sam wrestle with his thoughts. He looks so conflicted that Chío starts to wonder how he's going to answer. Up until then, even though she's been dying to ask him, she was sure she knew what his response would be.

Before he can, though, they hear a call from the beach. It takes a while to recognize her dad's voice, which makes Chío fear that they've gone too far out. Then she realizes he has a phone in his hand. Even before he waves them over, Chío's swimming in. She says "Let's go" almost as an afterthought, her mouth half-full of salt water.

When they reach the shore, her dad announces that he got a

call from Officer Badía, whom he had spoken to earlier at the police station. He told them to come in so he could show them some pictures of the body.

All of the lightness that the last few hours have provided flitters away. "Okay," she says, trying to mentally prepare. She dries off quickly and gathers her stuff. But when she picks up her bag, she feels her phone buzzing. She doesn't want to hope only to be disappointed. But telling the heart not to hope is just as effective as telling it not to be disappointed.

Isabel's name fills Chío's screen. It's a picture of the two of them from last year, before Isabel announced her trip. They've each got sprinkle-covered pistachio cones from Roys's. Chío wants to burst into happy tears as she answers.

"Jesus, Izzy, where have you been? Are you okay?"

Sam and her dad watch with wide eyes, smiles beaming.

They wait. But Isabel says nothing. There isn't even a sound before the phone goes dead.

11

El Nido, Philippines

Isabel marches down the hill from her hostel with one goal in mind: she will finally learn to ride a motorbike.

She never took Daphne up on her offer to teach her, too comfortable using the bicycle she'd come to think of as her own. Then there was her pet-sit in Saigon. The people she was sitting for—a Canadian couple who were traveling back home to Ontario for a month—had a motorbike that they said she could use, but Saigon was not a city to learn how to ride a motorbike in. It was a city for experts.

The closest she had come was splurging on a motorbike tour of the city. She had gripped the handles on the back of the seat so hard her knuckles had been sore the rest of the day. It had been thrilling, whizzing in and out of traffic, at times feeling like her knees were about to knock into cars, into light posts, into the many impressive items the other motorbikes could carry while nonchalantly cruising past her.

Now in her third month of bouncing around Asia, she feels it's time. She has some spare funds since she started tutoring kids in English online, and the two-lane highway that winds around this corner of Palawan feels like a great place to learn. Plus, if anything goes wrong, there is always the chance that she will be rescued by Ang Makahinga, the latest Super she's come to chase.

Isabel hasn't gone exclusively to places where Supers are rumored to exist. Yes, everywhere she goes she keeps her eye on people around her, as if at any moment they might accidentally reveal their powers by shooting lightning out of their fingers. But she allowed herself a few weeks of simple, random travel, trying not to focus only on Supers. A week on Langkawi Island in Malaysia, taking a scuba diving course, paid for by her cool aunt and uncle as a belated birthday present. Three days of eating in Singapore, just walking from one meal to the next, letting Sam and Chío pick what she would eat by sending them pictures of the stands at hawker centers.

Other than that, though, Isabel has remained committed to her goal. At times, she'd admit, she has felt desperate in the pursuit. Desperate to find one of the people that the forum talks about. Desperate to randomly bump into someone who can turn invisible or fly, or stretch their arms clear across the room, anything out of this world. Chío's voice, whether the real one or the one in her head, still chimes in to point out how unreasonable this all is.

This hike down the hill isn't that, though. This is learning how to ride a motorbike, which is entirely reasonable. After she signs a waiver, there's a minor mishap when, overconfident, she runs the motorbike straight into a hut by the side of the narrow road along the beach. The guy in charge calmly picks the motorbike up and rides it for her up the hill, then watches her practice a few times along the empty highway. Despite the earlier snafu, he gives a little nod and then lets her be.

Isabel rides a full loop, almost thirty miles, around the 490 highway or road or whatever it is, starting out from the town of El Nido to this corner of Palawan. She stops wherever she pleases, relishing the freedom. A hike in the woods to get to some waterfalls. Lunch at Duli Beach, a delightful tamarind soup called sinigang. She looks at people the way she's used to now, searching for Ang Makahinga's wrinkled face.

This time the image shared on the forum is not a blurred still from a cell phone camera or CCTV footage, but a well-lit portrait. There are various conflicting stories about who she is and what her powers are. One guy on the forum claims to have been rescued by her after a car accident, saying she was an old woman who breathed life back into him. Someone else linked to a story about a German scuba instructor who got the bends and was running low on oxygen when a mermaid-type creature pulled her oxygen mask off and helped her breathe. Others dispute these claims, saying they're ripped off from a manga series. Isabel has found herself not caring about the background work anymore, the theories of who or how these Supers came to be. She cares only about finding one. She imagines that the relief she will feel when she does will be a little like putting down her backpack after carrying it around all day, but with her soul.

Isabel returns the motorbike, triumphant. She doesn't ride it down the hill, but she still feels like she's succeeded in something. She has loved her travels, no doubt about it. There have been dark moments, to be sure. Her inability to find a Super has led to more and more spiraling as of late. Her belief that the world is more bad than good has not dissipated in the slightest. If anything, it's been further cemented. But for now, it is nice to feel like she has won something, that she has met a goal.

She returns to her hostel, excited for a dinner of pork sisig and rice. Marco in the kitchen makes the best she's had in all of the Philippines. She will eat and read a book on her tablet (a rom-com, to help the world feel brighter) and listen to the thunderstorms rolling in until it's time for bed. When she walks past the restaurant/bar area, she sees a trio of young guys at her favorite table, drinking San Miguel beers and playing cards. New guests who must have checked in while she was gone.

She waves to Marco and to Randy, who's working the desk and acting as server, then goes off to the employee cabin to shower and get changed. She grabs her tablet from her bunk bed and heads to the dining area, taking a seat a couple of tables away from the new guests. One of them smiles at her, and she gets a flicker of recognition. Probably someone she noticed at the beach earlier.

They're British, a little too loud. Isabel does the thing she's perfected in the last few months of generally lonely traveling: she holds up her tablet so that she can inconspicuously stare over the rim. A few times, one of them—the one with the sleepy eyes—catches her in the act and offers a smile.

It's only when Randy brings out her sisig and the short Brit asks her what she's eating that she realizes why he seems familiar. This was the trio she saw at the Tokyo capsule hostel arguing because they hadn't realized what the sleeping arrangement was. His name comes to her moments before he introduces himself as Gareth. She is both impressed with herself and completely creeped out by her own brain.

"Would you like to join us?" he asks, suggesting no one wants to eat alone. Isabel disagrees with that principle. She has always loved eating alone. It used to be her preferred time to be alone. But over the course of her travels, those words have come to hold some mystical meaning for her. She is constantly longing for people to say the words, to invite her into their lives, if only for a meal, a night.

Every time someone says "Care to join us?" an instant friendship forms. Her favorite nights throughout her travels have started with those innocuous words, often spoken precisely as casually as Gareth just has.

"Sure," Isabel responds, trying to be cool about it. She grabs her plate and her water bottle as Gareth stands to slide her chair over, next to him.

Gareth waves Randy over and orders another round of beers,

including one for Isabel. He also orders himself the sisig, though his buddies pick what every hostel offers for frustratingly unenthusiastic eaters: a burger, fries, a pizza.

"All right, then, lads," the loud one with glasses says. "Now that we've got a newcomer, let's get a different game going, shall we?"

"He's only saying that 'cause he's getting killed," Gareth says.

"Nah, mate. I was playing possum, that's all. You know how I like the comeback. This is just about being welcoming."

"Well, I hope you're ready to welcome a new ass-beating," the third Brit, Carl, says. "What are we playing?"

"How about a little twenty-one?" the loud one says. John, maybe? Something unimaginative, Isabel's pretty sure.

"Shit, if we're doing that, we'll need more beers." Gareth turns to Isabel. "No pressure, but it is a drinking game."

"I haven't hung out with many Brits, so correct me if I'm wrong, but pressure during drinking games is kind of *your thing.*"

"Our reputation precedes us," Carl says, with a touch of both pride and shame.

"No need to join us in drinking, but if you do, beers are on us."

"Oi!" John shouts. "You can buy beers for whoever you want, but don't offer my money away."

"I'll have one," Isabel says, laughing. "And I have no idea how to play, but I will do everything in my power to make sure you lose," she jokes, pointing at John.

"That's what I'm talking about!" John shouts again, which seems to be his baseline volume. He smacks the table and finishes off his beer. Gareth and Carl, meanwhile, gather the playing cards into a pile and set them aside. Isabel finally digs into the sisig while they explain the game.

She suppresses a bit of a moan. One thing she's learned during her travels is that, for all the complaints about globalization being too far-reaching, every country still holds treasures that the rest of the world hasn't woken up to. And Isabel has most often stumbled on the culinary kind. It has caused in her a deep longing for everything that's out of her reach because she is simply a traveler, a tourist. Everything inaccessible to her because of her lack of knowledge of the language, of the larger cultural landscape in wherever she happens to be that week, not to mention the cultural nuances that one can only understand after years of living them, or at least studying them.

"All right, everyone has their drinks ready, then," John says when the new round of beers arrives, along with Carl's pizza and his burger and fries. "Let's start the madness."

The game is simple, almost childishly so. You try to count to twenty-one as a group, but there are rules to remember for a few numbers to start. Instead of saying "seven," you all raise your glasses in cheers. You have to switch the order of ten and eleven. And if you make it to twenty-one, a new rule is added to a number. Every time you mess up, you drink. It's a communal game, which Isabel prefers, despite her earlier trash-talking.

After an hour, the boys have pounded several beers and are even louder. To their credit, they haven't pushed Isabel to keep up, and she is enjoying the pleasant buzz of her second beer, the boys' company. They remind her of Sam. Not that they are like

Sam, but they each have some of his characteristics. Carl is funny like him, and Gareth is thoughtful, at one time noticing her water bottle was empty and wordlessly going to refill it from the big jug by the bar. Though John's hair is darker, his curls are similar to Sam's, and his general build is too, tall and long-limbed. His fingers are short and stubby and show signs of basketball-caused jams, the knuckles swollen and bumpy, just like Sam's.

The game loses steam and they fall into conversation, the once-quiet lightning in the distance now accompanied by rolling thunder. The boys are on a gap year, and the four of them compare where they've been. Isabel quickly gathers that they are vastly different travelers from her. Even setting aside the obvious difference that they are not looking for superpowered humans while they travel. They seem to have chosen their destinations along a well-worn path. Which Isabel doesn't necessarily see as an indictment. Angkor Wat and Ha Long Bay are famous for a reason, true wonders that the rest of the world has recognized as worthy of seeing. That being said, the boys treat their Lonely Planet guidebooks less like recommendations and more like bibles. Also, though they are traveling on a budget, Isabel gets the sense that they can easily ask for more money from their parents. They're even going back home for Christmas before continuing on for another six months.

"I'm hoping for some of that sweet Christmas gift money," Carl says. "Forget the socks this year, Granny, y'know? I haven't worn socks in months." He lifts his sandaled foot as evidence.

"What about you?" Gareth asks Isabel. "Any plans for Christmas?"

Sam and Chío have asked her this too in the last week, to say nothing of her parents. Her mom even cried a little during their call a few days ago, which might be the first time Isabel has ever witnessed Dorah Wolfe crying over something that wasn't the happy pinnacle in a rom-com. She's usually the kind to get stoic when emotional, something Isabel inherited. "No chance, then?" her mom asked, her voice breaking.

Isabel might have considered it if they offered to pay for her flight, but her dad stayed silent throughout the call, somehow managing to be passive-aggressive without saying a word. She could feel his judgment in the silence, that she would dare choose anywhere else but the place they had chosen for her.

"I'm visiting a friend in Jakarta," she says to Gareth. She hopes they don't dig too much into her friendship with Mathilde, not wanting to get into it. . . .

"Sick," John says.

Thank god for men's inability to ask questions.

"I think I might go to bed," Isabel says. "Have to get up early to teach English to kids in China."

"You're working?" Gareth asks.

"Tutoring and behind the bar." She gestures with her head to where Randy sits on a stool, scrolling through his phone.

"Damn. We've never had a job between the lot of us, and she's working two while on holiday," Carl laughs.

John and Isabel join in, but Gareth watches her with eyebrows raised. "That's impressive."

Isabel shrugs. "Just trying to extend my ability to travel as long as possible," she says. "I had a nice amount saved up, but apparently if you don't replenish money, it just kind of disappears."

Later she lies in bed, hearing their voices carrying from the dining room. She wonders if they're talking about her, wonders if they'll hang out again. No matter how quickly these friendships seem to happen, they can just as easily dissipate. Someone she'll have shared beers and a night with will simply nod at her in the morning and continue on their way. Especially if they're already traveling in a self-sufficient group.

Taking advantage of having the room alone, Isabel thinks about Gareth and touches herself, thoughts of Sam involuntarily flitting in with the fantasy. She fades away to sleep, but wakes to the sound of a downpour. The storm has arrived, and it is right on top of her. And despite her thoughts about the cabin going up in flames because of lightning (she knows it won't), or that a mudslide will carry her down to the shore (the hostel is at the top of a fairly rocky hill, so it seems unlikely), what keeps her up at night is the opposite thought. That she is safe, though others are not. That the unbalanced ways of the world mean that money and luck protect her, while others are at risk simply because they have been born in different circumstances. For the first time since she started traveling, she allows herself the thought that she usually suppresses at all costs: this superhero theory is bullshit. They are not real. She is just a desperate, sad person trying to not fall fully into despair. Traveling under the guise of a fantasy will not change the ways of the world.

It takes her hours to fall asleep again, the rain hammering down on the corrugated roof above her, lightning flashing every ten seconds or so. She has to replay her day—triumphing over the motorbike, the pleasant time with Gareth and "the lads"—in her head to remind herself that good things can happen.

12

Mazunte, Mexico

Chío is still dripping wet when they arrive at the police station. Sam's got a hotel towel wrapped around his waist; as they enter the building, he puts on his shirt, which has been slung over his shoulder.

The energy is different this time, and Chío can't quite put her finger on what it is. It seems louder, there are more people talking at once. It's what Chío would expect from a police station on TV, not the quiet, sad place it was that morning. They stand by the door for a second, waiting for someone to call them over. A uniformed officer speaking into a cell phone hurries past them, saying "Permiso" as he goes.

Chío recognizes Officer Badía, tall with an ill-fitting suit and gelled hair. He's in the office visible through the window in the waiting room, talking animatedly to a man and a woman who have an authoritative air about them. Sam and Chío sit near the door as Santi goes to get the cop's attention.

It's just a precaution, Chío reminds herself. Isabel is very likely alive. She didn't answer the phone when Chío called back, nor did more check marks appear on recent texts Chío sent. But she called. She's alive.

"It's busy," Sam comments. His voice is quiet, no longer joyous the way it was earlier. Even if he is by nature more optimistic than Chío, it's hard to be exuberant when you're about to see pictures of a dead body.

Santi's standing at the window, getting ignored. Sam's leg is jittering nervously and Chío puts a hand on his knee to get him to stop. He smiles at her. "Sorry."

Then there's some muffled shouting coming from the other room. Chío can't catch most of it, but she does hear the word "incompetentes" getting yelled, after which the official-looking people storm out, slamming the door behind them. They both are looking down at phones as they pass by Sam and Chío on their way outside. Sam raises his eyebrows at Chío and she shrugs, not sure what that was all about.

Fifteen minutes later—though it feels much longer than that—Badía sends for them. They're escorted to a tiny office in the back of the building. There are two plastic chairs across from a wooden desk, behind which there's a slightly nicer chair. There's no computer or nameplate, just a legal pad with a handful of scribbled-on pages flipped over, and a pen on top of the fresh one. The walls are bare and painted a not-light-enough yellow.

The three of them remain standing behind the chairs while

Badía awkwardly shuffles past them. He makes a false start to sit, then notices they're all still standing, so he does the same.

"Do you want to take a seat?" Badía asks in Spanish.

Chío sees the folder in his hands, focusing in on it to the point she barely hears what he says, wondering what it contains.

"No thanks," Santi says, responding in Spanish too. Sam will have to guess what's going on from context. Hopefully, he's gotten more from high school Spanish than most people. "The quicker this goes the better, I think."

"Yeah, well," Badía says, and he throws the folder down on the desk casually. Some papers slide out. Not photographs. Chío realizes she's filling in the blanks using movies and TV, never a good idea. She closes her eyes, trying to ground herself. "Unfortunately," Badía continues, "we can no longer show you the pictures."

This breaks Chío's determination. "What?"

"What'd he say?" Sam whispers.

"There's been a development. We can't show you the pictures at this time. But we'd like to talk to you about your friend." Now he sits down and grabs the pen off the legal pad.

"What do you mean?" Chío says, her voice on the verge of both breaking and screaming. "Please. Just let us see the pictures. That's why we came."

Badía offers a tight-lipped smile and taps the pen on the desk a couple of times. "I understand. But something's changed. I can't tell you the details because it's an ongoing investigation. What I can do is take down some information about your friend, try to see if she's been seen around."

"We already did that," Chío snaps.

Her dad puts a hand on her shoulder. "We just want some peace of mind," he tells Badía. "Her parents are concerned," he adds.

"I understand," Badía says. "Unfortunately, we don't have pictures."

"Then go take pictures!" Chío yells. "It's a dead body, how hard can it be?"

Now Sam puts a hand on her shoulder, but he looks confused by her outburst. Which is what calms Chío down, the fact that he's missing everything that's happening. "I don't think they have pictures," she tells Sam.

He furrows his brow. "Do they not have a camera or . . ."

Chío does an exaggerated gesture toward Sam to say "See?!" and turns back to Badía, hoping he got the gist. He heaves a sigh. "You'll understand if we can't reveal too much right now. But we don't have pictures. And we can't provide any, for the time being. We just need you to tell us about your friend. Last time she was seen, any distinctive tattoos or scars, most recent contact—that sort of thing."

Chío scoffs and goes to her phone, pulling up her chat exchange with Isabel and clicking on the profile picture. She tosses the phone to Badía. "Her. Is it her? Please."

Watching his face for any recognition, Chío holds her breath.

She does it purposefully, taking in a good lungful, so that it can help buoy her throughout the next ten seconds. If Isabel is dead, she will know, and this breath might help her survive it.

Badía exhales again. He takes the phone, but it's clear he's only doing it to placate Chío. His eyes barely pass over the screen before he slides it back. "You can send us that so we have it on file," he says, taking out a business card and handing it to her.

Chío reads the email address on it, flicking the edge with her nail. She'd thought to bring their makeshift flyers, so now she reaches into her bag and tosses them onto the desk. Her dad squeezes her shoulder again, and instead of calming her down, it brings everything to the surface. Her fear and her sadness, her anger and her confusion, an overwhelming cocktail of emotions that doesn't present as tears, as she would expect, but as a desire to flee. She storms out of the office, feeling ridiculous in her still-wet bathing suit, her damp T-shirt. Her dad calls after her, but Chío can't stand to be in that glorified closet a second longer.

Outside, she suddenly loses steam, not sure what to do. She wants to hit something, wants to run, wants to curl up and cry. Instead, she goes to her recent-calls list and clicks on Isabel's name again. And again, and again. There is no answer. Then she has the illogical notion that her desperation makes it less likely that Isabel will answer. That she must be calm for Isabel to be okay.

Sam joins her outside. He leans against the wall of the police station, squinting at her through the late-afternoon sun, apparently trying to both be there for her and give her space.

She paces, still unsure what to do with her body to make herself feel better. Eventually she crosses the road to a convenience store and buys herself a soda and a bag of chips. When she exits, Sam is there, sitting on the curb. She joins him, and as she does so, she gets an idea. She pulls out her phone, opening an internet browser.

Chío senses Sam's eyes over her shoulder, but instead of asking what she's doing, he says, "Did you ever wonder if it was the stuff at school that did it?"

"Did what?" Chío asks, only half listening. She's scrolling through Actually Super, looking for anything about a Super being spotted even remotely nearby. She looks for Isabel's username in the comments.

"Made her leave."

After a long pause to open the bag of chips and click on a thread of comments about a Super in Belize, Chío responds, "I feel like she would object to that phrasing." She offers the chips to Sam and snaps open the soda. "She had something she wanted to do. There could be a lot to unpack about why it's what she wanted to do, sure. Kids at school being racist made me want to stay at home too. It probably didn't help that she had a conspiracy theorist at home. But thinking that something 'made her leave' implies that staying was the only thing she should have ever done. And as much as I don't believe in superheroes or superpowered people or whatever we're calling them, I disagree with that premise."

Another handful of chips, another sip of soda. She scrolls

through the forum, not caring about the discussions, the blurry pictures. She just wants to see Isabel's name.

"I always felt like . . . ," Sam says, apparently not done with the topic. He runs a hand through his hair, then reaches for Chío's soda, a gesture so nonchalantly intimate that it hits her how much she's missed him this year. How close they were before Isabel left, how that hasn't kept up. She watches his lips as they pull away from the can.

"There was this night," he says. "It's silly. One of our movie nights, you know. I think you had some school thing to do, so you left early. We were high and the movie wasn't great, and she just looked so . . . sad. All of a sudden. And she put her head on my shoulder and I thought . . ." Chío finds she's holding her breath, looking now at the mix of sand and pebbles on the asphalt at her feet instead of at her phone.

"I thought that maybe she was in love with me." He chuckles at himself, shaking his head. Then he looks at Chío, searching for confirmation. When she doesn't offer any, he continues.

"It's conceited, I know. But we fell asleep, and I woke up with our hands holding and I left without talking about it. We never talked about it, but I've been afraid this whole time that rejecting her might have sent her running." He shakes his head again and neither one of them acknowledges the fact that their legs are touching. This has been such a weird day, such a strange trip. Chío feels for the first time in her life like she might be living in a dream, some sort of simulation.

"I know it's probably not true. That it doesn't even matter if it's true or not. Because, like you said, it's not necessarily true that something made her leave. But when I catch myself thinking it was because of one night where we fell asleep near each other, I start to think about what else it could have been. That there *was* a reason, you know? And I just don't know what it was, so I'm trying to fill in the blanks.

"Sometimes I think maybe it was her dad. You know the way he is. Or maybe it was kids at school chanting racist shit during the election. Sometimes I think about all the ways human beings are fragile. How our psyches can be broken in so many ways. Or maybe not broken, exactly. Just fissured. Forever altered."

Chío sits with everything Sam's said, unsure how to feel about it. Her phone is in one hand, the soda can in the other. Goddammit, if Isabel would just answer a phone call, if she were just here, this would all feel normal again. She puts down her phone and grabs some chips, and when she finishes chewing, instead of thinking of what to say, she feels a wave of exhaustion. She closes her eyes and rests her head on Sam's shoulder. "Izzy's not broken," she says finally.

"No, I know," he says quickly, but can't find it within himself to elaborate, and neither can Chío.

They stay like that until Santi appears suddenly. He waits for them to look up at him, at which point he scratches the back of his head and says, "So, uh, I got them to tell me what's going on. You know, why they can't show us pictures. And it turns out that the body's gone."

Chío looks at Sam to clock his reaction, thinking maybe she

misheard. But he looks just as perplexed. “What do you mean, it’s gone?” she asks her dad.

“It was there and then it wasn’t,” he says, sounding aptly and totally confused. “It was in the morgue awaiting an autopsy. And then either someone came in and carried it off, or it got up and walked away. There is no body.”

13

El Nido, Philippines

Isabel wakes up to her phone's alarm going off near dawn and begins her latest routine. She gets changed and brushes her teeth, then takes her computer to the picnic table in the only thatched-roof hut that has an outlet near it. She goes to the bar and asks Marco for a cup of coffee and a glass of milk. To save money, she keeps a box of cereal with her things. The humidity has seeped inside the box, but a budget will turn any palate optimistic.

She tutors for two hours, mostly kids from mainland China. They are adorable six- and seven-year-olds, at times admirably hardworking, at times infuriatingly reserved and silent. Isabel often ends the sessions feeling like she is in no way qualified to teach someone English but with the mad, lingering desire to try harder.

Not long before she's done, Gareth and the boys emerge from their room, hair mussed, hungover. Gareth gives her a little wave, and she returns it with a smile, glad to be acknowledged. The last twenty minutes of her class go by at a crawl, Isabel feeling restless to join them. When she logs off, she has to run to the bathroom, and by the time she comes back out to the communal area, there's no sign of them.

Suddenly facing the day feels like an ordeal. What is she going to do? Another beach? Another bout of thinking about Supers with nothing to show for it, no steps to take but to peruse dubious posts online?

Her first thought is to march back down the hill to rent a motorbike again, to try to coax Ang Makahinga or any other Super with her recklessness, to be in obvious need of rescuing. Then there's a tap at her shoulder, and it's Gareth and his dopey smile.

"Hey. I wanted a day off from the lads. Want to go into town or something?"

Into town they go on another rented motorbike. This time the guy hands her the key and just raises his eyebrows, as if to ask if she's done crashing. She laughs in response, a little thrilled to have the interaction in front of Gareth, and to be the one who knows how to ride. She's thrilled, too, at his legs against her sides. She wants him to wrap his arms around her stomach to hold on, but he uses the handles behind him instead.

"My mum would kill me if she knew I was doing this," Gareth says at a red light. "The one thing she said not to do in Asia was ride a bloody scooter."

Isabel knows in that moment that if he continues to not be a dick for the next hour or so, she'll tell him everything.

She's had fun, yes, met single-night friends here or there. And she's opened up too. Confessed her reasons to people like Sienne, spontaneously, because she feels like she can't contain it anymore. But the only intimacy she's had is over the phone with Sam and Chío, and to a growing extent with Mathilde. This feels like it could come close. A hunch, maybe, but one that feels too good to not pursue.

She thinks of Sam, how he always knows where she is, not to keep tabs on her but because he gets some vicarious joy from her travels. Because he cares. How he sends voice messages throughout the day whenever something makes him think of her. A part of her brain goes: *Why is that not enough?*

Then she revs the scooter's engine, finds her balance, and takes off down the road. There's the hum of the motor, the wind in her hair, the whine of the tires on the road. Her brain is quiet among all this. There are no thoughts of those days with her grandmother. Of her dad's inherited mutterings about the ills of the world, just like Grandma. Different content, maybe, but the same idea. Mimicked and exemplified by kids at school, politicians on TV, everyone on the internet.

None of that.

Instead, there is the warm, humid air. The trees and their oversized leaves, the hills, the background of turquoise waters when the road curves.

They park at a random small beach in town, but choose to walk around before going to the shore. Isabel prefers it this way, the lack of pressure that comes from staring ahead instead of at each other. How the clip-clop of their sandals on the pavement makes the pauses comfortable.

They grab a convenience store coffee and pandesal. Every tourist office they pass tries to hawk a trip around the islands, to "secret" swimming holes that paradoxically are ranked in a top-ten list on every travel website.

"Have you been?" Gareth asks, motioning toward one of the posters.

Isabel shakes her head. In her longing to not feel like a tourist, she has opted out of most of these excursions, especially when they come with a week's budget as the price tag.

"Oh, you've got to! The boys and I did one. Bit busy, sure, but bloody gorgeous. Worth it."

"I dunno, I've got a pretty tight budget."

"Let me pay. It'll be like a date, if that's all right. You can pay for my beers back at the hostel."

Isabel resists, but only because of the price, the thought of having him pay so much when he's traveling too. However, she likes the idea of being next to him all day, a little world of two among a larger group of travelers, instead of just herself, the intimacy of leaning in to say something to each other over the whir of a speedboat.

So she says yes, and the day progresses exactly as she'd like. The boat is loud at first and the other tourists fall into silence. Gareth's knee rests against hers until they slow down to wind away around little rocky islands. They jump out and snorkel for a bit, Isabel feeling free in the water, trying not to think about the bleached coral, which looks sad and muted. She focuses on the colorful schools of fish, focuses on Gareth swimming serenely beside her, focuses on how moving through the warm waters almost feels like flying.

Back on the boat, to the secret swimming hole that's full of other tourists. They're given an hour to eat lunch and laze around on a corner of the beach that's at least a little farther out from the others. They grab their paper plates of pancit and lumpia and lie out on their quick-dry towels like all the other long-term travelers.

Here it comes, Isabel feels. The desire to unload, to confess what feels like her whole existence. But she holds off. They talk, instead, about home and travel and food. They talk about what they miss and what they don't, talk about family, though on this point Isabel mostly listens, not wanting to bring hers into this little moment of paradisiacal calm.

She can feel that intimacy she'd wanted building, can feel Gareth's appreciation for her growing, like a home being built around her.

After a while the conversation slows, creating a window. Izzy approaches the subject like she would if it were a wounded animal on the ground. Carefully, as if it might bite, as if she's not doing it at all.

"If you could have any superpower, which would it be?"

"Oh, you've asked my favorite question of all time," Gareth says, his hair tickling her cheek.

"Really?" She turns to look at him. He's got a smudge of sunscreen on his nose that he's failed to rub in.

"I've spent so much time thinking about it that I'm a little embarrassed to go on."

"No, please. No judgments, promise."

Gareth sighs as if he doesn't believe her and thinks this is going to derail the course of the day, but he's too excited to do anything but forge ahead. Somewhere nearby, a boat engine hums to life. They both turn to make sure it's not theirs. "The thing about superpowers," Gareth starts, "is that we're all so bloody unimaginative when we think of them. We have these pop culture references we rely on again and again—invisibility, superstrength, flight—but that's all based on some shit only a handful of people wrote in the sixties or whatever. Our basic idea of what a superhero can do, Marvel blockbusters notwithstanding, hasn't really changed all that much."

"Like vampires," Isabel says, giddy and breathless and trying not to show it. He sounds like someone from the forum. "We still think crosses and garlic and daylight, but if a hypothetical immortal bat-being could exist, why the fuck would it be freaked out by Christianity or alliums? It would likely be nocturnal, sure, but it would wake up at sunset with a hankering for bugs."

"Exactly!" Gareth exclaims, the most animated he's been, including the drunken game of 21 the night before.

"So, you think superpowers are more creative than we give them credit for?"

"Be still my heart, you said 'are,' " Gareth says with his dopey smile. He continues before Isabel has time to blush at her slip-up. "But yes. Absolutely. More creative, more specific, more subtle. If there's one thing that watching *Planet Earth* has taught me, it's that everything in nature is more exciting and unbelievable than human beings have the imagination for."

"You're saying superpowers aren't the cause of freak accidents involving spiders or radioactive waste, but just part of nature?"

"This is where I lose people."

"No," Isabel says, simply, quickly. She's the one who's hooked him onto the topic and is afraid he'll flee if she moves too suddenly. Like the line she's cast will snap if she speaks too much or too slowly.

"You sure?"

Isabel nods her head, propping herself up on her elbow to watch him as he speaks.

He looks at her and bites his lip. "I think with all that we know about nature, genes and their mutations, bacteria and the diseases they cause, the way the body can heal itself or fight off diseases—on top of all we *don't* know about the universe—I think it's perfectly reasonable to think superpowers are possible in nature, maybe even likely."

Isabel doesn't know whether to hold her breath and wait to see if he's joking or exaggerating in some way, or if she should loosen her lips and unleash her own tirade.

"Shit," Gareth says. "I know that look."

"I doubt you're reading this look correctly."

"You think I'm crazy."

"I believe in superpowered humans," she blurts. "I have for years." She bites her lip, waiting for him to laugh, waiting for him to admit he was just speaking hypothetically.

"You're taking the piss."

"That is such a weird goddamn expression. But no. I'm not."

Gareth sits up, his knee at Isabel's hip. His eyes are on the water, his hands digging into the sand.

Then he meets her gaze and grins. "I know one," he says.

14

Mazunte, Mexico

One last glance. And it feels all right to stare this time, because it is no longer undoubtedly death we're looking at.

Plenty of conversations could be had about why we think it rude to stare at death, to gawk at it, at least in some cultures. What is it about death that makes us want to look away, other than the mirror it holds up, the ticking clock it reminds us of?

Death, just like our acceptance of it, comes in stages. First, everything stops, yes. But it doesn't last long. Enzymes are released, cell walls get dissolved. Then—now—life again. Bacteria and organisms and insects. Gases and smells. The body grows, stiffens, leaks. Movement, of a sort.

Not that any of this would be comforting to Sam and Chío, even if they knew it, even if they had the presence of mind to think about it in those terms. The body is gone, but so is Isabel.

At least now Sam understands why there was yelling going on inside the police station. It is the only thing he understands.

Chío's sitting on the couch in her parents' hotel room, staring at her phone. Sam's in a chair, his feet on an ottoman, trying not to stare at her. He's afraid if he looks away, she'll fall apart, but if she catches him staring, she might too. Outside, the ocean pounds down on the shore. Children giggle and shriek in glee. Music is swept into the room by the wind coming in from the open balcony door. Life, out there, going on.

He looks at the beach, somehow still feeling the urge to be there, despite everything else. Before Chío can catch him staring longingly at anything that resembles fun, he grabs his phone and does what she does. He searches it for clues. For some unturned stone from under which Isabel will come scurrying out.

But the internet doesn't even have that many plausible stones, much less ones he and Chío have yet to look beneath. Isabel hasn't been online or answered any phone calls. She hasn't posted anything to social media in months, and googling her leads only to other Isabels, an actress with her name, a novelist with almost her name.

Mazunte hasn't been in any English-language news sources in months, and the last one was a travel listicle about off-the-beaten-path beaches. He does find one article in Spanish about someone drowning, but it's two paragraphs long, and after he runs it through a translator, it doesn't seem to have much info he doesn't already know.

He gets a few texts in his group chat with his basketball team, mostly memes and the chatter that follows. This leads him to click over to his texts with Isabel. He goes through the group chat the three of them have together, in case he missed anything the last three times he's scrolled through. Then he clicks over to his solo messages with Isabel, which he hasn't looked at in a while.

It only takes a few scrolls upward for something to spark in his mind. He shoots Chío a look as he realizes it. "Holy shit," he says, immediately going back to his phone and scrolling quicker.

"What?" She only gives him half a second to respond before she says it again.

"I can't believe I didn't remember this before," he says. "Isabel shared her location with me. I don't know if it's still working, but I don't think she ever turned it off."

Chío bolts off the couch and is at his side in an instant. Her hair hangs down over his shoulder, and Sam can tell she wants to grab the phone out of his hands and search for herself and is just barely managing to restrain herself. "When?" she asks. He's glad she's not berating him for forgetting, glad she's eager but not irate. Though he's not surprised.

"When she was hiking in Peru. I was curious about her route, so she shared her location. It didn't work while she was in the mountains, but I remember it coming back on when she had Wi-Fi. Last time I checked it, she was in Lima."

"There!" she calls out the exact moment he spots it too.

He clicks, and they both take a sharp breath as they wait for it to load. Of course, *of course* the phone has to think for a second. It can't just tell them right away.

And there it is.

A blue dot on a map.

It doesn't seem to be by the water, so Sam pinches his fingers out across the screen to zoom out. There are too many streets for it to be nearby, he can tell already. He's looked at the map of Mazunte enough times over the last year to have it memorized. There's not much there to memorize.

"It's Mexico City," Chío says.

"She's still there," Sam half says, half asks, relief tugging at his lungs, wanting to let in all the air possible again.

"We don't know she is," Chío says.

"If it's between thinking she's there or she's a dead body who disappeared from a morgue, I'm gonna choose to believe she missed her flight."

And he knows. He knows how many objections Chío could have to this logic. He has them too. But she swallows them and exhales. "Okay," she says. Then she swings into action. She calls her parents and tells them to come back up to the room. Sam can see them down at the pool keeping Fran and Liz company. Santi hangs up the phone and says something to Aída, then they both stand up. They say something to Liz, who has barely looked away from her book for the last two days.

A few moments later they're upstairs and Chío lays out her plan. She and Sam are going to go to Mexico City and track Isabel down. One of her parents can come with them if they need to, she says. And though they don't seem thrilled about it, they know their daughter well enough to guess that they won't be able to refute the many reasons she'll come up with for why her plan needs to happen. They call Isabel's parents with the update and see if they'd like to meet them in the city, but their passports are expired, and they seem to refuse to believe that anything terrible has happened. Dorah's voice is strained, but she follows Abel's lead in thinking Isabel is merely being irresponsible. They just ask to be kept in the loop.

When Chío opens up her dad's tablet to start searching for flights for that evening, Sam has to clear his throat to slow her down. "Um, Chío, you know that . . ." He trails off, self-conscious about saying what he needs to in front of Santi and Aída. "Well, I don't have a ton of money left. I want to be there with you, of course. But I don't know if I can pay for a flight, a hotel, and food and stuff in the city."

Chío doesn't even have to shoot her parents a look before she returns to the screen. Aída smiles at him and nods. "Don't you remember?" Chío says. "You are Chío Guzmán-Stein too."

They barely make it onto a six p.m. flight out of Huatulco. The whole drive there, Chío stares at Sam's phone, watching the blue dot as if it will disappear if she loses sight of it, even though she's already taken screenshots, already saved the location onto her own phone. During the brief flight, she hangs on to it despite its uselessness, falling asleep with her head resting against the window, jolting awake when she thinks she feels it buzz in her hand.

When they land, Chío joins the rest of the passengers in crowding the aisle, even though Sam remembers her ranting about that very thing in their group chat with Isabel. She speed-walks ahead of him and her dad in the airport, calling a car on her phone before they're anywhere near the exit. Instead of inputting their hotel's address, she sends them straight to the blue dot.

No one says a word the whole time until they're five minutes away, the only sounds coming from the city traffic and the pop radio station the driver keeps at a low volume, plus Chío's leg jittering against the door. Then she says, "I hope she's fine so I can kick her ass."

Sam laughs, and that's how he knows he's an optimist. This whole time, he's been sure that Isabel really is fine. That the cab is going to pull up to an Airbnb and Isabel is going to have a perfectly rational, albeit annoying, reason for her two-day disappearance. She got food poisoning and missed her flight and couldn't find a phone charger. Or maybe she had to stay in the city to be near the U.S. embassy because she's waiting for a replacement passport and she'd dropped her phone in water and was waiting for it to work properly again. He doesn't think about Supers, because the truth is that no matter how much he supported Izzy, wanted to believe her, wanted her to be right for her own sake, the concept that Supers exist has never really slipped into his consciousness. His brain rejects it no matter how much his heart wants to embrace it, no matter how much he went on the forum to feel close to her, no matter how many of their arguments he read.

"Servidos," the driver says, pulling up to a street corner near a park. They're in a hip neighborhood, judging by the number of restaurants and bars they recently drove past. They're not at a hospital, not at a police station, not at a morgue. These seem like good signs.

Chío is out the door already, Sam's phone in hand. Sam and Santi thank the driver and pull their bags from the trunk while Chío takes a few steps toward a building, then backtracks and looks at its neighbor. "I think this is it," she says.

A storefront on the first floor looks like electronics repair. Above that there's three stories of apartments. Isabel goes to the small door adjacent to the business and starts reading the names listed beside the intercom buzzer. What she's looking for isn't clear, since it's unlikely Isabel's name will be there. She uses her phone to call Isabel's again. When there's no answer, she starts buzzing every name in the building.

"Hija," Santi says gently.

No answer on the first, so she moves right along, still calling Isabel. Sam steps up to the storefront, but there's a steel curtain down and there's not much to see. If Chío were her usual rational self, she'd have already reached the conclusion in Sam's brain, and probably in Santi's too.

"Chío," Santi says, joining her and putting a hand on her shoulder. "Don't you think that—"

"Sí, Pa, lo se. But I'm gonna try anyway, okay?"

A voice comes through the intercom, and Chío switches

back to Spanish to ask about Isabel. Five minutes later she's gone through everyone in the building who will answer.

"Come on," her dad says. "We'll go to our hotel, we'll get some food, and we'll come back here tomorrow morning when the shop opens. We'll find out more then."

Chío breathes in deeply and rests her forehead against the wall by the intercom. "Izzy, where the fuck are you?"

15

El Nido, Philippines

The first time Isabel stumbled onto the part of the internet that believes in superheroes, she was sixteen and probably depressed. The world had seemed particularly gloomy at the time, sure. Aside from increasingly common climate disasters and a global pandemic, more and more people around Dearborn and in the world in general, or at least on the internet, had proved to have a secret brain similar to her dad's. And the louder they were about these secret thoughts, the more comfortable her dad seemed to feel admitting he agreed.

So that was basically where her mind was at when she found a video of a guy swimming with whales and apparently communicating with them. At first, she'd clicked on it looking for a surface hit of dopamine, something gentle and good that could replenish, however momentarily, her feelings of hope. She hadn't been expecting the audio narration on the video to claim that the man's ability to stay underwater for a long period of time and to communicate with whales were both genetic mutations: superpowers.

It wasn't like she believed what she heard. The video was impressive, and she knew she could believe in someone communicating with wild animals without having to believe that it was a superpower. But she was curious about the person in the video, about the person who uploaded it. It was, if nothing else, a distraction. Something to chase on the internet for a few minutes.

She hadn't expected to chase for hours, hadn't expected to find a niche forum that hooked her attention the way it did, and she definitely hadn't expected what she'd felt when she finally put her computer aside. The lightness, the way her thoughts stayed at bay and let her fall asleep and weren't there to greet her in the morning.

When Gareth says he knows a Super, Isabel's heart starts pounding, and then she feels a flood of that same lightness. "You're not lying, are you?"

"I'm not."

"Where? How?" A giggle bursts out from deep in her belly. "You better not be fucking with me."

"I thought you were fucking with me, remember?"

Now they're beaming smiles at each other. Isabel can't help thinking, *What are the odds?* Then she realizes she has more pressing questions that Gareth has yet to answer. But their boat guy appears and says they have to go.

Isabel and Gareth gather their things hastily. "You haven't

answered yet," she says. "How? Who? Where? You have to tell me everything."

And under the protective humming of the boat engine, he does. He answers every question she has, tells her the Super's name is Rick. "Rick?" Isabel says, laughing. "That's a terrible name for a superhero."

"That's just his person name, as far as I know. His superhero name would probably be a little more grandiose," Gareth says. He lives in Sydney, and Gareth met him a few months ago in Bali. They'd been playing soccer on the beach, then he'd offered to buy him and the lads some beers. After a few, the other guys had called it an early night, but Gareth and Rick had kept talking. A little drunk, Gareth had pushed the conversation to the topic he always did, prompting a confession from Rick.

Gareth tries to tell her more, but the boat accelerates and drowns out his voice.

When they get back to shore, they climb aboard Isabel's motorbike. She puts the key in but she has to know. "What is it? His power."

Gareth scratches the back of his head, grinning sheepishly. "It's, uh, hard to describe," he says, but immediately follows it with: "He can replicate organic matter, I guess. Maybe that's not technically it. But he bloody cloned a lime. Or made it grow? I don't know, it was bonkers." The way he's stumbling over his words, she can just tell his excitement is real. That he's actually seen what he's recounting.

Gareth's hands hold on to her hips on the ride back, and Isabel purposefully goes slower, her mind abuzz with endorphins. She wants to stretch out what she's feeling, especially with Gareth so close to her and the beginnings of the sunset on the horizon. She almost crashes the scooter on the hill down to the rental place, and Gareth yelps, then they both laugh.

Walking back up to their place, they are quiet at first. Then Isabel says, "I want to meet him."

Gareth doesn't answer right away. He waits until a truck passes on the highway, then they cross it to get to the stairs up to their hostel on the hill. "I'll message him, see if he's around. If I remember, he's a little cagey about letting people know—when he's sober."

"Thanks," she says, and she wants to reach over and squeeze his hand, but that's not something she knows how to do. Riding the scooter was a boldness that was easy to try out. This one, not so much.

They reach the top of the stairs and pause, suddenly shy. Isabel doesn't know where to look, doesn't know which of her many thoughts to focus on. She wants to grab her phone and call Sam and Chío, she wants to post a long rambling message on Actually Super, she wants to start looking for flights to Australia, wants to let out a whoop of excitement, wants to kiss Gareth.

"I think I'll get changed," Gareth says. Her heart sinks the slightest bit, but she tries to buoy it with all her other thoughts. Her face must reflect the sinking, though, because Gareth smiles and says, "I was thinking we could have dinner together. Work out when you could go visit Rick. Get some more of that sisig, which I've been dreaming about all day. I need to thank you for convincing me to try it."

"I can't believe you've been eating pizzas throughout Asia."

"It's the lads, you know. They're squeamish."

"No excuse," she says.

The conversation peters out and they go their separate ways to get changed. Isabel suddenly regrets the lightness of her luggage, the haphazard way she packs. Everything is wrinkled, especially the one dress she brought with her, which she hasn't worn since she got to El Nido two weeks ago. There's a new German guy volunteering who's on his phone in his bunk, so Isabel decides to go off to the bathrooms to get changed, maybe sneak in a quick shower and hang up the dress to give it a chance to straighten in the steam.

At dinner, Gareth is wearing an equally wrinkled short-sleeved shirt. His friends are sitting at a different, farther table and they surprisingly limit their teasing to a couple of comments throughout. There's plenty of good to focus on: the sisig, Gareth's dopey smile, the fact that she knows exactly where to find a Super, the fact that she's found someone else who believes. Giddy, they spend part of the dinner planning the logistics of getting her there. Mostly, Isabel is thankful for the lightness she feels. Here, on this hill on the island of Palawan in the Philippines, up the road from the laxest scooter rental place in existence, Isabel is not thinking about the harm people do to the world and to each other. She is not thinking of concentration camps or conspiracy theorists or the balance of the world. She is as light as a joyous thought, light as a breath.

Isabel follows Gareth and his buddies to Manila.

She hadn't spent much time there before heading to Palawan, she reasons, and it's the best place to catch a flight to Sydney, which she starts looking for as soon as Rick responds to Gareth's email about having a friend who wants to meet him.

"Do me a favor," Chío says on the phone. "Take a picture of Gareth's passport when he's not looking and send it to me."

"I'm not doing that," Isabel says. "I will ask him nicely for a picture of his passport, because he's a good person and he'll understand."

There's a pause on the call, then Sam says, "I still vote for doing it in secret. Seems a little more fun."

"I promise you that when we're in Mexico, we can heist something. But I'm not gonna make Gareth the focal point of one."

"Because you two are smushing faces?" Chío teases.

"Ew," both Isabel and Sam say.

"Also," Sam adds, "taking a passport photo is hardly a heist. If we're going to be doing anything like that in Mexico, I want to make sure we're all on the same page for what qualifies as one."

Isabel is finally feeling exactly how she was supposed to throughout this trip. She's enjoying exploring Manila, its sprawling expanse, its food. The malls, even, don't seem like vacuous shrines to capitalism. They are social hubs, they are places to watch the curious lives of human beings on display. Funny how much easier it is to see things that way when her thoughts don't interfere.

At night she either works the desk at the hostel—it's come to feel like a certain home, how similar these places are, how similar are the guests that show up—or hangs out with Gareth, sometimes with his friends too. They gather around a laptop in the hostel's common area and watch a movie while gulping convenience store beers, or they venture out to a dive bar.

Isabel's even doing well financially. She has learned how to make her money last. It's an easy balance of self-control and the desire to keep doing this. The boys seem ready to go back home for Christmas in a few weeks, but she is nowhere near ready to stop. Especially with her first real encounter on the horizon.

Australia will deplete her bank account at a much faster rate than Asia has, so she keeps teaching English online, even though the only things on her mind are Supers, and, admittedly, Gareth.

On the day that Gareth and his friends planned to go to Cebu, Isabel finds a $150 one-way fare to Sydney for three weeks later. The boys had invited her to come along, but she decides she's going to get to know Manila, and save her money. Gareth watches as she fills in her passport information to buy the ticket. His friends are packed and ready to go, casting impatient glances his way.

"Go," Isabel says. "I'll have time to see you before I leave."

"No," Gareth says. "That's not what I'm thinking. I'm wondering if maybe . . . if I could come with you."

"To Australia?"

“Yeah,” he says, eyebrows raised adorably. “I reckon it’d be good for you to have someone you know with you. And since I know Rick and everything, maybe it’d be all right if I help introduce you. He can be a bit rough around the edges.”

“Hmm,” Isabel says, sensing there’s more he’s not saying.

“And I like spending time with you. So, I’m not ready to say goodbye.”

It is not the first time they kiss in daylight, but it’s the first time they do it in front of his friends. Isabel feels a twinge thinking about Gareth coming with her, something not entirely joyful. But she chalks that up to companionship being beyond her comfort zone, and she latches on to the excitement of Rick, of having Gareth there with her, and of getting to make out more.

“Go,” Isabel says, “before John and Carl start hating me. I’ll send you my flight info so you can book the same one.”

He kisses her again, and she watches him go, wondering how much of the lightness she has been feeling is tied to him.

16

Sydney, Australia

After three days of walking the city, grimacing at the cost of everything, and being subjected to a roller coaster of emotions due to Rick's flakiness, Isabel is finally about to meet a Super.

At this point, she knows everything about Rick, having interrogated Gareth repeatedly, but hopefully not to the point of being annoying. She posted vaguely about the planned meeting on Actually Super, leaving out Rick's name, since he had only agreed to meet if they promised to keep quiet prior to the meeting. Mathilde messaged her a bunch of exclamation points, then expressed her hope that he was, for lack of a better term, actually Super.

Others on the forum speculated about who it might be that she was meeting, floating the names of some suspected Supers in Australia. None of their theories came close, from what Isabel could tell. Which makes her wonder how good the forum is at finding Supers, how many there might actually be out in the world that this small group of internet sleuths have no idea about. Of course, the lack of details about Rick fits with what people on the forum have come to expect of Supers. Too much information available publicly would be a red flag.

She and Gareth get off the mostly empty train near Bondi Beach. They walk in silence, hand in hand until Isabel feels her palms get clammy and she pulls back. That's a new thing, holding hands while they walk. She tries not to think too much about what it means, only that it feels nice when they're doing it.

Gareth is leading them with the help of his phone, and when he looks up and says "This is it," Isabel can't help but want to double-check him.

"This?"

She expected a cute bungalow. A nice condo, perhaps. The house they're standing in front of is a sleek modern building that reeks of money. Aside from being a Super, Rick is also a software developer, so Isabel knows she shouldn't be entirely surprised. But something feels off, even if it's just her expectations.

Gareth shrugs and offers a reassuring smile. "You ready?"

It takes her a second to nod, at which point he reaches for the doorbell.

Rick answers a few moments later. And he is almost shockingly normal. He's a thirty-three-year-old man in a rumpled black T-shirt and jeans; his general vibe doesn't really scream superhero. It screams man who used to be into binge drinking but now is very much into the stock market and a specific diet from back when human beings mostly died in childhood.

"Fuck me, you're younger than I remember" are the first words out of his mouth.

"Um," Gareth says. Isabel doesn't say anything.

Rick barks out a laugh and then opens the door fully to let them in. "All right, children, come on in. It's a nice night, so I reckon we could sit outside." The house is about what Isabel would have expected from its exterior, but once again it's not what she's always pictured a Super's home would be. There's a lot of sleek furniture and glass, and somewhere in the house a TV is playing what sounds like a rugby game. Isabel reminds herself that there's all sorts of people in the world, and just because she wouldn't hang out with this guy based on seven seconds of meeting him doesn't mean anything.

"I know we talked about this beforehand, but I went ahead and had my people draw up some NDAs, just for my own peace of mind. I'm sure you understand." He says this as they walk through the kitchen and to the sliding glass door that leads to the backyard. Although instead of a yard, it's a pool, complete with a little babbling waterfall. "Did I make you sign one of these before?" he asks Gareth.

"Um, no," Gareth says.

Rick shakes his head at himself. "Must have been drunk." Then he points at the two separate stacks of paper on the glass coffee table. A pen sits atop each pile. "Read that over, let me know if you have questions. I'll go grab us some drinks. Beer? Wine for the lady?"

"Beer's fine," Isabel says, annoyed at the comment but mostly trying to wrap her head around this meeting.

She and Gareth ease down on the two-seater, each taking a sheet of paper as they do. "An NDA?" Isabel says out loud, her eyes already scanning the page.

"It kind of makes sense, though, doesn't it? How else could he stay under the radar?"

"I guess," Isabel says, reading on. There's a lot of legal jargon she doesn't understand, and some stipulation about how any piece of art that could be reasonably interpreted as inspired by Rick's likeness would belong to him, but could be optioned for a fee of no less than fifty thousand Australian dollars. She won't even be able to post about her exchange on Actually Super without putting herself at risk of getting sued for way more money than she could ever hope to make. She mentally notes to delete the post she put up a few days ago, disappointed that she won't be able to tell Sam and Chío, won't be able to confirm a Super's existence to Mathilde.

There's a queasy feeling in Isabel's stomach as she reads, but she tries to reassure herself that what Gareth said makes sense. This is how Rick and other Supers have managed to stay hidden for so long.

Rick comes back out a minute later, holding three craft-beer bottles, which he places on coasters on the table, a big smile on his face. "All good, any questions?"

"Can we see it before we sign?" Isabel asks. "Your . . . power?"

Rick uses a lighter to pop open the beer bottles, a weird move considering he's at home and ostensibly has an actual bottle opener. "Sorry, but no. We can chat about travels, I can show you my record collection, we can have a laugh, but no discussing anything other than normal stuff until those are signed."

He plops himself down on the chair across from them, leaning back and crossing his legs. Isabel looks at Gareth, who also seems put off by the NDA, though not quite as much as she is. He feels her gaze and tries to offer a reassuring smile before he picks up his pen and signs. Isabel wants to text Chío and ask her what she should do, but it's four a.m. in Michigan, so she signs it too. Before she slides it across to Rick, though, she snaps a couple of pictures for future reference.

"Smart," Rick says. He grabs the papers and sets them aside, then he claps his hands and says, "All right. A demonstration is now in order."

Isabel's heart starts racing. This is it. This is her proof. She braces herself against the love seat as Rick gets a focused look on his face, then raises his hands up and points them at Gareth. He starts wiggling his fingers.

Gareth flinches involuntarily, and Rick immediately breaks out into guffaws. "I'm fucking with you, mate! It's not going to shoot out of my fingers." He leans over and smacks Gareth on the knee. "Silly bastard. Though I do get a kick out of doing that every time."

"I know," Gareth mumbles, trying to brush it off.

Oh, Isabel thinks. *This guy's a dick.*

But she pushes the thought down, because there's a more important word to describe him. "How does it work?" Isabel asks.

"I don't know the science of it. Don't really care to, you know? Just happy to have it."

"I just meant . . . how do you make it happen?"

"Right. It's like a muscle, really. A skill I had to finesse. Which is something all those comic books got right, at least. The training montage. Spider-Man shooting jism or whatever it is on the rooftop, trying to practice. I sometimes wish I would have taped myself. Would have been a laugh." He takes a swig of his beer, shaking his head at the memory of himself.

Rick stands up and goes back into the kitchen, where he starts rummaging around, opening and shutting drawers in a way that seems a little performative. Isabel wants to roll her eyes at Gareth, but maybe this is part of what she must go through to see her dream come true.

Over the last few weeks—years, really—Isabel has tried to imagine what this moment would be like. It was impossible not to romanticize it occasionally, but she always wanted to make the daydreams as uncinematic as possible. No explosions or shimmering lights, no sweeping score in the background, no excessively handsome or fit Supers.

Rick is testing her ability to stay in the present, but it is in remembering those fantasies that she realizes what this moment is. How much it will mean to see this in person. She knows what the power is, but until she sees it for herself, it is hypothetical, it is still a fantasy that Chío could disprove. When Rick comes out with a bowl of strawberries and a flowerpot, she's equal parts confused and intrigued. "Right," Rick says. "Please hold your applause until the end." He gives a shit-eating grin, then rips off a small chunk of a strawberry and drops it into the dirt in the flowerpot. He pops the rest in his mouth and wipes his hand off on his pants.

Isabel and Gareth both scoot forward, gazing at the dirt, waiting for something to happen. Rick buries the small strawberry chunk, then digs his fingers into the dirt around it. "I thought you said it didn't shoot out your fingers," Gareth mutters.

"Fair play," Rick says.

For a moment, nothing happens, and Isabel is sure that she's being scammed somehow, that she's being made a fool. That she has been a fool this whole time. A scared child, worried about the world she's growing up in and grasping at whatever might make her feel better about it.

Then there's movement in the dirt. It's slight, almost a trick of the eyes. At first, she thinks it's just Rick moving his fingers around. But then she sees a sliver of green. It's just a pinprick of color that all of a sudden is growing brighter and bigger, like the sun rising over the horizon. Isabel looks at Rick's face, expecting to see a smirk, some sign of a ruse. But his is an expression of sheer concentration, like an athlete focused on a task, an artist lost in a specific world they're trying to make real. She looks over at Gareth, whose face is lit with orange by the evening sun. His eyebrows are up, his lips curled at the edges. He shoots her a quick glance, and she can't help but return the smile that blooms across his face.

When she brings her gaze back to the flowerpot, there's clearly a stem rising from the dirt. It begins to crawl upward, and for one last moment, Isabel's mind tries to convince her that she's being tricked. That Rick's hands are maneuvering a stem that was hidden in the dirt.

Then a leaf sprouts from the side of the stem. And another. Right before her eyes, the strawberry plant grows in fast-forward. More stems appear, followed by more leaves. Her heart starts pounding in her chest, her hands start to sweat, her legs are jittering. "Holy shit," she says right as the first little white bud forms. Her mouth turns into a smile as she speaks, and it won't leave.

Those buds open into flowers, then fall away a petal at a time. Isabel wants to reach out and grab them but is frozen, watching. Now a different kind of bud starts to grow. When those buds start turning into white hearts, their tips just starting to blush red, Isabel barks out a laugh and claps her hand over her mouth. The plant keeps growing, the stems lengthening, the strawberries going from white to green to a plump and juicy red.

Rick pulls his fingers out of the flowerpot and claps his hands together to get the dirt off them. "Pretty cool, right?" he says. Then he plucks one of the strawberries off the plant. "Just wait until you taste them. Best strawberries in the world, if I do say so myself." He leans back in his chair, strawberry juice dripping through his knuckles.

Isabel can't move at first. She's still got a smile plastered on her face, and now there are tears threatening to push out from her diaphragm. She lowers her head to stare at the ground in wonder and compose herself. It's true. She wants to run out of the room and scream, she wants to hug Gareth, wants to call Sam and Chío. She wants to run to her father and shove it in his face, wants to bring her grandmother back from the dead and make Rick repeat his trick for her so she can see there are still marvels in the world.

Instead, she reaches for one of the strawberries, turning it around in her hand as if she's never seen one before. It feels completely real. She rips it in half, and the smell is instant and strong and unmistakably strawberry.

"What'd I say?" Gareth says, nudging her with his shoulder. It seems like he's going for confidence, though the quiver in his voice gives away the wonder he too is feeling.

Isabel can only laugh, and she bites into the strawberry. It's the last reservation she has. Despite it all, how long she's wanted this, she won't let herself have it until she can prove it's real. Until even Chío with a lab at her disposal would be satisfied.

She bites down, and she knows right away that it is the best strawberry she has ever had. And it was grown in front of her eyes in a matter of seconds, with nothing but a scrap, some dirt, and a person's fingers. Now she wipes at her eyes, because the tears have snuck past her while she was tasting magic.

17

Sydney, Australia

It is only when Isabel has finished chewing and swallowing, when she has had a moment to catch her breath, when her mind has wrapped around what she's just seen, that she is hit with a deeply uncomfortable realization. Gareth is starting to giggle to himself, almost hysterical, his hands covering his face. "Fuck me," he says. "I knew it, I bloody knew it. A part of me thought I'd imagined it last time. But fuckin' hell."

But Isabel's giddiness isn't taking over. She looks around the house again, looks at Rick, taking in the furniture, the pool, the watch on his wrist. "What is it you do for a living again?" she asks.

"Really?" Rick scowls. "That's your question?"

Gareth is still laughing, possibly not having heard her, borderline manic. She watches him for a moment to make sure he's okay, then looks back at Rick.

"I guess I'm wondering how you use this power in your everyday life."

"Well, grocery shopping's a lot easier, I'll tell you that," Rick laughs. When Isabel doesn't join in, he rolls his eyes. "All right, I see you're not keen on jokes." He raises his hands defensively. "I go grocery shopping less, it's true. It's a neat trick at dinner parties, among those who've signed forms, of course."

"You don't do anything . . . bigger with it?"

"I own a farm about an hour away. I visit just often enough to make sure our yield's decent, you know what I mean? A little extra income. I don't want to raise too many suspicions, though, so my main gig is in software. I'm better at it, believe it or not."

Gareth is just now catching his breath, his eyes almost glazed over. He sits up, his leg bumping against Isabel's. He starts bubbling over with questions. "Does it hurt? Does it take energy out of you? How much can you do in one go?" When Rick doesn't immediately answer them, Gareth seems to wake up to the newfound tension in the room. He turns to Isabel. "Did I miss anything?"

"I meant *good*," Isabel says to Rick, ignoring Gareth. "Do you do anything good with it?"

"What would you have me do?"

Isabel leans back, unable to look at him. She fixes her eyes on the strawberry plant, which is still very much real. This man conjured food from a scrap in a matter of seconds, and he is spending his time working for computer companies and beefing up a farm's output for profit. She can't help but let a scoff escape.

"No, please," Rick says, putting his beer down forcefully on the glass. "I'd like to hear it. You have this ability that I have, what do you do with it?"

Isabel can feel the rage building in her stomach. She still can't look at him. Gareth, meanwhile, is sitting at the edge of the seat, and he puts a hand on her shoulder while speaking to Rick. "I'm sure she didn't mean it like that," he says.

Isabel moves her shoulder away from his hand. "Don't speak for me," she says quietly.

"No, I know what she meant," Rick says, grabbing his beer again. "I've heard this lecture before."

They fall into an uncomfortable silence. Gareth is peeling the label on his beer, biting his lip. Rick pulls out his phone and starts scrolling. Isabel still has a little red stain on her finger from the strawberry. She puts it absently in her mouth, feeling tears of a different sort climb up her chest.

"You have a gift," she says simply, trying to swallow the tears. "A goddamn superpower. And you're using it to make money and perform tricks for teenagers."

"I ask again," Rick answers, still scrolling through his phone, pretending not to be bothered. "What would you have me do?"

"Feed people!" The anger's pushed out the tears. She notices both Gareth and Rick flinch a little at her volume. "Do you not know that there are places in the world where children die by the thousands because they don't have enough to eat? Do you not know that the production of food uses up precious water we're running out of, that shipping food from one place to another comes with climate-changing emissions that lead to food being harder to grow and then to more famine? Hell, trees! Just make a bunch of trees. Go to Brazil and repopulate the Amazon, which we've decimated."

Isabel's never been much for anger. Even as her father fell deeper into conspiracy theories, most of which were rooted in poorly disguised antisemitism, her instinct had never been to yell "But you're Jewish!" She's much more familiar with responding to enraging situations with hurt. When a group of kids at school were caught etching racist epithets into a bathroom stall, Isabel did not stick a finger in their face and shame them, though they certainly deserved it. She didn't feel the kind of anger that made Chío attend school board meetings and advocate for anti-racist changes to the curriculum. She did not get quiet and moody like Sam and work her anger out on a basketball court.

Anger, to her, is an elusive emotion. One that she studies from afar, sometimes with a sense of voyeurism, but more often than not with a sort of detached horror, like it's some terrible thing she's watching on TV.

So, it's no surprise to her that she already feels it waning, being replaced with despair, her old friend.

"You have this incredible gift that could change the world, and you are sitting in your fancy house making people sign contracts." She gestures at his stupid sleek glass coffee table, with its rings of sweat from the beer bottles. The NDAs aren't even on it anymore, the realization of which almost makes Isabel laugh at herself.

There's so much more she can say, so much more to rant about. But Isabel suddenly feels exhausted, and the thought of having to trek back to another hostel is what pushes more tears out. She wipes at them and then looks up at Rick, waiting for him to call her naive. To say it's not that simple. Maybe there are perfectly logical reasons why he can't do any of the things she just yelled at him for. Maybe she does not yet have all the information. Maybe he's . . . better.

Rick reaches for his beer and takes a long pull from it. Isabel tries not to cry anymore, tries to raise her chin at him. But she doesn't have the energy.

"All right, mate," Rick says, directing his words to Gareth, not Isabel. "Best if you two go."

18

Mexico City, Mexico

After a night of tacos (more for Sam and Santi than Chío) and restless sleep, they wake up and go get breakfast across the street from the electronics store, which only opens at eleven. Even though her chilaquiles are delicious, she can't finish more than a third of what's on her plate.

Sam takes a walk to explore the neighborhood, and Santi goes to a nearby bookstore, but Chío doesn't want to go anywhere. She orders another Americano and keeps her sights fixed on the storefront, as if Isabel might walk out at any moment. If she looks away to grab her coffee cup or because a noise catches her attention, then anything in her periphery automatically becomes Izzy. It's a roller-coaster morning of hope and tiny little heartbreaks.

At ten to eleven, a young guy shows up and unlocks the steel curtain, then disappears inside. Chío's heart races right up until he flips the sign out front to OPEN thirty minutes later. As soon as he does, Chío's on her feet, Sam and Santi following behind.

Chío explains the situation to the guy, who vaguely remembers Isabel coming in. He says he can't give them the phone without the receipt, which makes Chío want to throw a fit, but Santi puts a hand on her shoulder. He uses his Latin American sweet-talking technique, the one he constantly employs in restaurants, in banks, all over Michigan. It always embarrasses Chío, until it works. Which it almost always does.

The guy slides the phone across the counter, and Chío snatches it as if he might change his mind. He says that when Isabel brought it in, not only did it have a badly cracked screen, but it wasn't turning on for her at all. He told her he wasn't sure he could do anything but fix the screen, since the phone seemed to have water damage, and she said that was fine, but then never came back.

"How long ago?" Chío asks.

The guy looks at his computer. "Four days."

Chío's not sure if she's encouraged by that or not.

"She called me. Yesterday."

"That was me. A mistake," he says. "Sorry."

Chío's heart sinks, and she focuses on the phone. Thankfully, Isabel never changed her screen passcode, and Chío is able to get in right away, searching for clues in Izzy's texts, her phone calls. There are no immediate clues that place Isabel anywhere other than Mazunte, but Chío finds the address of a nearby hostel where Isabel was scheduled to stay until her flight.

At first, the guy doesn't want to let them leave with the phone, but Santi re-explains the situation with some more sweet-talking and adds a tip to Isabel's unpaid bill.

The rest of the day is a goose chase of sorts, following a digital ghost. The hostel confirms she's checked out, and none of the people working there remember seeing her since. "I think she kept her bag in the storage room for a few hours before her flight," one girl says with an unhelpful shrug.

Sam then figures out how to check on Google Maps if Isabel had her location activated at all times. She did, so they can see where she'd been in the city before she left her phone. Taco stands, coffee shops, the Frida Kahlo Museum, the subway, Xochimilco. They go to as many as they can within the city, and call the rest. They show baristas and servers her picture, but even Chío knows this is a long shot. That in a city of many millions of inhabitants and constant travelers, plus a horde of white remote workers setting up shop in the last few years, one girl is hard to remember. Unless she was shooting lasers out of her eyes or something.

While Santi's on the phone with the airline trying to confirm whether or not Isabel was on the flight, Chío is on the phone with her mom back in Mazunte to see if there's any news about the body. The police there have not been forthcoming, so her mom says she'll call back after doing some pestering.

"It's a little unnerving, isn't it?" Chío says at a churro spot looking out at Parque México, not far from their hotel. An afternoon thunderstorm is about to roll in, the dark gray clouds providing a dramatic backdrop for the green trees and the purple jacarandas that line the park. "How easily we can lose touch with a person. Assuming she's still out there and okay, if she doesn't have a phone to call or an address to stop by at, she could just"—she makes a butterfly motion with her hand—"she could just disappear."

Her dad's caught with half a churro in his mouth and a dulce de leche drizzle on his chin, so he has to gather himself before he can answer. Sam has taken over Isabel's phone, reading through emails and texts. It feels strange, but they've managed to bury the guilt of betraying her trust beneath the avalanche of other shit going on.

"We'll go to the U.S. embassy," Sam says. "She's left a trace. Just 'cause we can't see it or don't know how to find it doesn't mean it's not there."

"Wow, that's a good idea. Why hadn't I thought of that already?" Chío says, tearing off a chunk of churro and dipping it in chocolate. She whips out her own phone and starts looking for where the embassy is. It's a long walk or a short cab ride away. It's currently closed to "U.S. citizen services." Does that apply to them? There is a phone number for emergencies, and she's about to tap on it, but her dad puts a hand on her wrist.

"We have an appointment in the morning," he says.

"You called already? Why didn't you say anything?"

"Because going to the embassy is a last-resort move. And I know you. You wouldn't have been ready to admit we're at our last resort until you'd actually exhausted everything else." He pauses as a loud truck rumbles by, then sighs deeply and pulls Chío in for a hug. At first, she wants to tell him not to comfort her, but it occurs to her that he might be doing it for his own comfort too. "I might not have been ready either, to tell you the truth."

They move to a nearby café with an awning right before the rain starts pouring. In the Midwest, storms that pound down like this exhaust themselves after fifteen minutes or so. But the rain just keeps coming. Santi puts in earphones to catch up on his podcasts and rest his eyes while Sam and Chío pass Isabel's phone back and forth, trying to get something useful from it.

Eventually it calms down enough to walk hurriedly back to their hotel, where they shower and, Chío assumes, wait for the next day to come. She calls her mom again, who offers a sigh and says, "Nothing, honey. I don't get it. They won't tell me anything."

When Chío starts changing for bed, her dad shakes his head. "You're in one of the best food cities in the world. I know your mind is on other, bigger things, but it would be a waste to skip a meal here. You two should go out."

"And you? You're gonna skip a meal?"

Santi laughs. "I've been sneaking so many tacos throughout the day, I can't take any more."

"You have?" Sam asks, and Chío's heart warms a little at the hurt in his voice. Sam's biggest fear is being excluded. She'd almost forgotten that. Remembering now makes her think about the past year, how often she left his calls or texts unreturned. How often she opted to stay at home rather than meet up with him at Roys's.

"I dunno," Chío says. "I'm a little tired. And I'm not sure my appetite is all there."

"Give yourself a night off," Santi says. "Worrying will not answer your questions about her. Worrying will not be what brings her back. Go be young in this fun city, live the way she has for the past year. Just for a night. Maybe putting yourselves in her shoes will help."

He walks over and kisses her forehead, and as if by magic, she starts feeling more hungry than tired. Then Santi steps over to Sam and wraps him up in a hug too. "Sorry I didn't tell you about the tacos."

Sam laughs, and to Chío's surprise, he returns Santi's hug, even leaning his cheek on her dad's shoulder for a moment before the two step away from each other. "I have an idea for where to go," Sam says to Chío. "I was thinking of sneaking away, but since your dad has a point, you want to come with?"

So, the two of them basically re-create a night that Isabel had a week before, which she had texted them about. They go to a sit-down, no-frills taco spot that's blindingly orange but prepares the most genius thing Chío has ever encountered: a taco where the meat is wrapped up in a thin layer of fried cheese. Isabel had sent them a picture of herself eating it, and even though they'd both pretended out of jealousy that it didn't look that good, it is exactly as good as it looked.

From there they go where Sam had intended to sneak away to: a lucha libre arena. "Why didn't you mention it?" Chío asks him.

"Because I feel guilty thinking of anything fun."

Whether the guilt will come later or not, they do have fun watching Mexican-style wrestling. In an arena full of people screaming at masked men performing acrobatic maneuvers in the air and women with powerful legs flinging each other across the ring, it's hard to not have fun. Chío and Sam get themselves beers and popcorn, which the attendant hands over with a few packets of hot sauce. An hour and a half goes by without Chío thinking about Isabel being dead. She thinks about Isabel, sure. But it's about how her friend has been doing this for a year. That whatever her reasons or motivations, she has seen so much of the world. The worry is there, beneath everything, like a winter's chill that she can't beat but can momentarily forget.

Afterward, they go try mezcal for the first time. "Holy shit," Sam says, coughing. "There is no limit to what people can bring themselves to enjoy."

"Kind of inspiring, in a way," Chío says. It's not like she's loving everything going on in her mouth, throat, and chest right now, but she doesn't hate it either. Something she hasn't been able to take advantage of during this short vacation (interrupted by potential tragedy though it may be, it is still technically a vacation) is her love of new experiences. Each new experience to her is like a scientific experiment. Or, more accurately, each is a data point. What the experiment is, what the hypothesis is, Chío's not quite clear yet. But she loves the gathering of data.

Now she makes another face as she sips the mezcal and she looks around the small patio bar. There are two other tables with Americans, which doesn't surprise her. She did a fair amount of reading about the city when Isabel was first headed here, and she knows how popular it's become with American travelers after years of being synonymous with danger. It's a Tuesday night, so it's not exactly packed, but the street they're on is still lively. Families are taking after-dinner strolls in the boulevard, a couple of friends on bikes chat at a stoplight.

"Remind me who Gareth was?" Sam says.

"The guy she went to Australia with. Why?"

Sam reaches in his pocket and pulls Isabel's phone out, handing it to her after swiping through for a few moments. It's an email from Gareth. "I didn't think much of it when I read it at the churro place. But it's been in the back of my mind and I'm trying to figure out what's weird about it."

"Is it in Comic Sans?" Chío asks, cracking a smile.

"Wow, a joke," Sam teases, knocking his leg against Chío's.

" 'Hey Izzy,' " Chío starts reading out loud, but quickly makes an aside. "I can't believe she let other people call her Izzy."

"I know."

She reads on. " 'Thought of you the other day, wondering if you're still traveling. I decided to stick around these parts after Christmas. Parental guilt is strong, isn't it? Anyway, did you hear of the guy in Peru? Doesn't make you sign NDAs, and not much of a prick either.' " Chío looks up from the phone. "An NDA? Why would Izzy have signed an NDA?"

"Yeah, I don't know. I had to google what it was. It's weird, right?"

"Yeah," Chío says. She takes another sip of mezcal, a buzz coming on, which, scientifically, she thinks, might be the trick to enjoying it. Her mind is scouring her memories for what Isabel said back in December when she went to Australia, what she and Gareth did. She knows they were looking for a Super, but Chío never heard anything about it and figured it was another disappointment for Isabel.

"Did Izzy ever write him back?" Chío says, taking note of the date of the email and then clicking over to the SENT folder. Before she can read too far, though, she hears a phone ringing. At first, she tries to answer Isabel's phone, then rolls her eyes at herself and scrambles for her own. It's her mom calling. Chío shows the screen to Sam, then picks up.

"Hola, Ma."

"Chío," her mom says, and there's too much emotion in her voice. Chío's heart starts pounding, and she's already sitting down, but she wants to further brace herself. "Where are you?"

"At a bar with Sam. Dad knows. What's going on?"

There's a pause at the other end, and Chío knows that her mom is just trying to figure out how to say what she has to say, but every millisecond feels eternal and heavy. "Jesus, Mom, please, just say it. What did you find out?"

Her mom takes a deep breath. "It's good news," she says. "I think." Chío relaxes just the slightest bit, giving Sam the most reassuring look she can manage under the circumstances. She would put the call on speaker, but she's nervous she'll miss her mom's update, lost to the sounds of the city and people chattering over music. "She's alive," her mom finally says. "It was her in the morgue, they think. But also, she's alive."

When Chío hears the word "alive," she has to lean forward onto the table in relief. But the table's a little wobbly and the motion sends Sam's mezcal spilling all over them. "What?" Sam says as he reaches for a napkin.

"Shit," Chío says, but she says it with a smile, says it with relief coursing through her, says it like a blessing.

A server comes by with a rag and helps a very confused Sam, who keeps looking at Chío. She looks around for a napkin but her brain is still processing the words and doesn't register the dispenser nearby. Isabel's alive. Nothing else matters. The server asks if they want more to drink, and Sam says "Sorry" in English, then looks at Chío for a translation.

Chío tells the server, "Sí, otro igual." Even though Chío still has mezcal in her little glass.

On the phone, her mom says, "Chío, are you there?"

"Yeah, sorry. I'm here. Tell me."

"Did you say you were at a bar? Do I have to fly over there and kill your father?"

"Dad says teenagers being exposed to alcohol by their parents before they reach drinking age in the U.S. is key to avoiding the kind of reckless binge drinking so common in American college kids."

"I hate how smart you two are," her mom says, laughing, the relief clear in her voice. Sam is still pretending to clean up the table, even though it's fully dry, and the server is coming by with a fresh round of mezcal. Aída is about to elaborate, but Chío tells her to hold on a second while she fishes her earphones from her purse so Sam can hear too.

She's alive! Chío mouths to Sam, whose eyes widen in surprise and joy. His free hand goes to the shot glass, and he sips, smiling even as he winces.

Chío's mom explains what she's found out. The police in Mazunte were working under the assumption that someone had come in and stolen what they believed to be a body. Who knows why someone would steal a body, but that wasn't the important bit. There were no security cameras at the morgue, but a convenience store nearby had an ATM out in front. And that's how they found out that no one had broken into the morgue. The body had broken out.

Or, as it turned out, Isabel had. They have no idea how it is that she's alive, what mistake was made, but there was a clear image of her walking past the camera. Aída hasn't seen it, but Officer Badía used a copy of the picture Chío left to confirm that it was her. They're all confused in Mazunte, but right now they're looking for a living girl, not a dead one. And that's all that matters to Chío.

19

Luang Prabang, Laos

Isabel has had enough of people.

After Rick, she briefly considers going back home, and sleeping until she forgets. Maybe she can just slink back into her old, typical Dearborn life and apply to colleges.

She's not entirely sure why she doesn't. It feels too soon to admit failure. Or maybe it's the thought of what she'll do with her life if the trip is over. She can't imagine working at some restaurant job for a few months while she fills out college applications. All those days in Dearborn, waiting for Sam and Chío to get off school, having to go back home and have dinner with her parents. Seeing her dad on his phone, on his computer, knowing what he's reading. Not being able to tell Sam and Chío. Or worse, telling them and not having them believe her. Not having them understand why this is a failure.

Maybe Isabel doesn't want to go back to that world when she knows the one she'd been looking for actually exists. Maybe she's mad at that world for bleeding into this one. This Super world is supposed to be a hopeful one, and part of her spends the next few weeks embarrassed that she'd never even considered the possibility that Supers could exist but be dicks, for lack of a better term. How had she never considered that in all her hoping for Supers to come around and right the balance of good and evil, they might be there already, tipping the scales the wrong way?

Or maybe she simply doesn't want to go back because she likes traveling. The world, she enjoys. Movement and languages and cuisines. How big and beautiful the planet is, its contours and valleys and the colors it flaunts in nature. It's just the people in it that cause her grief.

An old movie she watches on her computer one day sums it up pretty well. A store clerk says to his friend, "This job would be great if it wasn't for the fuckin' customers." That's how Isabel feels about Earth right now.

So, she looks for isolated places to go. Beautiful but hard-to-reach corners of the world. She doesn't care if there are Supers nearby or not. Now she would actually prefer if there weren't any around. It's the first time on her trip that she picks her next location without even consulting the forum, which she can't bring herself to log on to.

After Sydney, she was supposed to go to Jakarta to spend Christmas with Mathilde. But she can't bear the thought of trying to be cheery without being able to talk about what happened with Rick. She could break the NDA, sure. It's highly unlikely that

Rick would ever find out. But the truth is, she doesn't want to talk about what happened. She doesn't want to think about it. She cancels on Mathilde, pretending she's decided to go back home for a bit, dodging questions about how it went in Australia.

The last two days in Sydney are sullied, and she and Gareth walk around the city quietly, talking only about where to go next. They sit at the beach and put their earphones in and don't hold hands. Then he has to fly back to Manila to catch his original flight home for Christmas, and they kiss goodbye without much passion, promising to stay in touch and meet up during the second half of Gareth's trip, when he'll be in South America, where she's planning on going before Mexico. It's an unceremonious end, and Isabel is glad it has come.

She goes to Laos for two weeks of volunteering at an eco-hostel. The man who runs the place is friendly and mostly absent, and even though the duties he assigns her are way more than what she had signed up for, she's gotten very used to being flexible in these situations, and she likes being too busy to think.

The hostel is ten miles from the nearest town, which is exactly what Isabel wanted: distance. She texts Sam and Chío when there's an internet connection, which isn't often. She tells them Gareth went back home for the holidays and that maybe they'll meet up again down the road, but she hasn't texted him in days, and every time she thinks of him, all she can think of is Rick. Mostly, she reads, she takes strolls in the forest, she spends time with the owner's family, who speak no English at all.

She watches the matriarch cook meals: papaya salad with

a fistful of chilis, ground chicken heavy with herbs. They slay a duck one night as a special feast just for Isabel, and it reminds her of her intention early in her travels, when she wanted to connect better with locals. Now that she's trying to avoid thinking about Supers, about Gareth, there's a lot of mental space to fill. And if she doesn't actively fill it with other thoughts, then Rick is quick to show up; her whole failed worldview is there to greet her. Her dad and her grandmother are there to scoff at her naivete, that she would dare to think the world was anything else but what it is: cruel. "Can't make flowers grow from shit, sweetie," she tells herself in her dad's voice. And even though Chío's voice shows up to say that's exactly how flowers grow, it doesn't make her feel any better.

So, what she's thinking about instead is whether she's lived up to her own ideals of travel.

She's tried to at least learn how to say "hello," "thank you," and "please" in every language she encounters. "Water" and "beer" and the numbers up to ten are ideal too, though that's been harder in countries where she's spent less than a couple of weeks, or in big cities, where people are quick to switch to English. She's stuck to the goal of reading at least one book about each country, but has she interacted more meaningfully with those places? Has she done a good job learning about local customs and culture? Has she been a traveler instead of a tourist? Or, perhaps more accurately, to what extent has she been both?

With New Year's having just passed, Isabel has made a resolution that has nothing to do with Supers. If not a resolution, exactly, then an intention, a concept that Sam shared with her after he'd seen it online. And her intention for the rest of her travels—or the rest of the year, whichever is longer—is this: cause no harm. Or, at least, try to cause the least harm possible. She's not sure anymore if she wants to hold the world accountable for being good. She doesn't think she's given up on searching for Supers, but the emotional wound Rick caused is still fresh, and she shies away from thinking of them for now.

After exploring Laos for a few more weeks, Isabel decides it's time to see another part of the world. She has fallen in love with Asian cities and their food, the beaches and the motorbikes, the noise, the quiet, the curated aesthetics and the grime alike. She could spend years in Southeast Asia alone and never get sick of it. For now, though, a change of scenery is in order. She wants to go somewhere with fewer people.

She finds a ridiculous six-layover itinerary involving four separate bookings that gets her from Laos to the most remote place she can think of: Patagonia. It saves her a few hundred dollars but spans three days of travel, with overnight stays at two different airports, including in Atlanta.

It's strange to be back in the U.S., however briefly. Despite the rush of joy she feels understanding so much of what is said around her, she actually feels more like a fish out of water back in her home country. There are so many televisions playing sports, so many flags, so many T-shirts advertising brands, universities. Everything once familiar to her is both nostalgic and cringeworthy. She knows it is the most "study abroad" thought she has had, but she looks around the Atlanta airport and has trouble believing that she ever lived here.

I can't believe this is the closest you've been in four months and you're not even gonna swing by Roys'ss's's's', Sam texts.

If you can convince Roy to open up in January, I'll hijack this next flight and come see you by the morning.

Jesus Izzy don't text that from an airport, Chío writes. *Also, I can't believe you're gonna see my homeland without me there.* Then, after another minute: *Also also, his first name is Roys, please spell accordingly.*

Again, I will hijack a plane to come pick you up, if you're willing to come.

Bitch, I have midterms, Chío texts.

Gross. See you in a couple of months, then, I guess!!!

Chío responds with a middle-finger selfie, her tongue sticking out. Isabel misses her so much in that moment that she stops at a flight board and looks to see when the next plane to Detroit is. It leaves in two hours, which would be plenty of time to at least try and snag a spot on the standby list. Instead, she goes to an entirely different terminal, and finds a comfortable enough corner of carpet to lie down on.

This is when it's hardest. Controlling her body's learned bedtime routine of scrolling through Actually Super, controlling the nighttime thought pattern of the last few years. She has to distract herself by watching TV shows on her laptop, hoping she'll get carried away to sleep before the thoughts slip in.

20

El Chaltén, Argentina

Isabel climbs off the bus that she's been on for the last twenty-four hours, the final leg of her journey to the tip of the world. She's incredibly happy that she decided to splurge on a shower at the Atlanta airport, but her sense of time is completely warped, and that feels like a million years ago. The landscape throughout the drive has added to her disorientation. It started out pretty enough, with mountains and cliffs and trees, but it turned barren a few hours in and stayed the same until the short night. Add in jet lag and the lack of a bed for days, and Isabel is feeling loopy, to say the least.

She picks up her backpack, thankful that she hasn't had to carry it while on the bus. El Chaltén is a cute little town, a mix of no-frills hostels and cabins, a few fancy resorts, and a whole lot of hikers. On her walk to the hostel, she realizes she blends in with them.

Her weeklong stay was an expensive rate for a bunk in a shared room, but Isabel is hoping that in a few days' time she'll find some under-the-table work and cheaper accommodations.

Following a screenshot she captured, Isabel takes a handful of wrong turns. She blames technology as much as she blames her lack of sleep. After ten minutes of doubling back and recrossing the highway three times, it would be easy to be annoyed at herself. Her body is crying out for a shower and a real bed. But there's something wonderful about where she is. What a privilege it is to point at a spot on a map and be able to get yourself there. Physically, financially, there are so many ways she is lucky to be in this mountainous, isolated part of the world. It helps, too, that it's lovely out, relatively warm and sunny with a pleasant breeze. The snowy peaks of El Chaltén itself, the mountain that colonizers redubbed Mount Fitz Roy, are covered by clouds, but impressive nonetheless. Something about her journey here feels miraculous.

It is in this exhausted gratitude, only ten minutes away from her newest temporary home, that Isabel notices a woman carrying a canoe. It would normally be impressive, albeit just in a normal-feat-of-strength-still-within-the-laws-of-physics kind of way. She's walking in the same direction as Isabel, but because she's carrying all that weight, Isabel overtakes her pretty quickly. At first, Isabel simply admires the woman's strength and the fact that she goes canoeing in the Patagonian wilderness. But then the woman shifts the canoe from one shoulder to the other, and Isabel realizes that the woman's fingers aren't curled over the rim of the canoe. They're flat against the sides, and seem to be gripping the surface the way a lizard scales a wall.

The woman sees Isabel and gives her a smile. Isabel returns

it and immediately glances away, feeling like she's been caught. She shifts her gaze to the ground and speeds up, but the image is seared in her brain. An object that heavy, held up by fingertips. She knows nothing about carrying a canoe, but there's something counterintuitive about it.

Isabel glances once more to be sure she's not imagining things, making something Super out of the ordinary. The woman is looking over at the mountains in the distance, and Isabel has a clear view. Just as she thought, the fingers are pressed flat against the edge of the canoe. Maybe it's just perfectly balanced, Isabel thinks, realizing how strange it is to find herself rooting against witnessing a superpower. The woman feels eyes on her again, and when their gazes meet, she winks at Isabel.

The woman with the canoe is not the only one, but the ensuing sightings are less ambiguous. On an early-morning hike to catch a sunrise view of Chaltén, Isabel thinks she sees a guy on the trail drawing drops of dew from various plants. His hand is to the ground, cupped and angled toward his reusable bottle, though there is no apparent water source. She sees his container filling up and has no non-Super explanation for what she witnesses. By the time she gets close enough to take a better look, his bottle is full and he continues on his way.

At a little pizza place with happy-hour deals for people coming back from a day of hiking, Isabel sits and reads a book, fighting the wind to keep the pages and the napkins down. Two girls about her age are playing cards and drinking beers. Their hair isn't flapping about as much as hers. When they catch Isabel looking over the edge of her book, one of them snaps her fingers and immediately the cards fly off the table, after which they give up on playing.

Baader-Meinhof phenomenon, Chío will later tell her it's called. It's as if now that she's seen a superpower in action, Supers are suddenly easier to spot. The curtain has been drawn, it seems, and now she is allowed to peek behind it. She still hasn't told Chío about Rick, but the Chío that lives in Isabel's head tries to rationalize what she's experiencing. What's more likely than suddenly being able to see a bunch of Supers existing around her is that she wants so desperately to believe in them that she's allowing her mind to play tricks on her.

What should be a dream come true feels far from it. Isabel does not find herself running toward these suddenly plentiful suspected Supers, but away from them, as if their mere proximity causes pain. The memory of Rick is still fresh in her mind, she supposes. His cockiness and his wealth, the small, selfish life he was happy living despite his abilities. She worries that behind every inexplicable thing she witnesses is another disappointment, and a part of her does not believe that she could handle it. There is still a flutter of joy every time she thinks she recognizes one, but she is quick to stamp it out.

When she is on the phone with Sam and Chío—easier now on

this side of the world, where the time difference is slight—she talks only about travel, about her day-to-day life, about what they will do in Mexico. Chío is thrilled by this, Isabel can tell in her voice. Sam picks up on it too, and tries to broach it when they talk one on one, but Isabel changes the subject.

She only calls home when she knows her dad is at work, or likely to be in front of the TV watching a game. Speaking to him always brings more thoughts of Rick, and so she'd rather try to fake cheeriness with her mom, who keeps asking her if she's sick.

"I can hear it in your voice," she says. "I always know when you're sick."

"I'm not sick," Isabel responds, annoyed, feeling antsy to return to a podcast, a movie, anything that drowns her thoughts out and does not pretend to know her better than she knows herself.

Throughout the next two weeks, Isabel goes into every restaurant, bar, and hotel looking for work. While she waits for people to get back to her, she explores the many hiking trails available right from town. When she sees something that her brain can't necessarily make sense of, rather than go investigate, Isabel looks away. She is here, at least for the time being, for isolation. To be far from people, Super or not.

21

Mexico City, Mexico

After she hangs up with her mom, the first thing Chío does is reach for the mezcal. She does not know why people punish themselves with alcohol as a celebration, but any good scientist knows that reason does not exist in a vacuum; emotions are always tangled around it.

"Good news?" Sam says, his face breaking out into this huge smile that makes Chío want to hug him and tell him she loves him, tell him she's missed him, tell him the world is a weird and terrible place that sometimes can be a true wonder. She settles for clinking glasses with him and sipping on mezcal.

She relays what she learned, and although they still have no clue where exactly their friend is, or what exactly is going on, they know she's alive. There is evidence of it now. They can try to wrap their heads around the rest later. For now, Chío wants to celebrate, and Sam is not about to object. They clink glasses every time they drink and take a bite of the orange slices sprinkled with chili salt. Even though they're still pretty full from the glorious cheese-wrapped tacos, they order guacamole topped with crickets, because Sam thinks it'd be criminal not to try. Chío, a bit more of a picky eater, doesn't object because she's in a good mood, and she read that insects are a sustainable food source that might become more and more necessary in a climate-changed world, so she might as well start getting used to it now.

Chío's practically dancing in her seat, which is the only thing she can do to keep from screaming out loud that her friend is okay. Sam laughs, but it's mostly at the recognition of the same relief in him. They look out at the boulevard, watch the cars go by. Sam thinks about what other kids at school are doing for spring break: video games at home, road-trip family reunions, some of the guys from the team in Florida. He'd much rather be here.

"Why didn't we see each other more this year?" Chío asks.

Sam does not throw his blame at her, though he easily could. He shakes his head at a street vendor that's come by selling candy. "We talked a lot."

"In the group chat with Izzy. Doesn't count."

"There were some video calls mixed in there," Sam answers. Chío shoots him a side-eye, and he puts his hands up defensively. "Okay, yeah, fair."

"Answer the question."

The truth is, neither one of them has an answer for this. They threw themselves into their own things. Sam had basketball, and Chío had school, her family. A few times, they went to Roys's and talked to Isabel, if the time difference worked out.

Early in the school year, just a week or so after Isabel had left, Sam and Chío went to a movie together. They laughed about how it was going to be weird, promised themselves that they wouldn't let it get weird, and then it was weird.

They kept starting to speak at the same time, and laughing at the fact they did that, even though it was really only funny the second time it happened. The dynamic had been thrown off. Sam didn't know how to be around Chío, what he normally said to her. So, he started talking about basketball practice, for lack of anything better to say, knowing he was boring her but not being able to stop himself.

Finally, the theater plunged into darkness, and they didn't have to speak. In the dark, it came back. The silly jokes, the popcorn sharing. The ease returned, except that Sam was constantly aware of Chío's body next to him, of where her hand was, how far away her leg was from his. When the movie was over, they sat still throughout the end credits, the way the three of them used to. Sam remembered fleeing Isabel's that one night, suddenly piecing together why he'd been in such a rush to leave.

He and Chío had a running gag throughout the movie about what different characters would sound like if they got poked in the stomach, and as they read the long list of names of people who had worked on the movie, Chío reached over and poked Sam's stomach. He let out an "Oof," which sent Chío into a fit of giggles. Sam waited a little bit, trying to hide his intent to retaliate. Which, of course, didn't work. Chío had her hands up and scooted to the opposite edge of her seat, waiting. When he finally attempted it, she caught his hands in hers. Not wanting to poke without consent, Sam laughed and stopped trying, but Chío kept his hands in hers, not wanting to let go, saying she didn't trust him not to poke. And so they sat like that for another minute, Sam's hands in Chío's, watching the rest of the names. By the time the credits finished rolling, his fingers were resting on her stomach and the silence between them felt both sacred and fragile.

"You promise you won't poke me?" Chío finally whispered, as if the theater were still chock-full of people.

"I promise," Sam said.

Now, in Mexico, Sam shrugs and tells Chío, "My guess is that we hadn't figured out how to just be the two of us together, and that was a little too weird. So we looked for things we were already comfortable with, hoping it would just eventually work itself out."

Chío nods at this, but doesn't look at Sam, her eyes on a group of hip-looking college-age kids passing in front of the bar. "I'm glad we've figured it out," she says.

They finish their drinks and pay the bill with the money Santi gave them for the night, then they follow the latest group of cool people headed somewhere nearby. It turns out to be a club of sorts, the music barely audible until they reach the doorway leading up to some stairs. Though Sam has no interest in it, he will not deny Chío anything right now.

It is dark and crowded, and while he hasn't entirely grasped the exchange rate yet, Sam knows the water bottles he pays for are extremely overpriced. But the bar has a DJ playing fun eighties music, and Chío wants to dance, and this is where he wants to be. She leads him by the hand to the dance floor, which has a wall of windows looking out at the city. Yesterday he was in Mazunte, waiting to see if a dead body was Isabel. Now he's here, in front of Chío, smelling mezcal's smoky remnants on her breath, watching her eyes light up.

So, let us gawk.

Not at death, this time, but at life. At the sweat forming on Chío's brow. How a few strands of her hair have come loose from her bun. How she closes her eyes in order to feel the music, and her body follows the beat. What a thing to witness: bodies responding to music. These unrelated phenomena: compressed air, beating hearts. How like home they are to the other.

Through a cracked window, a breeze comes in, swirling the air around and everything it carries with it. Oxygen, bacteria, viruses, pollution, little particles of scent from the hot dog cart outside, making mouths water, stomachs rumble. There are tapping feet and hands tracing invisible shapes in the air; there are bodies pressed together, moving apart, pressing together again. Inside those bodies, livers process alcohol and drugs, intestines suck nutrients from late-night dinners, the brain responds to chemicals and proteins and hormones, sending out signals to the rest of the body. There are traumas swirling in the back of the minds of the people on the dance floor, joyful memories, fantasies playing out in real time. There are bodies skilled at dancing from the sheer repetition of the act, others just blessed with a natural inclination toward it. Hearts beat, pumping life itself through the veins and arteries to which they're attached.

Sam and Chío, two living, breathing beings no longer carrying the burden of their friend's death, get closer. They touch hands, something happening in the air between where their eyes meet that science right now can't measure in any way. Which isn't to say nothing is happening.

That's simply what we know. What life is up to in those little nooks and crannies that we don't have names for, we can only guess at.

Sam wakes up in the hotel bed to the sounds of men at a garbage truck sorting through glass bottles. The room is dark thanks to the thick curtains, so he has to feel around for the cup of water his body is dying for. He swallows half the glass in three gulps, feeling it cool his insides as it goes down. He lays his head back on the pillow, and once he's quiet again, it hits him that there are two other bodies in the room with him.

Santi is lightly snoring on the far side of the room. Right across the gap between the two beds, Sam can start to make out Chío's shape beneath the comforter. She's on her side, facing him, one leg sticking out from beneath the covers. Memories from last night trickle back, like a dripping faucet. Should he feel guilty about what happened?

The dance floor, the sweat, the way their hands found each other again. Which of them had been the one to initiate the kiss? He can't be sure, and it's not because of the mezcal. By then he'd sweated it all out. One moment they were looking at each other and laughing, and the next they were lip-locked, just a before and an after, the transition nonexistent. The same way life was before Isabel and after Isabel.

He and Chío walked back to the hotel hand in hand, the city quiet and peaceful around them. "Had you thought about this before?" Chío asked, all smiles.

He nodded and lobbed the question back, but Chío didn't respond, instead asking whether they should cut through the park or not. They kissed again in the stairwell of the hotel, then slipped into the room quietly, taking turns in the bathroom brushing their teeth, then saying goodnight with a silent hand squeeze before going to their respective beds, Chío sliding in next to her dad.

Now, though, he does what he's done every morning since Isabel left. He looks for things to talk about with Isabel, tries to predict which of the suspected Supers she'll go after next. It's a habit more than anything. Isabel slowed down her posting quite a bit after she left Asia. Not just on the site, but on social media too. Sam only does it while his brain wakes up. He tries not to judge the people on the site too harshly, which was much harder early on, when Isabel first told him about it. It got easier when he started thinking of those people as other Isabels, real human beings who need to believe in something.

He gets up quietly, glancing at Chío as he scoots past to use the bathroom, phone still in hand. He shuts the door behind him and takes a seat, since he's not into the chaos of peeing in the dark, and turning the lights on sounds even worse. Inertia taking hold well beyond the time he needs to pee, he sees a post that catches his eye. A sighting *in Mexico*?

Even before he clicks over to it, his heart is racing. There's a sizable difference between hearing last night—through Chío, through her mom, through someone else—that Isabel is alive and seeing photographic evidence.

There it is. A grainy picture, like so often happens in these posts. But even if he didn't know Isabel intimately, he would have recognized her pretty quickly. He zooms in, trying to spot the birthmark on her wrist. The angle of the shot isn't quite right, though.

It's not like he doubts it's her. He did last night, at least somewhere deep down. That part of him that was beginning to accept one of his best friends was dead and he was going to have to wrap his mind around it. He'd been scared of hope, despite how he'd been acting. Now the picture proves that it was right to hope. It's part of a brief article from a Puerto Escondido newspaper. There's a little description of what happened. A body found on the beach, a teenage girl. The body went missing, this photo surfaced, police are still investigating.

He closes his eyes and allows himself a smile, then decides to read the comments on the forum. These people aren't always connected to reality in the strictest sense, but they are good at guessing the why of things. They are creative masters of logic, of making outlandish conjecture follow some sort of reason. It's pretty impressive that they've already heard of this story, honestly, even if it has nothing to do with Isabel or Supers.

What Sam wants to know, now that the bigger question of whether she's alive or not has been answered, is how. A big screaming *how* that did not feel in the least bit important last night, but now is the only thing on his mind.

A soft knock on the door startles him into dropping his phone. "Sam, you okay?" It's Santi, whispering through the door.

"Yeah, sorry. I'm good."

"Street tacos get you?"

"No," Sam says, embarrassed and standing to flush. "Just got stuck."

Santi chuckles. "Been there."

Sam washes his hands and passes Santi awkwardly, flopping back onto the bed. Chío is still out, so he starts reading the comments, expecting a bit of silliness and some left-field posts too. But the very first one, the one that's been voted up by other users, says it simply. It's a question, not even a statement. Despite it all, he's actually surprised he hasn't asked it himself yet, even if just in his head, where Chío can't judge him for it.

Kinda looks like Isabel from Michigan, no? Any chance our old friend is a Super herself now?

22

El Bolsón, Argentina

Isabel feels like she's losing her mind.

El Chaltén is at its peak tourist season, and all the restaurants and bars have hired everyone they need already. Isabel takes on more Chinese students, and she got a little Christmas money from her parents, so she can afford to stay around long enough to do all the day hikes in the area. When she's not teaching English, she sticks to herself and her books and her earphones.

She keeps seeing things that would have thrilled her a month earlier—a woman sneaking off the trail and literally blending into her surroundings to pee; a man running his hand through a stream and coming away with dozens of pieces of plastic—but instead of her heart swelling, instead of running toward these people as if they were her salvation, she still finds herself retreating. The bruise lingers.

Part of her doesn't believe that she's seeing what she thinks she's seeing. Why would it happen now? Why would there be a higher concentration of Supers in this remote corner of the world? And the rest of her, which does believe, which continues to flutter with hope and validation when she witnesses these acts, knows that what she sees is not enough. Supernatural abilities were only part of her worldview, only part of the hope. As it turns out, they were not the most important part.

One day, the wind ruins everyone's plans, and the town is busy with hikers with nowhere else to go. The common area in her hostel is loud with conversation, people bonding over the weather, their previous hikes, going from coffee or maté straight to beer. Isabel's in a lounge chair reading, or at least trying to read instead of eavesdropping on the three girls sitting on the couch nearby.

Two are from Singapore, the third a solo college student from Wisconsin, who Isabel gathers is Korean American. The Singaporeans are telling the Wisconsinite about a place up north in El Bolsón, which they call the quietest, most magical hostel they've ever stayed at. They try to convince the Wisconsinite to go, but she's on a limited winter-break trip and doesn't have the flexibility of schedule. This, Isabel has learned over the last few months, is the thing that most commonly sets Americans apart from other tourists from wealthy nations. They travel in shorter spurts, trying to pack everything into the tiny window allotted to them.

Since she can't focus on her book anyway, Isabel cuts in and asks about the hostel. "Quiet and magical sounds great."

Which is how she ends up in El Bolsón.

It's actually a bigger town than El Chaltén, but sleepier, at least where the magical hostel is located. It's a little outside of town near some vineyards, farmland, and a surprisingly fantastic gelato spot. Though she was suspicious of how quiet it would be in a room with seven other beds, she has to admit she's immediately enamored with the place. Everyone reads, they take turns making their own dinners, the common area is soft with chatter. The hikes are less beautiful than in El Chaltén, less impressive. But Isabel is no alpinist, and she is happy to walk along dirt roads seeing cows and sunflowers to arrive at some modest waterfall if it means she will not run into anything Super along the way.

This is exactly what she's thinking on her day hike to a waterfall as two dogs start barking madly at her, stirring her from her thoughts. She doesn't spot them at first—they're the exact same shade of light brown as the road. But then she sees them, at the end of a driveway a little bit up the road. She stops in her tracks, hoping they won't think of her as a threat. They keep barking, though, and it's not the friendly kind of barking. One of them, the smaller one, but with longer, matted hair and the meaner bark, bares its teeth. Isabel immediately searches the ground for a stick or a rock.

A gray, fist-sized stone catches her attention, and she kneels down to grab it, keeping her eyes on the dogs in case they come running at her. Although she doesn't know what she would do in that case. She can't imagine herself hitting a dog with a rock, even if it's to protect herself. She could try to run—she's in the best shape of her life with all the walking these last few months, but will that matter at all? In shape does not mean suddenly faster than a dog.

The dogs stop barking for a second, maybe reconsidering how intimidating Isabel is. She sidesteps, thinking that if she gives them a wide enough berth, they'll calm down a little. Except they don't seem to agree on what qualifies as a wide enough berth. One of the dogs takes a step forward, full-on growling now. The other starts barking, startling her, and the rock in her hand goes flying in their direction. It's not far enough to hit them, or scare them off, but too far for Isabel to walk over and pick it back up.

"Fuck," she says out loud.

She stands there for a moment, wanting to find more rocks but too nervous to take her eyes off the dogs. She takes a couple of steps back, hoping that will help them feel less intruded upon, but the dogs just follow.

Isabel takes a breath, inadvertently whining in the process, and tries backing up again, but the dogs move forward into the space she's given up. The road behind her is quiet, hot and dusty in the late-morning sun. Isabel leans down to grab a fistful of dirt and pebbles, and that's when the larger dog starts running at her, teeth bared so far back she's starting to wonder if the dog is part wolf or coyote or just an asshole of a dog.

Before the situation presented itself, Isabel would have thought that her instinct would be to run. She doesn't know why that's her assumption, that when it comes to a fight-or-flight response, she's one that would choose flight. But her immediate response is to toss her fistful of dirt at the charging dog's face, and then brace herself. She feels in her bones that she's about to get bitten, experience some pain. Yet she knows her best chance right now is to fight back.

The flung dirt slows the dog down for a moment. It yips and stops in its tracks, snapping its mouth and blinking a few times. But the smaller dog starts running, and the first one has recovered, and now they're both milliseconds away. Later, she'll remember the sound of the car approaching, but in the moment it doesn't register.

She hears the car door close, though, and then the footsteps. That all happens so quickly she barely perceives it, what with the dogs advancing at full speed again. She doesn't think she's going to die; the fear is not that specific. She pictures teeth, foaming mouths (though they're not, currently). Adrenaline is pumping and her muscles are tensing, and she prepares to do whatever she can to get away.

The dogs, however, never arrive. A wind sweeps past Isabel—or at least that's what she thinks is happening—and picks the dogs up off their feet. The dogs growl and bark one more time, then start to whimper as their legs scurry uselessly in the air. Isabel tenses, preparing to flee, expecting whatever it is her brain is doing to snap away and the dogs to fall on her.

It never comes, though. What happens is that two teenage boys, speaking Spanish, approach with no urgency, laughing. Isabel can't quite catch what they're saying; they're speaking way too quickly and the accent is very different from what her app has been teaching her, and it's not even the same one she hears at Chío's house.

Her eyes only momentarily flit away from the suspended dogs—which are still whimpering—in order to assess what's happening, to look for a net or whatever it is. Even after Rick, even after the little unexplained sights she's been seeing throughout Patagonia, she wants her mind to go toward natural explanations. Or, rather, quotidian ones, since maybe superpowers are within the realm of nature.

But no. One boy is standing over her, probably checking to see if she's okay. The other one, wearing the national Argentine soccer jersey, is talking to the dogs, his palms held out in front of him in a strange way. It's as if he's holding on to a rope, but there isn't anything in his hands. From his body language, it's clear that he's not actually trying to communicate with the dogs or anything. He's taunting them, laughing at their whimpering.

The boy near her asks, "¿Estás bien?" which she does understand.

"Sí," she says, realizing that her body's still tense. Her knees are bent, and her hands are up, like a high school wrestler preparing for a match to start. She tries to relax, standing straight, letting her shoulders loosen. "Gracias," she adds, but she's still watching the boy air-holding the dogs.

"No te preocupes," the boy near her says, but she's not really listening.

Almost as soon as she starts to concede that she's witnessing something actually Super, Soccer Jersey tugs at the air and the dogs are yanked forward too. They let out actual cries this time as they stumble, snout-first, onto an invisible ground. "What's he doing?" Isabel says, the fear in her stomach easing, though it's replaced by something not entirely better.

"¿Estás bien?" the boy asks again.

"Wait, don't," Isabel says, stepping toward Soccer Jersey as he starts to whip his arms around his head. She tries to run, tries to intercede. But she's still shaky and the boy is too quick at whatever power it is he has.

The dogs get flung backward through the air. It is not just a move to clear them away. There is malice in the motion, a degree of flaunting. Soccer Jersey feels powerful and he wants the animals to know it.

One lands with a cry and immediately limps back toward the driveway they emerged from. The other, the meaner one, doesn't move for a moment, wheezing in the dirt road. The boys laugh and exclaim, celebrating, high-fiving.

Isabel can't contain herself. She rushes at Soccer Jersey and shoves him hard in the chest. "What the hell did you do that for?"

Confused by her reaction, they stop laughing. Soccer Jersey tumbles backward, and the other boy steps between them. "¿Qué te pasa?" he screams. "¡Loca boluda!"

She doesn't care, though, doesn't care that they were trying to rescue her. Doesn't care that he is being open with his abilities. Doesn't care how scared she was a moment ago. There is helping someone, and there is flexing your muscles over a weaker creature.

Isabel heads up the road, wanting to check on the dog. The boys are yelling something or other at her, but Isabel ignores them. It's not dead, at least not yet. She stands over it, not wanting to scare it, not wanting to disturb it, and still a little wary herself of those teeth. Its eyes follow her, and she raises her hands, slowing her gait. When she's almost at its rear legs, she kneels down, feeling the strange urge to put a hand on it.

The dog growls, maybe at her, maybe at the boys still shouting at her. She turns to look at them briefly, but just waves her hand to tell them to go. They share a confused look and say something to her, but she doesn't bother to respond, wanting them to go away.

When she looks down at the dog again, her hand is closer to its fur than she realized. Hesitating, knowing this isn't the most advisable thing to do, but feeling like the dog needs comforting, at least, she lays her hand gently on it.

Instead of snapping or growling, the dog immediately springs up and trots away, running normally. Isabel is frozen in place, watching the dog, which disappears down the driveway without looking back. Then the boys honk the car horn to get her to move out of the road. Soccer Jersey gives her an annoying smirk as they drive past.

23

Dearborn, Michigan

It's a sweltering day and Isabel has just turned twelve. She's a few hours away from hosting a birthday slumber party, and in a few months her grandmother will die from a stroke. They don't know about the latter, clearly, and are choosing to celebrate just the two of them with an ice cream outing before Isabel's friends arrive.

Isabel is in her room, reading and waiting for the doorbell to ring. She's excited about the party, about her friends coming over, few though they are. She's excited, too, to have this old tradition of ice cream with her grandmother come back. Nostalgia has softened the overall impression Isabel has of her grandmother. The years of her grandmother's grumblings about the world have given her an aura of automatic gloom, though that's something Isabel will come to realize only later, and it's nothing but a vague feeling sitting beneath the love she still feels.

For now, Isabel just knows she can't focus on her book. Her

mind is racing with thoughts about the upcoming school year, how grown-up sixth grade sounds. She's hoping her dad will order enough pizza, hoping that they'll find fun ways to fill the day.

Eventually her grandma arrives, and Isabel runs downstairs. As of late, her grandma and her dad have been arguing, though they try to avoid doing it in front of her. Something about Judaism, so Isabel assumes Grandma's upset they're not practicing enough, or something along those lines. Later, she'll piece together that her grandma knew about her father's secret brain, that it had already started showing itself back then, before Isabel could pick up on any signs of it. At the time, it was just adults arguing, something uncomfortable that she could do nothing about.

Isabel receives a birthday lipstick-kiss on the cheek, and after a bit of standing around the kitchen—thankfully, no bickering, no tension to the air—the two of them leave.

"New place or old favorite?" Grandma asks with a smile.

Isabel feels her muscles loosen. It's a good sign, she thinks. Grandma's mood is light, airy. She plays music in the car on the way into Detroit, and they go to a new, pricey gelato place with inventive flavors that are worth every penny if you've got enough spare pennies. They sit outside beneath an umbrella, and a breeze comes in from who knows where to make it exactly the right temperature for ice cream eating.

Grandma talks about her week, the movies she went to see. She's been going to matinees twice a week for years, and while Isabel is starting to notice that Grandma just likes to complain about almost all of them, it's fun to hear her tear the movies down. Now that Isabel thinks about it, the only time she consistently hears her grandmother laugh is when she's recounting plot holes and wooden dialogue.

Taking her last bite of a strawberry-balsamic gelato, Isabel wonders why she doesn't spend more time with her grandmother. *This is lovely,* she thinks.

Then comes the car ride back home, and Grandma starts flipping through radio stations. She lands on a news story, and Isabel feels the tension creeping through her, sucking the air out of the car. Isabel fiddles with the air-conditioning vent.

"What other movies have you watched?" she asks.

"Shh," Grandma responds, turning up the volume on the radio. The story is about a world leader who is allowing thousands of acres of natural reserves to burn down because it'll clear the way for economic development. Shutting her eyes and leaning her head against the window, Isabel tries to think of anything else. The topic itself is depressing enough to fill Isabel with dread, but there's a threat hanging over the news report, and that's her grandmother's commentary.

The story ends. They cut to commercials, and Grandma changes the dial to a classic rock station, turning down the volume. Isabel breathes a little easier, opening her eyes and fiddling with the air vent again so it points away from her.

Then Grandma clears her throat and says, "It keeps tilting, Izzy. I thought maybe it would correct by now. There were days here or there, years, maybe, when I thought the worst of humanity was over." She turns on her blinker to change lanes, the motion almost insultingly casual. "Don't get me wrong. There are good people out there. They exist. And they are fighting. I do believe that."

A pause here, one long enough that it almost lets in space for hope.

"But they're fighting a constantly losing battle. They've been losing so long. They're outnumbered, and now I see it. They will never be able to balance things out, to tip the scales. The good, unfortunately, are just not strong enough to win the fight." She scoffs. "I've seen that for a long time, I just didn't want to believe it."

Now she turns to look at Isabel, a brief glance, just a second, not the prolonged kind that drives Grandma wild with frustration when she sees it in movies. "It's best you know that when you're young. So that you don't spend all that energy on hope. So that you don't get surprised over and over again by the disappointment."

Without waiting for a response (just as well—Isabel does not feel prepared to provide any kind of one), Grandma sighs deeply and parks the car. When Isabel climbs out, she says "Bye" as normally as she can, wondering if she should cancel her slumber party. Grandma blows her another kiss. "Happy birthday!" she calls out.

24

Mazunte, Mexico

Chío expects the town to be a circus of reporters. While she does see a news van drive past them on the highway from Puerto Escondido, it's almost a little disappointing when their hotel is exactly the same as before. Three groups of people are waiting to check in; two young girls with their hair braided walk past, eating mango from a plastic cup and dripping water on the lobby floor. It feels like Chío's living in a different universe from everyone else.

The night before only adds to the sense that she might be dreaming. It's been just four days since they arrived, and she can't believe that's when she thought she was going to see Isabel, when the whole superhero thing might come to an end. In texts, Isabel had said she didn't know where she was going next, and Chío felt like that had somehow been proof that she was coming back, despite the lack of Isabel's college plans, despite how she never once said she missed Dearborn. Just four days ago, Chío thought she was going to have a fun beach vacation, deliver a moving and poignant speech, and then go back home with her friend group intact.

Now she and Sam have made out. Isabel has been dead and then not, and Sam thinks it's because Izzy's a superhero. He actually said those words out loud.

The two of them hadn't had much time to talk privately until her dad left them alone to take a walk at the airport. Their uneasy silence broke quickly when their eyes met and both of them burst into huge grins.

"So," Sam said, eyes flitting shyly away, then coming back to her. "You wanna talk about it?"

Chío thought for a moment, but her brain quickly became crowded and muddled, joy confused with worry and guilt. "Not now, I don't think. Let's find Izzy first."

He nodded slowly. "Okay," he said, and Chío wondered if he was disappointed. Then he pulled out his phone and showed her the forum, the article. Maybe there was something to the question someone had posed.

"Think about it," he said. "It kind of makes sense."

"It absolutely does not make sense."

"If we're living in a world where people do have superpowers, then it's the only explanation for her being dead and then not."

"There are so many things wrong with that statement that I don't even know where to begin," Chío said, not wanting to be mean, but not wanting to sugarcoat it either. She had a brief, horrifying image of Sam going down Isabel's same road, of losing him in the same way. “First of all, your assumption that we’re living in a world with Supers could be—and absolutely is—wrong. Secondly, we don’t know for a fact that Izzy was dead—”

“She was in a morgue.”

“Just because she was caught on camera near the morgue doesn’t mean she was the body in the morgue.” She shook her head, frustrated at Sam, that he would do what everyone else does and assume that logic can be molded without being scaffolded by facts, that facts themselves are malleable to the story you’d like to believe. “We can come up with as many explanations as we want, but without any supporting evidence, theories aren’t theories, they’re just blind guesses. Especially ones that assume the world is different from the one we actually live in.”

“You don’t know for a fact that this world doesn’t have Supers, though,” Sam said, grinning.

Chío rolled her eyes but couldn’t stop herself from smiling at him. “Fair enough,” she said. A couple walked in front of them, carrying large hiking backpacks. Chío thought of Izzy the day they saw her off at the airport. “My point is, I don’t want to throw out wild guesses. Even if your theory is right, it doesn’t help us find her. That’s all I care about for now. Finding her. Everything else can wait.”

Now in Mazunte, Chío and Sam get changed hurriedly so they can go back to the pinned spot on the beach. Her mom is going to call every hospital in the state of Oaxaca, and her dad is going to the police station to see if they’ve flagged her at any bus stations or hotels. Izzy's parents are doing what they can from Michigan, in touch with the State Department, trying to track her credit card purchases.

Chío and Sam sit on some daybeds at a restaurant about twenty feet away from the spot and order lunch. Sam pulls his trunks halfway up his thighs, applying sunscreen to the paler skin above his knees. The hairs there are sparse and delicate, like carefully placed garnishes. Chío can't help but stare and wonder how long this attraction has been sitting within her, waiting to pounce. Or is it completely new, birthed by mezcal and last night's hope?

"Get my back?" Sam asks.

The sun is in front of them, its rays not as harsh, for it's late afternoon already. Chío suspects Sam just wants her touch, and though her first instinct is to call him out for it, she pictures the act of touching him again and it is undeniably pleasant. So she does just that, him sitting on her bed, her legs on either side of him. She lets her fingers linger, feels the muscles that basketball has shaped into his back, his shoulders. Seeing the freckles on his back makes her blush, makes her heartbeat feel thunderous. They are such intimate little flecks; she wonders if anyone at all has seen them this close up since his parents did when he was a little kid. Sam and Chío don't say anything in those thirty seconds or so; it is just the waves and her fingers on his back, the wind rustling the pages of the book she brought, the coconut scent of sunscreen.

"Thanks," Sam says when she's done, his voice indicating that he might have experienced the same thing she just did.

They lie side by side, their hands playing with the sand beside them. Chío keeps her book on her stomach, as if she might be able to bring herself to read it instead of looking at every person on the beach and trying to spot Izzy. At one point, Sam reaches over and hooks his pinkie in hers, and they don't mention that either, but they don't pull apart until a server comes by to see if they want anything.

It is only after they order a late lunch and Sam is halfway through a michelada that they remember: they have Isabel's phone.

"Will she be able to find the spot?" Sam asks.

"She was or is in Mazunte," Chío responds. "It's not that big of a town, she'd pass by here eventually."

Despite that, she's immediately restless, and for the next hour they take turns walking up and down the beach while the other stays put. Then they pay their bill and start walking up and down the beach together. Sam keeps trying to distract her with pleasant conversation, but each lap they take and each time he speaks brings her one step closer to desperation.

"I just don't understand," she says, interrupting Sam in the middle of some half-funny diatribe. "This doesn't make sense. Where the hell is she?"

Sam starts to speak, but seems to think better of it.

"What?" Chío says, a little more aggressively than she means to.

Sam has his shirt off still, slung over his shoulder. He grabs it now and absentmindedly wraps it around his arm. "I just . . . ," he sighs.

"What?" she repeats.

"I think you're a little too caught up in things making sense. I know you're a scientist. I know that's your whole worldview, and for the most part I think it's the right one to have. I believe in science."

"Science isn't religion, it doesn't need you to believe in it. It's just the name we give to the discovery of truth."

"Yeah, I know." He kicks at the sand, sending a softball-sized splatter into the wave that comes lapping at their ankles. "That's the thing, though. There are things left to discover, right?"

"Sure," Chío says, sensing where this is going, and not loving it.

"So, that means that there can still exist a whole bunch of stuff that won't make sense to us. Theoretically, it *has* to. This whole thing with Izzy, the Supers, you were right. I didn't believe her. I thought she was just exaggerating for the sake of the story, because she needed something big to chase after to get out of Dearborn, to get away from her dad, to get out of the U.S. I thought that once she was out, the whole Super thing would float away. But then it didn't, and instead of waiting for her to give up on it, I tried putting myself in her shoes. I started going to her site, and . . ."

Chío stops walking to watch Sam.

He stops, too, turning to face the ocean, unwinding the shirt from his arm and looping it back onto his shoulder. In the water, two kids are flinging wet sand at each other, laughing wildly.

"I missed her," Sam goes on. "And that helped me feel close to her, you know? Made me understand her mindset a little better, at least. We had our group chat but I wasn't seeing you as much either. There was an Izzy-shaped hole, and the only way I knew how to fill it is what made her go away."

He takes a deep breath, bends over to pick up a plastic wrapper poking out from the sand, and shoves it into his pocket. "Look, I'm not saying I think it's scientific fact that there are actually superpowered humans out there. But something is going on that we don't understand, and instead of forcing those events to fit into our understanding of the world, I think it could be helpful to accept that they might be beyond our understanding. It's what Izzy would do. Or is doing."

Chío wants to push back against all of what he's saying. At the logic, at the assertion that she wasn't around enough to help him fill an Izzy-shaped hole, that a website could do that. But for whatever reason, she doesn't. Maybe it's the emotion coming through in Sam's voice, maybe it's the fact that she's emotionally exhausted from the past few days. A girl tanning on a towel to the right flips over onto her back, and for a second Chío's pulse quickens, but it's not Izzy. Of course it isn't.

Chío steps into the water until she's ankle-deep, the crashing waves reaching her knees. Sam follows, standing close enough that their shoulders touch, and Chío takes advantage of that to lean into him. "Okay, so, how do we find her?" she asks.

"Put up the Bat-Signal, I guess?" Sam says, resigned, his tone suggesting that he knows it wasn't funny but that he has nothing more to offer than jokes.

"Weren't you listening to her? Batman doesn't have powers."

"Right, of course." Sam laughs and puts his arm around Chío. He smells like sunscreen, and Chío sinks further into him, wrapping her arm around his waist.

They stay like that for a few minutes, sun on their skin, looking out at the horizon over the ocean, until Chío once again gets restless. They take one last lap up and down the beach and then plop down on the exact spot Izzy had pinned on the map, logic be damned. Sam wades in the water, gets another beer from the nearby restaurant, brings a bowl of guacamole to snack on until dinner.

The sun sets.

It rises again.

Chío wakes up and goes back to the spot, where an hour later Sam arrives from his hostel with a coffee and a croissant. Chío makes calls every few hours, the voices on the other end already tired of hearing from her. She keeps Isabel's parents in the loop, maybe more than she needs to, given that there are no updates. They sit on daybeds and talk, occasionally touch, swim, order food. At night they sit with Chío's family and laugh as if everything's normal, and then she and Sam sneak away to the beach to kiss and talk and sit in heavy Izzy-less silence.

They repeat this for the last two days they have left in Mazunte. Isabel has survived whatever happened to her, it seems, but she has broken her promise to them. It's clear until the end, but Chío doesn't admit it until she boards the plane that will take her back home.

25

Huaraz, Peru

It is four in the morning and Isabel is the lone passenger in a large white passenger van. Up front there's a driver and the man who will be her guide for a twelve-day trek through the mountains.

Ever since the incident in El Bolsón, Isabel has retreated even further from people. She signed up for as many shifts of English tutoring as the service she uses would allow. Because of the time difference, this has resulted in a wonky schedule that keeps her away from others. Plus, her bank account is the heartiest it's been since her travels began.

She stayed the rest of the time she'd paid for at the adorable, magical hostel in El Bolsón, then she started going on hikes, keeping earbuds in so others wouldn't be tempted to strike up conversations. She worked two weeks picking Malbec grapes in Mendoza during their harvesting festival, then flew to Lima, meaning to get to know the city. But the airport was overrun with people, so she looked for an overnight bus somewhere remote, and now here she is in Huaraz.

Having hiked almost every available trail in the Huaraz area and gotten accustomed to the altitude, she feels capable of going on and on. And with that confidence, the thought of twelve days away from civilization sounds fantastic. She's only a few weeks away from meeting up with Chío and Sam, but she has a stopover in Mexico City first and feels like she needs to get away while she can.

Now the van arrives in front of a nondescript hostel that looks more expensive than where Isabel is staying. Isabel closes her eyes and rests her head against the window, thinking it'd be a good idea to sleep. But curiosity takes over, and she waits to see who emerges from the hostel, who she will spend the next two weeks with. Two blond women in their early twenties emerge, decked out in gear that tells Isabel they are much more serious hikers than she is. They hand over a paper to the guide, and in the dim light provided by the van and the overhead streetlights, Isabel tries to make out completely irrational things. Can these women crush others with their thoughts? Can they set things ablaze? Do they want to?

The driver leads them to the back of the van and arranges their bags beside Isabel's, then slams the door. They climb in through the sliding door, each offers Isabel a muted, accented "hello," and the van rumbles onward. The five-hour drive is dreamlike after that. She's not sure how much she sleeps, how many stops they make for more people. The sky outside the tinted windows lightens very slowly. Isabel opens her eyes only to change songs on her phone, which, since she's opted not to have a SIM card, is mostly good for just music and pictures. She's happy for the disconnect, and sent texts to her parents and Sam and Chío before to let them know not to worry.

After about an hour of winding roads, they come to a sudden halt. The sky is brighter, though the sun isn't fully up yet, as far as Isabel can tell. She looks around and sees that three guys have joined her and the two blond women. They all put away their earphones and rub the sleep from their eyes as the guide slides open the door and starts handing them little cups of tea poured from a large thermos.

Despite the hikes she's taken and the time she's spent in the mountains, Isabel still finds the landscape striking. The snowy peaks, the brown jagged inclines, the green valleys below.

Isabel takes a cup of tea and stretches her legs. The air is chilly, her breath coming out in big clouds. She looks around at her companions. The Latino guy is on his own, taking pictures of the mountains, his tea at his feet. The other two look like they might be a father and son—both look exhausted in the same way, their hair mussed from sleeping in the van. The women are rummaging through their bags, speaking in what sounds like hushed German.

Now the guide approaches her with a plastic container. "Breakfast," he says with a smile. He's significantly younger than she assumed at first glance, close to her age. Her first thought is a sense of panic that this is who she has to trust to lead her through the wilderness for so long. But the truth is, he's probably better at finding his way around these mountains than she is at finding her way around Dearborn.

"Thanks," she says.

"Your name was Isabel, yes?" He's got a bit of an accent, and a lot of warmth in his voice, like he's already talking to a friend. He's attractive too, with beautifully dark, kind eyes; his whole vibe is generally pleasant, and Isabel suddenly feels very happy to be in this particular part of the world.

"Yup," she answers him. "What's your name?"

"Ezequiel," he says, the second syllable pronounced "eh," not "ee."

"Nice to meet you," Isabel says. They both look at the majestic mountains. The Latino guy who was taking pictures comes over and points his phone, all smiles and laugh lines. He looks to be in his thirties, and has an absurd amount of energy for having taken the same four a.m. van ride. After a few snaps and a selfie with her and the guide, he goes over to the German girls.

Isabel takes a bite from the orange slices in her breakfast container, then turns to Ezequiel. "Do you do this hike often?"

"Twice a month, usually. Sometimes just once."

"You like it?"

"I love it. This is my home. I grew up in a village just behind that mountain," he says, pointing. "We will pass by it and have lunch on day three."

"And you don't get tired of it? Leading tourists around the same route?"

"Well, I take a few different hikes. But look at it," he says, gesturing grandly with a sweeping motion. "How can you get tired of this?"

Isabel takes in the sight. She draws a deep breath and has to admit that it's a fair question. Especially with how few people are visible from up here.

The group has breakfast and finishes their tea as they take pictures of the sunrise, none of which do any justice to the view. Then the driver honks them a little goodbye and continues up the road, while two men who've appeared with horses come by to pick up their bags and carry them ahead to the first campsite.

Ezequiel gathers the group and explains again the general trajectory of the hike, plus what they can expect for the day. Isabel doesn't care much about the plan, so her mind wanders, studying the others. *Please don't be Supers,* she finds herself thinking. *Please don't be terrible.*

No matter how much she's done it over the past weeks, though, she has not gotten better at sussing out if a stranger is good-hearted or not, just from their appearance. Observing someone long enough might give some hints, sure. But watching a bunch of people standing around listening to descriptions of a trail and altitude changes doesn't offer much in the way of a peek into their souls.

When they start hiking, Isabel is closest to Ezequiel, and so she's ahead of everyone else in the group, even though she expects herself to be the least qualified to lead the way. They all seem like serious hikers, not teenagers looking to escape civilization and happy to pay a precious thousand dollars to do so in the mountains.

She can hear the others behind her starting to make small talk, and though she's curious about Ezequiel, she's happy to just listen in and let the sound of her footsteps take over her thoughts.

ꟹ

The first day is an easy one, hiking-wise, at least relatively. Just a few hours at a slow pace for the altitude. There was definitely a point as they were ascending to the Cacanapunta Pass that Isabel was wondering if she'd made a terrible, terrible mistake. But a quick rest and a hearty snack later, she'd recovered and was feeling rather elated with herself, proud of the way she could push herself physically and not entirely hate the experience.

Now they've set up camp near a lagoon. The two German girls opt to stay by the official spot near the restroom, as do the father-and-son duo. There's another group near there, though, and better views down the hill by the lagoon itself, so Isabel decides to set up her tent there. She struggles with the fabric for a while, until Ezequiel shows up and helps her make sense of the equipment she's borrowed from the tour company. Isabel feels a flush of embarrassment, but there is no judgment in Ezequiel's offer to help. He seems to want to do only that, nothing more.

"It's hard when it's not your tent, no?" he says kindly.

Once her tent is staked, he sets up the gas stove and starts preparing dinner for the group. Isabel's exhausted but feels strange watching him do everything, since he not only walked as much as they did (if not more, doubling back every now and then to check on the stragglers), but was carrying a heavier bag too. "No, it's okay," he assures her. "You rest." She insists, though, and finally he says that she can go up the hill to tell the Germans that dinner will be ready in twenty minutes.

While Isabel was looking forward to reading alone outside her tent and enjoying the view of the Huayhuash peaks until sleep took over, the group ends up gathered inside a tent that shields them from the wind, eating and chatting. The cold increases dramatically once the sun dips below the mountains, but only the German girls go back up the hill for an early night.

Tomás, the picture-happy solo traveler, is the chattiest among them. Born in Mexico, he currently lives in San Francisco, working as a nurse for elderly patients. The father-and-son duo are Belgian, a little on the reserved side until Tomás coaxes more out of them. "I love that you're traveling together, it's adorable," he says. "Do you do these hikes often?"

The older man, Ricard, takes a moment, looking at his son, Jacques, who stares down at the ground. "We haven't spent much time together the last ten years," he says. "This is kind of a reunion. To be honest, I don't do much hiking." Isabel can see his son suppress a smile—at least she thinks that's what she sees. "So now I'm here, trying to catch up. Emotionally and literally." He barks out a laugh. "Sorry for being slow."

"Oh, my heart broke and healed itself so quickly," Tomás says. "Beautiful, I love it, I wish my dad were here too." He laughs, but it's clear he's not joking, and that he doesn't even care to pretend it's a joke.

Tomás is disarming conversationally the way Ezequiel is in his presence. Isabel doesn't think it's a superpower, just a character trait, a run-of-the-mill skill that makes her feel even more at ease.

That night she sleeps deeply, pulled into dreams by her body's exhaustion and a sense of peace that she has, at least for the moment, escaped Supers and the thoughts they bring.

The next few days are perhaps some of the best Isabel has had on her travels. There's something about having nothing planned for the day but a methodical moving forward. Looking down at her feet to make sure where she's stepping and then looking back up and getting a stark reminder of the physical beauty of the world.

They get one miserably rainy day, and they opt to scrap one of their more relaxed days of exploration in order to avoid hiking in the gross weather. Isabel sits in her tent and reads, listens to music, naps, anticipating the moment when Ezequiel will come by and tell her a meal is ready. She thought she was done with people entirely, but these days are proving that's not the case. Maybe it's because none of them have any superpowers (other than Tomás's knack for conversation), or maybe this particular group is just fun to spend time with. Even the German girls, who keep to themselves and seem generally serious and prone to complaints, have been disarmed by Tomás and the shared experiences they've all had in the Andes.

There are moments of exhaustion and frustration, of wondering what the hell she is doing spending money on walking in the middle of nowhere. Her body has never worked so hard, and when she lies down at night, she can feel the tiredness in her bones. Every now and then she stumbles, or some rocks she steps on go tumbling down the side of the mountain, rolling and rolling without ever seeming to come to an end. Even the thought of a sprained ankle seems ruinous, despite Ezequiel's satellite phone and the donkeys and horses that carry gear from campsite to campsite.

Mostly, though, it's beautiful. Her mind is clear and happy, and she relishes the wonder that she can cast up pleasant memories whenever she wants to. She can fantasize! What a brilliant skill brains have for fiction. Why has she been so obsessed with telekinesis or invisibility when her brain has the capacity for imagination? Why has she let her brain control its fictions when she can take the helm too?

A cheesy line of thinking, but the mountains seem to provoke sentimentality. Or maybe it's Tomás and his chattering, Ezequiel and his listening, the two Belgian men walking together for the first time in years, each step a reconciliation. There's a lot she doesn't know about them, but everything that they've revealed seems to point at that: pain getting buried beneath healing, the slow march toward recovered intimacy.

On the seventh day, Isabel is walking near them, listening to the pleasant lilt of their French. They're lagging behind everyone else, as usual, Ricard because of his age and inexperience. Sometimes Jacques goes on ahead, but mostly he sticks around his dad. They've been hiking for three hours already, ascending to get to a pass between the mountains. They haven't stopped for lunch yet, which means it's coming soon. But Ricard is struggling through the switchbacks, and he takes off his pack and sits on a rock to drink water. Isabel and Jacques do the same, but after a couple of minutes, Ricard still isn't ready to go. He says something in French, which is easily understood to mean he wants them to continue on without him.

Jacques argues for a while, but eventually they keep going. He looks over his shoulder every thirty seconds or so, causing Ricard to yell out, "Je suis pas encore mort!"

"What was that?" Isabel asks.

"He is telling me to stop being annoying," Jacques says, smiling.

They catch up with the others, who have paused at the top of the pass for lunch and to take in the view of a turquoise lake below. Even the German girls are smiling and chatting, lamenting the fact that the trek is already more than halfway done.

Isabel has watched how Ezequiel knows which of the many trails to follow, and she admires how familiar he is with the land. Isabel knows the highways in Dearborn, knows the streets of her neighborhood, knows the parks pretty well. But not the place itself, not Michigan. Unfair to compare Dearborn to this place, sure, but she wonders if she would have cared to stay home if she knew it as intimately as Ezequiel knows these mountains.

Aren't you forgetting something? the Chío voice in her head says. *You didn't leave Dearborn because you didn't know its streams. You left to hunt Supers. Now look at you. Hiding in the Andes so that you don't come across them.*

Fortunately, she's distracted from this line of thought by the group packing up their things. Ricard hasn't gotten there yet, and Jacques looks worried until they see his dad's bright red jacket at the bottom of the hill.

"I will bring him lunch," Ezequiel says. "We have a lot of walking, so we shouldn't wait." He tells them to go through the pass and stick to the left to descend, saying he'll catch up and that the trail should be easy to figure out. Just in case, he gives the German girls a map, since they're the most experienced hikers, and points out the path they need to follow.

For the next hour, the group is chatty, feeling energized from lunch and the fact that they're not climbing up for the moment. Tomás takes dozens of pictures of them, his phone at full charge thanks to a solar battery. Then he gets tips on going to the Amazon from the German girls, who'd been there a few weeks before.

The chatter keeps Isabel from sinking into her thoughts, but eventually it dies out and everyone's natural pace separates them. Isabel knows that Chío's voice will be returning soon, if not her own natural tendency toward fatalistic thoughts. She tries focusing on the view, on her steps, on her breathing. But the thoughts sneak in anyway: *The world is even worse than you imagined. You can run away from the realization all you want, hide wherever you like, it's still true. Supers are out there being as shitty as everyone else.*

Isabel hears footsteps behind her and sees Ezequiel coming up. She smiles and says, "Hey."

"Everything good?" he asks, flashing a thumbs-up.

She nods. "Yes. Is Ricard okay?"

"Maybe a little altitude problem, but nice and slow and he will be okay," he says, another easy smile. Isabel thinks about Gareth, and in that moment realizes that she's developing a little crush on her guide. To her disappointment, he picks up his pace and goes ahead of her, probably to pass along the information to Jacques.

Isabel's left with her thoughts again, but she picks up her own pace to catch up to Tomás and get him talking, thankful that he's always nearby and able to provide a distraction. He indulges her for a while, telling her about his job in San Francisco, caring mostly for elderly people with mobility issues, often with Alzheimer's as well. It's a nice reminder to Isabel that there are entire professions meant to help others out, and it's enough to put her back at ease until the end of the day.

At the campsite, Isabel sets up her tent and chooses to huddle inside against the cold with a book until dinner is ready. When Ezequiel strikes a knife against a pot to let everyone know food is served, Isabel comes out and realizes that Ricard still hasn't caught up to the group. She can sense the worry on Jacques's face too.

The mood has shifted, and everyone stares into their bowls

and then looks toward the trail, hoping for a flash of his red jacket. Jacques shovels his dinner into his mouth, then starts pacing, going back the way they came for five, ten minutes at a time, coming back looking more and more worried. Ezequiel tries to calm him. "It happens. There are many trails, many ways to go. It does not mean he's lost, he's just not with us."

The reassurances don't do much, especially as nightfall approaches and Ricard still hasn't come. They can see a local villager headed their direction, and when he arrives, Ezequiel speaks with him in what Isabel assumes is Quechua. The man shakes his head a few times, and Isabel hopes that she's just reading into it, but when the man departs, Ezequiel says, "No. But he will spread the word to others on the trail. Meanwhile, I will go back and look. There is a town close by, and there is a chance he went there. It's too late to go there tonight, but we will go tomorrow." He puts his hand on Jacques's shoulder, saying the next words just for him. "He has his tent, he has water, he has food. He will be okay. These things happen, the next day we find them and we all laugh."

Jacques nods solemnly and thanks Ezequiel, looking only the slightest bit comforted. Isabel imagines that it's like turbulence on an airplane: if the flight attendants aren't nervous, you shouldn't be either. But she's not about to say that to Jacques, since it probably won't help to hear. The group tries to small-talk for a while, but conversation doesn't take, and then everyone begins to retreat to their tents, offering Jacques a kind platitude as they go.

In her tent, Isabel wants to go straight to sleep. But her

thoughts are running rampant, Chío's voice prodding her about Supers, her grandmother's voice cursing the world. She starts to think about Jacques and Ricard, and how she would feel if it were her dad out there in the wild, left to his own devices through the cold night. She tries to really picture it, imagining that she'd feel nothing. That her innate love of her parents, or at least of her dad, was conditional and had dissipated in the years since he revealed his secret brain. And while that may be true, there is a sinking feeling in her stomach imagining her dad in physical danger. She remembers that dog in Argentina on the ground, its whimpering. How things that bare their teeth can still be hurt.

She keeps tossing and turning and drifting into restless sleep. After a few hours of this, she unzips her sleeping bag and throws on the jacket she bought just for this trip to face the cold and goes to pee, grabbing some toilet paper and a ziplock bag for the waste.

It's freezing outside. A slight wind whistles through the tall grass, causing the tents to flap. There's a sliver of moon helping light up their campsite, but Isabel's thankful for her headlamp, since the terrain is rocky and uneven. She only really needs to go to the nearest bushes—even if anyone comes out while she's peeing, they'd have to point a hearty light right at her to see anything at all. But she's always been weird about strangers hearing her pee, and so she sleepily heads out a little farther than she has to.

Watching her steps carefully, she chooses a spot between two bushes, at the top of a little slope that'll make the angle easier and keep her pants dry, crucial when it's freezing outside. As she squats, she finds herself impressed by her mind's steadfast ability to berate her with its usual complaints.

You were so stupendously wrong, it says, ignoring the cold on her bare legs, the creepiness of the howling wind.

"Yeah, well," she says out loud, her voice barely a whisper. Isabel sighs, tired by her inner monologue at this point, more annoyed than anything else. The clouds blow in front of the moon, throwing everything into a deeper darkness, so she closes her eyes.

And that suddenly strikes her as a perfect response to everything her brain tries to tell her, everything her grandmother used to whisper about. The great imbalance of the world tilting toward cruelty and destruction, all the things people do to each other. *Yeah, well.* It almost sounds like wisdom this late at night.

Isabel laughs to herself and opens her eyes. The clouds have moved again and the white light of the moon is reflecting off a snowy peak in the distance. Isabel turns to look at the campsite to her left, thinking about Tomás working with elderly people, providing care and companionship. She thinks of Ezequiel spreading his joy and reassuring Jacques. Thinks of Jacques and Ricard attempting to mend their relationship.

There was Rick and the jerks in Argentina, but there was also Hatori, or whoever it was that pulled her to safety in the Tokyo subway. There was the woman who rescued people from the building in Hualien, and Daphne sitting on the couch with her making her feel at home, and Shu-ling helping her make the flyers. There was Gareth being sweet, and Sienne checking that she got back to the hostel safely. There've been dozens of kind people in the past months—hundreds, really.

The world is generally evil. Yeah, well.

There is hate and destruction and a lack of humanity among human beings. A losing battle, sure. But who, other than Isabel, is keeping count? What does it matter what the score is? There is good and there is evil and there is no actual way to keep track, no definitive answer other than what Isabel might feel at any given moment.

As she pulls her pants up, Isabel revels in this little epiphany. She's been wanting an epiphany for so long, ever since Rick. Some groundbreaking realization that could make it all feel okay. She had just never put it together. Who cares who's winning? There are kind people out in the world, people good down to their core. No matter if there's more or fewer of them, they exist. What else could matter?

She feels giddy, elated. She can't imagine falling asleep right now, and for the first time all week she wishes her phone were able to put her in touch with Sam and Chío. She wishes there were somewhere to go, a way to enjoy this elation.

Instead, she stands there, feeling the cold flush her cheeks and drain the sensation from her fingers. Then she remembers she just peed where she's standing, and instinctively sidesteps. When she does, though, her left foot lands on a loose rock, which slides out from beneath her. She tries catching herself, shooting her arms out. But thanks to the angle of the slope, when her shoulder hits, her head follows, smacking into the hard rocky terrain. The last thing she notices when everything starts to go black is that she's still falling.

26

Dearborn, Michigan

Back in Michigan, Sam and Chío are both met with a numbness they can't shake. It's supposed to be a time of big emotions. Everyone else at school is definitely feeling them. People are celebrating college admissions with parties, couples are breaking up, friends are desperate to spend every waking moment together. Song lyrics are scribbled on the white space of shoes, on desks, on bathroom stalls, dripping with sentimentality. Isabel is old news. In their minds she disappeared long ago.

Sam sees his basketball teammates focus on the playoffs. And while basketball was a salve for him this past year, now he's suddenly lost interest. For the first time all year, he skips a practice, choosing instead to go to Chío's house after school. This is his solution for the numbness: Chío. He gravitates to her as if her presence alone can make sense of Mexico.

Chío's solution is to research. She doesn't even know what she's researching per se, but she has to find a hypothesis, some hint that Isabel is out there in the world. She needs to know what happened, and why the hell Izzy has not even contacted her and Sam. When she's not doing last-minute studying for her AP exams, Chío is reading news articles from Mexico. She's reading any scientific study available to her via the school's library, any title at all potentially about superpowers. Cells replicating, new medicine that improves human function, discovery of new species of plants or animals. Anything that could even slightly provide an explanation. Scientific or not, but at least rational.

She spends hours going through Isabel's phone for clues. It would feel like more of an invasion of privacy if Isabel had secret conversations, friends she hadn't told Chío and Sam about. Her text conversations with people line up almost exclusively with where she was when she met them. They are quick bursts of friendship, plans and inside jokes, gone as soon as Isabel or the other person moved on. A few of them checked back in on her occasionally, or vice versa. She sent someone named Maude a picture of a zucchini on a grill with exclamation marks, to which Maude replied with a crying-laughing emoji.

Chío spends so much time trying to find out where Isabel is that she barely processes the changes that are coming her way. Graduation, college, the start of her pursuit to become a full-fledged scientist. The fact that she'll have to spend time away from her family, the fact that she and Sam will no longer be around each other. Wherever she is in the world, Isabel does not know that Chío and Sam have hooked up. That when Sam is over at her place, studying for his tests on her bed, Chío will look over at the exposed inch of skin as his shirt rides up and want to slip in next to him. That sometimes she does exactly that, overwhelmed by everything she's found online and everything she can't find, and wanting to madly kiss it all away. To focus just on Sam's lips and arms and the way he holds her when she's exhausted herself and becomes overwhelmed with tiredness. He wipes a thumb against her cheeks as if she's crying, but she hasn't since they got back.

Her family walks on eggshells around her, which is annoying, even though she can't blame them for it.

One day, about three weeks after Mexico, Sam tells her that he's going to see Izzy's parents. She thinks it's too grown up of a move, uncomfortable, awkward. But she doesn't want to make Sam do it on his own, and despite Izzy's dad being a raging idiot, she did always like Izzy's mom, and she feels bad for her. It is kind to show up, and, admiring and begrudging Sam for the idea, she goes along.

It's strange to be back at Isabel's house after a year. It looks the same, which shouldn't be a surprise. Except there aren't tea mugs by the side of the sink, no plate with a smear of dulce de leche, which Isabel fell in love with at Chío's house and used to have as an afternoon snack with two cookies. Chío thought being in Isabel's house would cause her to miss her friend more than before, but this house no longer feels like Isabel to her. Chío now pictures Isabel in hostel lobbies, in beach hammocks, in the world's subway stations. She pictures a ghost, not a girl living in a three-bedroom house in Dearborn.

They sit on the back deck, since it's a nice day out. It's turned into a whole reunion, not just Sam and Chío but their parents too. The mood is exactly as strange as Chío would have guessed: tense, awkward, everyone's movements and speech feeling staged, too carefully thought out.

"Have you heard anything?" Chío asks Izzy's parents as soon as there's a break in the initial small talk about college.

Sam's parents look down at the ground, true to their confrontation-avoiding ways. Sam himself looks at Chío, but she meets his eyes, trying to communicate that it's a fair question, that she doesn't aim to pick at wounds, she just thinks they could have heard something and hadn't thought to bring it up.

"There's a nice lady at the State Department we've been chatting with," Izzy's mom says. "They're still talking with authorities in Mexico. Unfortunately, unless she enters the country again, they don't really have a way of flagging her passport for other travel, so we don't even know if she's in Mexico anymore. And even if she enters the U.S., they might not be able to tell us right away."

"They say she's not a security risk, and since she's an adult, there's nothing else we can do," her dad chimes in, taking a swig of his beer. Chío doesn't really want to get him started on his whole anti-government thing, so she doesn't ask any follow-up questions.

"You haven't heard from her?" Izzy's mom asks, her voice

carrying just enough hope in it to break Chío's heart. "Social media or anything?"

Chío shakes her head.

The mood threatens to go from uncomfortable to somber, and Chío is fine with that. They should all be somber. They should all be losing their minds. The first, shocking scare of Isabel being dead might have passed, but that doesn't mean it's not still in the realm of possibility.

Sam compliments a dip on the table, asks how Izzy's mom made it. She responds with a recipe, offering to share it with him, though Sam has never once shown an interest in cooking. Chío's dad makes a joke to that effect, and they all laugh, relieved at the tension dissipating.

After two weeks of numbness, though, Chío would rather have the tension. She cannot stomach the thought of all of them being here any longer without keeping Isabel the center of attention. "Is that it, then? Do we just"—she stands up, though she's not going anywhere—"I don't know, leave her for dead?"

"Chío," her dad says, his voice pleading.

She's about to shoot back with something else, but she notices Isabel's mom tearing up, and the fire goes out of her. Sam's eyes meet hers and he gives a little head shake. She knows he's right, but she can't stay here and move on. "I'm sorry," she says. "Is it okay if I go up to her room? Just for a few minutes."

"Of course, honey," Isabel's mom says, her voice strained. Then she looks at Santi and smiles and says she's okay, it's all okay.

Chío's already up by then, heading to the sliding glass door that leads into the kitchen. Ignoring the lack of tea mugs, she lets muscle memory guide her through the living room and to the stairs, doubling back to go down the hallway to Izzy's room.

She hadn't even paused to consider the fact that it might look different. Izzy's not dead, it's not like there was some memory that her parents had to preserve of her. As soon as she left, they moved in some boxes that had probably been in the way in the basement. Izzy herself had taken down her posters, given away most of her books. Chío had been with her when she did that, sorted through to find the ones she wanted before taking the rest down to the library to donate.

Part of her thought that maybe she could go through all Izzy's things, search for clues, like some amateur detective. It now strikes her why she's been on a kick of listening to mystery audiobooks since she got back. Through her numbness, she has been clinging to the idea that there are clues out there for her to solve, that there will be a satisfying resolution. It was comfort she didn't even realize she needed.

The bed, at least, is unchanged. Chío walks over to it, remembering Izzy falling out of its clutches the day she left. She remembers all the nights they spent together watching movies, grabbing popcorn one kernel at a time, not by the fistful, so as not to spill any on the bedspread. She plops down on it, feeling so heavy with sadness that she can't bear being on her feet any longer.

She lies down facing the wall and waits for the tears to come.

They don't, though, and soon she senses someone else in the doorway. Turning over her shoulder, she sees it's Sam, who gives her a little smile, then comes to the bed and sits at the foot of it. The bed creaks under his weight, and then she feels his hand go to her ankle. It's exactly the kind of touch she wants at the moment.

"I think what sucks the most is that I'm *angry* at her too," Chío says. "Above it all, the confusion, the worry, there's this layer of anger that she hasn't told us anything. Hasn't reached out. She can. She could."

For once, Sam doesn't stick up for Isabel, doesn't point out the abandoned phone, doesn't make excuses. He just says, "Yeah. I know."

"I want her to be okay. But if she's okay, she's being such a dick right now."

"Super Dick. There's a superhero for you."

Chío manages a laugh. "I don't know. I'm pretty sure that one's taken."

"A few million times, probably."

Chío closes her eyes, suddenly tired. She remembers how they used to joke about Isabel's bed being so comfortable she couldn't escape it. She had even believed it, to an extent, despite spending many a night on it and finding it no more or less comfortable than her own bed. Then she had dismissed the idea when she learned about Isabel clicking around on Actually Super every night. Now, though, the bed feels almost magical, the way it's pulling her to the edge of sleep so quickly. “I just hope she’s happy,” Chío mumbles into the pillow.

Chío wakes up some time later, drool drying on her cheek. She’s not sure how long she’s been out, but Sam has left her alone and closed the door. She can still hear voices downstairs, though the sunlight coming into the room has changed. Sitting up, she runs her hands through her hair and gets her bearings.

That’s when she remembers what Isabel said back when she first announced her trip last spring at Roys’s. Once the shock had mellowed and Sam was trying to ease the tension with jokes, he asked why Supers would hide. “I don’t know,” Isabel had said. “But I imagine that if I had a superpower, I would try to help as many people as I could while being as invisible as possible.”

“Would you tell us?”

“If I was Super?” Isabel had thought for a while. “Chío obviously wouldn’t believe me if I said it, so I’d have to prove it. I might try to prove it and then run away somewhere and wait for you to chase after me so I’d know you still love me.”

Chío reached over to steal Sam’s napkin and throw it at Isabel. “If that’s your way of guilting us to drop out of school and come with you, it’s not happening.”

“I don’t know, I’m listening. I don’t want Izzy to think we don’t love her,” Sam said.

"So, if you're invisible, how do we chase you?" Chío asked.

Isabel had taken a spoonful of her ice cream, pensive. "I'll send out a signal. Something subtle enough to be cool, but obvious enough that you'll know where to find me."

"Nothing cooler or subtler than Roys's," Sam said, holding up his cup.

The conversation had shifted then, Chío doesn't remember to what. But her heart is racing with hope and she tidies up the bed and sprints down the stairs. She smiles as best she can at everyone to apologize for disappearing, then when they all say it's fine, she asks Sam if he feels like getting some ice cream.

27

Huayllapa, Peru

Almost as soon as Isabel opens her eyes, she knows that she's in an unfamiliar room. It's plain, the walls white, sienna curtains on the lone window pulled tight but not keeping the daylight out. There's a bedside table with a lamp, and an empty chair off to the side. Someone nearby—in a different room, maybe—is playing a video. The door to the room is cracked open, letting in more light.

Despite the throbbing headache, the first thing she thinks of is Ricard. She looks around her as if there might be an answer, as if he might be lying in an adjacent bed. Pushing herself up onto one elbow, she finds a glass of water on the bedside table, and she drinks thirstily from it. Her body's a little sore, but aside from the headache, nothing hurts enough to scare her. As she sets the glass back down, she notices her phone plugged into the wall, and she reaches for it.

It picked up Wi-Fi at some point, because there's a slew of notifications on the screen, but it's not currently connected. There are emails from places whose mailing lists she's somehow managed to subscribe to over the past few months. Announcements for improvements at the Bangkok airport, 15 percent off her next rideshare in Australia, they miss her at a coffee shop in Singapore. There are texts from Sam and Chío, asking if she's back in civilization. She rolls her eyes at that phrasing, but is happy to see them check in on her. Then she realizes that they sent those messages the day she was supposed to get back to Huaraz. There are even some missed voice messages from her mom, who only remembers that app function when she's worried.

Isabel exits back to the main screen, and when she sees the date, her head hits the pillow. She's been out for a few days. Or, no, that's not exactly right. Now she remembers waking up here and there, someone in that chair next to her. Another flash of a different room, brighter, a doctor with a gruff voice speaking to a nurse. Closing her eyes, she can picture herself in the mountains, the moon shining its light on the snowy peaks. God, did she really hurt herself while peeing? Is she still in a hospital? There are other scenes in her mind, but she can't tell if they're memories or dreams. Being carried on a gurney, someone changing her bandage.

After going through the rest of her notifications, Isabel leans back and tries to sleep again, but she's clearly done enough of that lately and she's up for good. She wants to tell people she's okay, but she doesn't know where to start, feels too overwhelmed.

After a few minutes, during which Isabel tries to remember

what happened after she fell, as well as muster the energy to use the bathroom, she hears footsteps that sound like someone is headed to the room. She's thankful, if not for the answers she'll get, then at least for a break in the monotony. She expects to see a nurse or a doctor, someone who will greet her somewhat uninterestedly and fill her in on her ailments in Spanish she'll only catch pieces of.

Instead, she's pleasantly surprised to see it's Ezequiel. He steps through the door quietly, but he's focused on a plastic bag he's rummaging in. He's moving toward the chair by her bed in an automatic way, which tells her it's not the first time he's come to see her. He sits and is pulling out an apple when he notices her watching him, and he startles, the apple jumping from his grip and rolling on the floor toward the bed.

"You're awake," he says, smiling slightly, eyebrows raised. He looks even younger now, cuter too, his hair wet from a recent shower, and it's flopping down his forehead and over his ears. He's not in hiking gear either, just jeans and an alpaca sweater.

"What happened to Ricard?" she asks.

Ezequiel furrows his brow, as if that was all so long ago he doesn't remember. "Don't you want to know what happened to you? Where you are?"

"I'm okay, right? More or less? I'm not in a ton of pain, I can move everything. So, I'm okay?"

"Yes, I think so."

"Then let me hear about Ricard first. That was the last thing on my mind," she says. It's not exactly true, but it is what she's been thinking about for the last hour, and she needs to know.

"You're not hungry?" Ezequiel asks, offering her the bag.

She's not sure why he's stalling, but she takes the bag from him anyway. Inside there's some fruit, a bag of plantain chips, some nutty granola-looking thing. She grabs the plantains and hands him back the rest of the goodies, which he sets aside. Then he squats down to retrieve the apple he dropped earlier and rubs it on his shirt.

"I'm sorry," he says. "It's good to see you awake. We weren't able to call your family. You didn't put an emergency number on the paper you signed, and your phone was locked. It connected to the internet in Huaraz, but we couldn't answer messages for you." He reaches for her phone, presumably to hand it over to her.

Isabel waves him away. "It's okay. I'll tell them in a little bit. Is Ricard okay?"

Ezequiel leans back into his chair, relenting with a smile. "Yes, he is okay. He had made it to town the night before, but there wasn't a way to tell us. The next day someone came on the trail with a note for Jacques about where he was staying. Nothing bad."

"Like you had said," Isabel points out.

"Yes." Ezequiel draws out the word. "Usually, it isn't bad. Every now and then it is, though." He looks at her meaningfully.

"So, they had a happy reunion?"

He nods. "It was very sweet to see. Lots of tears, especially from Tomás," Ezequiel says, letting out a chuckle. "Ricard and

Jacques hugged for a long time. The people who Ricard stayed with are building a hostel for travelers. They didn't even want to take his money for a night, but Jacques gave them all the money he had, enough to build a new room and a bathroom for their hostel. More tears, more hugging. It was all very nice. Except . . ."

"Except I was now missing."

Ezequiel says nothing.

"I don't like peeing where people can hear me," Isabel sighs, and opens the bag of plantains, thinking his silence is him trying to bite his tongue on calling her irresponsible. "My friend Chío is going to yell at me so much for doing that." She reaches in and grabs a chip, the flavor exploding in her mouth and awakening her hunger. Has she even eaten in the past week? "So, how did you find me? How long did it take?"

At this, Ezequiel takes a deep breath and leans forward, his elbows on his knees, his face angled toward the ground, in thought. "Not that long," he says. He's not meeting her eyes anymore.

Isabel decides not to press him, to let him come to what he needs to say on his own. She wonders if he's going to yell at her, if he's going to beg her not to sue (though she's pretty sure she signed release forms and that suing is much more likely to happen in the U.S., not that she would even think to do that anyway). She recalls, instead, what it felt like when she had that midnight epiphany before stupidly tripping herself into oblivion. The feeling comes rushing back. *Yeah, well.*

"I need to tell you something," Ezequiel says. "It's going to sound strange. But it might help you understand everything—" He stops himself, standing up suddenly enough that Isabel thinks he's going to run off. He's just checking to see if there are other people in the hallway. She hears him shut the door to the room and then he's back.

"When we made it to town, it wasn't just a happy reunion with Ricard, and hoping you were there too. We knew you hadn't just gone off and left your tent up, we knew you were hurt somewhere. The reunion? It happened only after I found you at the bottom of the hill. You were in the clinic here. Thankfully, the doctor was only an hour away. Jacques was happy to see his dad not just because Ricard was okay, but because he had seen you hurt a couple of hours before and he had worried the same had happened to his father."

"Did I really look that bad?" Isabel laughs. She can tell she has some lingering bruises, but other than her head, nothing hurts enough to make her think she had been seriously injured. She grabs some plantain chips, even though it feels incongruous to the moment. The hunger is building up quickly and she almost wants to shovel them into her mouth. She also feels a swell of emotion thinking of the father and son hugging. There is no scoresheet, she remembers. No one is keeping track except herself, and she's been counting all wrong.

Ezequiel scoots the chair closer, and his expression turns very serious. "You might have died if I hadn't found you quickly enough. Although . . ." He trails off, starts over. "It wasn't just luck that helped me find you." The way he's holding her gaze, it's like he's searching for something in her eyes, like he's trying to read her thoughts. "It was something else. And the only reason I will tell you what it is, is because I think you already know."

Now he has Isabel's attention. She crinkles the plantain bag, her breath catching in her throat. "You know?" Ezequiel asks, reading something in her expression.

When Isabel says nothing, Ezequiel sighs and runs a hand through his hair. "Okay," he says. "I think you know, but I'm going to say it anyway. I am not like everyone. I can find people."

"In the mountains," Isabel says.

"Anywhere. Where you fell, you were hidden. It would have been very easy to miss you without helicopters, without a whole team of people, dogs, maybe. Except one of the reasons I do what I do . . . yes, I know the mountains, but I also do it because people get hurt out here. They get lost. And when that happens, I am the one that can find them quickly enough to help. You understand?"

Isabel nods, but for some reason she's resisting the leap he wants her to make. Maybe because she sees the leap that follows after that, and she's scared, still, of what comes when she takes that leap. "You have a talent, then."

"No," Ezequiel says quickly. "It is not just a talent." He considers her now, maybe trying to figure out if he's got this all wrong. *Yes,* she thinks, *you do.* But even in her thoughts the denial sounds desperate, thin. It is not the resolute rejection Chío would send her way every time the idea of Supers came up. "It is something supernatural," Ezequiel goes on. "A gift from God, or Pachamama, or the universe, or my own body. I cannot explain it. And I think the reason you are alive is because you have a similar gift, or power, or talent."

Now there's no inner monologue. Her brow instinctively furrows. "What? No."

"There was a lot of blood, Isabel. A lot." He stands up, his half-eaten apple in his hand. He walks to the window and sets it on the sill, pushing the curtains open slightly. After he looks out for a few moments, he turns back to her, leaning against the wall beside the window. "I've been walking the mountains since I was eleven. I've seen a lot of accidents. A lot of injuries. And I'm not a doctor, I know that. But your head, Isabel. The blood. You should have been dead a long time before I got to you. Before any of us even woke up." Now Isabel turns to look at her lap, at the blanket covering her legs. She plays with the frayed edge of the fabric.

"You didn't know?" Ezequiel asks.

Isabel can't come up with a reasonable answer. Nothing feels reasonable at the moment. "What did the doctor say? A doctor saw me, right?"

"Yes. He said you had a concussion, nothing bad. He saw you a long time later, maybe twelve hours after you fell. I think you had a lot of time to heal by then."

Now a laugh escapes her. "I've been going to the doctor my whole life. I get colds, I got salmonella when I was little, I sprained some ligaments in my finger once playing volleyball. If I could heal so quickly, how would no one have seen it until now? How could I not know it?"

Ezequiel shrugs, then returns to the bedside chair. "I don't really know. I'm not a scientist, I'm not a doctor. I walk in the mountains. I know the mountains, that's it. I know what I see."

Isabel takes a sip of water, sitting up in bed, almost wanting to feel more pain than she does, wanting to be normal. Why, after all this time of hoping for Supers, would that be the instinct?

"I have only one guess," Ezequiel adds.

Isabel raises her eyes to him, and she wishes it were Chío that was about to speak. If Chío said it, whatever it was, Isabel would believe it, would think it plausible. It would feel factual, and comforting. She doesn't want guesses anymore, doesn't want hypotheses.

Ezequiel thinks for a moment, then continues. "There was a time I remember when the mountains suddenly started making sense. Each hill and valley, each trail. They no longer looked like each other. My uncle, he calls it 'el despertar.' The awakening. One day you are following someone else through the mountains, you are looking at the trails and at the map and you have no idea what you're doing, you are lost. The next day, though, you do it again, and now it all makes sense. You can see the differences in the world, you know each mountain's shape, each bend of a river. You can tell, even, which way the wind will come. Maybe *when* it will come. After that, after you wake up, everything changes. You can see yourself on a map in your head, everywhere you go you know where you are. Even in places you're not that familiar with, you can see the way the mountains work.

"I think this, whatever we have—"

"I don't have anything," Isabel says, but her words lack conviction.

"It works the same way," Ezequiel goes on. "It's almost like a word you didn't know before and then you see it all the time. You know that?"

Isabel closes her eyes, leaning back onto the pillow. "Baader-Meinhof," she says. After a pause, during which she can hear the wind outside blowing, making something whistle, rattling the window against its frame, she continues.

"But that's psychology," she says. "It doesn't mean things that shouldn't be possible are all of a sudden possible. It doesn't make things more common than they really are. It's just a quirk of human psychology. And it doesn't apply to other people. Doctors, for example. Why wouldn't they have seen it in me?"

"Because they have never been in the mountains," Ezequiel says. "They don't know what they're looking at."

The answer quiets Isabel. It echoes the logic that people on the forum use all the time, the logic that Isabel herself clung to for years, the only argument that Chío could never refute. Science has not discovered it all.

She sits with this conversation when Ezequiel leaves, saying he has to go to a bigger town for the day. He introduces her to the owners of this hostel, Jaime and Rosa, who turn out to be the people who hosted Ricard while Isabel was knocked out or maybe dying.

Isabel showers, checking herself for bruises. In the bathroom mirror she gets the first glance at the wound on her head. It's just above her left ear, a one-inch cut that hardly seems like it could have been life-threatening. But Ezequiel has no reason to lie. And how could he even know to lie about this specific thing? If you're looking for normal, normal is what you see. Same thing with good, same thing with evil.

After she gets dressed, she gets the Wi-Fi password from Jaime, though she manages to understand, with her minimal Spanish, that the internet comes and goes. She sends off texts to Sam and Chío and her mom: *I'm alive! No internet where I am. Talk soon!* Then, as promised, the signal weakens, and though her phone shows a bar, she can't do anything internet-related. She walks around the little village, smiling at the few people she sees. She finds a patch of sun to sit in and look at the mountains that tried and possibly succeeded in killing her.

She thinks the thought facetiously, with no intention of ruminating on whether she's a Super or not. It's ridiculous. But once it's there, the notion is hard to shake, and she can't help but follow it down the path where it leads her. That she has been Super this whole time. Why is that any more ridiculous than Supers existing? If there is anyone tipping the scales one way or another, why not her?

If it's true, what she is, what could she do with it?

That night, she's sitting in Jaime and Rosa's cozy living room in front of a fire, eating a delightfully hearty potato soup, when Ezequiel returns. He greets them warmly and joins them, acting as a translator. Isabel tries to offer to help with the dishes, but they insist she sit on the couch and rest, even though she feels fine, and then they leave the room.

Ezequiel is in a chair next to her, drinking some tea, and he reaches over to put another log on the fire, his hands perilously close to the flames.

"Can I ask you a question?"

"Of course," he says, his face illuminated by the flickering light.

"If you have this . . . ability, supernatural or not, why are you here?" She curls her legs up, tucking them beneath the heavy blanket Rosa had brought over for her.

"Where would I go?" He doesn't say it the way people in Dearborn would ask her why she was going somewhere that wasn't in the U.S. He says it like he's ready to really listen to her answer.

"I don't know. You could go to disaster sites to track down survivors. You could go to cities and track missing people. There's probably a lot of money to be made finding people."

Ezequiel takes a sip from his tea and puts his feet up on a little stool. "Maybe someday. Some of those things are not so easy. There's a storm in the U.S. and people missing. Okay. I need to go get a passport, which would be a hundred soles that aren't going to my family. I also need a visa, which is more money, more time, a bus to Lima, hotel, food while I am there. And that is if

I get approved." He waves his hand, like he could go on and on but doesn't care to. "Anyway, I help here. I know the mountains, which makes it easier to find the people I can sense who are lost or hurt. Somewhere else, maybe I hurt myself, get lost on the way. Are there many more people that need help? Yes, of course. There will always be more. As long as you're trying to help some, I think that is the best we can do."

Isabel watches him as he watches the fire. He catches her looking and smiles, then turns his attention back to the crackling logs and his tea. "You know," she says, "if I had met you a year ago, my life would probably be very different today."

He laughs, even though he can't possibly know why. They sit in silence for a while, listening to Jaime and Rosa cleaning up and chatting in what Isabel again assumes is Quechua.

"So what do you think I should do? If it's true. If I can heal myself. Or if I can't die. Whatever my power is. What do I do with it?"

Ezequiel really gives this some thought, like almost everything he responds to, not answering with a quick platitude. "You are not close to your family?"

Isabel sort of shrugs, uses a Spanish phrase she's learned recently and loves the sound of. "Más o menos. Let's say mostly no."

"Pe, it's easy, I think. You find the people you love, and you spend time with them, and you help whoever you can who is nearby. You help as much as you can."

Something in the fire pops. Outside the wind whistles on.

"And what if I'm not actually Super? What if it was just a lot of blood and I was lucky? What if I would put myself in a dangerous situation thinking I'm invincible?"

"No one is invincible," Ezequiel says. "Your gift, who knows what shape it has. But I think that if you put yourself in a dangerous situation to help others, it will probably be worth it. You have to choose how much danger is okay. I understand if you don't believe me, though." He looks at her, and she believes that much, that if she chooses to never do anything Super in her life, she will receive no judgment from him.

A few minutes pass, then Jaime and Rosa come by to say goodnight. They tell Isabel through Ezequiel that she's welcome to stay as long as she needs to. She thanks them profusely, then asks Ezequiel if there's a way to get back to Huaraz, or maybe Lima, the next day.

"Yes, of course. There's a bus to Cerro de Pasco. From there you can get to the capital. But there is no hurry, you can stay as long as you need to. They say you are always welcome here."

"Yes, thanks," she says. "But I have a flight to Mexico I have to catch."

28

Mazunte, Mexico

Isabel has a lot of time to reflect on the minibus ride to Cerro de Pasco, the seven-hour drive to Lima, the overnight stay in a not-great hotel near the airport, the flight into Mexico City, all the sitting and waiting in between. Isabel keeps her earphones away, neglecting the podcasts and audiobooks she's used to distract herself this past year, the noise she uses to silence her too-loud thoughts.

She has a video call with Chío and Sam from Lima, thinking she might confess it all in front of them. But it's strange to say something so big to a little screen, or at least it feels that way to her now. She'd rather do it face to face. Maybe by then she'll have figured out some logical way to test out her supposed power without killing herself, something reasonably scientific that Chío can get behind.

Until then, though, now that she's landing in Mexico City, days away from seeing them, Isabel feels a swell of gratitude for her life. The fact that she still has it. The fact that this past year has been generally devoid of bad luck. And almost completely devoid of evil.

Isabel is no longer concerned with doing the math.

Instead, she walks around this new city, thrilled to be doing exactly that again. She walks through Parque México, enchanted by the dog walkers who have lined up a dozen pups and have seemingly hypnotized them into lying still, off their leashes, despite the other pets being walked, the birds and squirrels flitting about.

She eats freshly fried potato chips covered in hot sauce and lime as she walks through the tree-lined boulevards, looking at the delightful mix of old-style French architecture and street art. After her two-and-a-half-week pause, she teaches an English class again, and she's surprised by how much she enjoys watching the children. Despite their silence and learned obedience, she can see a twinkle in their eye as they absorb the language, can see the moment when they're proud of themselves for having grasped a new word. It is a wonder that humans can acquire languages, a wonder how children grow their knowledge.

Whether it's because of her epiphany or her near-death experience, Isabel feels elated during her time in the city. She takes a food tour, reveling in the varied tacos and other dishes she samples, and is struck by the injustices that some Mexican restaurants in the U.S. and around the world have perpetrated on the cuisine. She packs into three days a week's worth of activities, at least judging by the hit her budget takes.

On her last day, she gets caught under an awning waiting for a thunderstorm to pass. After thirty minutes, when the rain shows no sign of slowing, she takes off running for the nearest refuge: a three-story bookstore and restaurant. As she runs, though, her phone goes flying out of her hand, hitting the edge of the curb before sliding into a puddle.

She curses for a second, then laughs at the situation. A server at the restaurant tells her where she can get it fixed, so when the rain stops an hour later, she goes. The repair guy says it will take a few days and she says okay, thinking she'll come back to the city to pick it up later, since she won't really need it in Mazunte and she bought a round-trip flight anyway. Or maybe the phone is dead and, unlike her, cannot return to life.

The thought catches her unawares, makes her giggle. Is she technically a zombie? She wonders if her heart stopped beating at the bottom of that hill in Peru, longs to sit with Sam and Chío and have a too-impassioned discussion on the topic. She'll soon get to do just that, and it adds to her giddiness. Though maybe giddiness is to be expected after a near-death experience, after being told that she might be better at surviving than most people.

What if she really is? What if instead of just causing no harm, she can go well beyond that? Rescue lives. What if during all her years spent worrying about the dangers that befall others, she had an ability that could help her to save them?

Through lucha libre and mezcal and the post-rain walk back to her hostel, Isabel thinks about what she'll do the rest of her life, if it'll just be this: exploring places around the world, finding ways to make money in order to keep it going, helping people along the way. What else could she possibly want from life?

Twelve hours later, she's at the beach where she'd dropped the pin a year before. She looked at the map often during her travels, whenever she was feeling lonely, whenever her mind couldn't help but look forward to the reunion with Sam and Chío. So, even without her phone, she has found the spot, or at least one close enough to it.

For so long she had hoped that during the reunion she would be able to confirm to them the existence of Supers. Then Rick happened, and she wasn't sure she'd ever say it. Now here she is, a day away from seeing them again, and she is going to announce that she is maybe one herself, without providing any evidence other than a cut on her head. It has scabbed and is healing, but not supernaturally quickly, as far as she can tell.

There is no way Chío will accept the version of events Ezequiel told Isabel. Even Sam would look shyly away, say Isabel's name all soft and worried. And he'd be right to.

She digs her heels into the sand, watching the other beachgoers. If only there were some easy way to test out her supposed power. She tries pinching her forearm to make it bleed, imagining that it'll be like a movie and she'll watch it clot and heal on fast-forward. But it hurts too much to actually break the skin, and she gives up. Her next thought is to text Sam and Chío to brainstorm ways to test it out, but then she remembers her phone is in Mexico City.

So she does what a beachgoer does. She wades into the water, diving under to avoid the waves. She comes back out and lies in the sun, reading. She looks at people passing by, buys a too-dense muffin from the ridiculously attractive Argentine couple who smell like weed. Although she mentions she was recently in Argentina, they don't seem very interested in chatting, and she lets them continue on down the beach.

Her mind wanders. She thinks about invincibility, rolling the concept around in her head like a hard candy she's savoring. But then her mind leads her to Sam, that night when she was feeling so bad and needed him there with her and he comforted her. Why, she wonders, did they never talk about it? Why did he flee in the morning without a word?

She thinks about where else she might go after Mexico. Or, rather, where in Mexico she should go. She met one couple, she forgets where, who were also traveling long-term, and they had nothing but great things to say about the country, all the towns and mountains and beaches to explore. Waterfalls and forests, too, beauty of all kinds.

Like each of us, but especially because she might have so recently brushed against it, she thinks of death. She marvels at the fact that she hasn't known too many people who died. Her grandmother, of course. There was a kid in middle school too, but she didn't really know them, struggles even now to remember their name. What a strange thought it is that death will come. Not just for every person alive, not just for herself. But that it'll rear its head time and time again throughout her life, if she's lucky enough to avoid it herself. Her parents, older relatives, former teachers, people she's yet to meet. And if she is what Ezequiel thinks she is, then she will probably see a lot of it, again and again. If she will put herself in dangerous situations to help others, that is.

Everyone at the beach, she realizes, holds memories of dead people. The way her grandmother lingers still in her mind, whispering, muttering. What a strange thought, beautiful, almost. How death has its finger on everything and life carries on. People, sure. But in the sand too. The tiny pieces of reef and shells that once held living organisms, long dead now. Who knows what else. Traces of bodies lost at sea, recently or a long time ago. Maybe Chío would know enough to refute that, but at the moment it seems plausible to Isabel. Human history buried in this sand.

The line of thought makes her more comfortable with Ezequiel's diagnosis, or whatever it is. Death and life, after all, are entwined completely, like the ocean and the shore. There is no hard line between the two. There are waves lapping at the sand. Maybe that's all she is. Not the sand or the water. The shore.

Her stomach grumbles, the dense muffin having done nothing to quell her hunger, but she's enjoying the beach too much to pull herself away. She runs into the water, her gratitude swelling. At all of it. The planet and its wonders. People. Life. The time she exists in, which allows her to experience more of all of it than others in history could ever have dreamed. The winning lottery ticket, being born where she was, to financially stable people who didn't completely fuck her up psychologically. Sure, a little. She'll grant the Chío voice in her head that much. But everyone's a little psychologically fucked up, in one way or another. There's a lot to take in in this life, and it's truly remarkable that anyone alive is ever doing anything but processing what it means to be alive, processing everything that has ever happened to them, good and bad and traumatic and elating.

A man walks down the beach selling paletas, and Isabel runs back to her things to get money for one. Enjoying the cold and the sweetness and whatever berry flavor she's tasting, she picks up her book to read, but her mind is still too busy marveling at it all.

When she really thinks about it, supernatural abilities existing in the world is not really all that remarkable. There is life, and there is death, and those two things feel so highly improbable that anything that happens within them feels entirely possible. Why not? In a world with sunsets, one of which she's witnessing now, why not a sweet Peruvian boy who can find people hurt in the mountains? Why not a man who can grow fruit from seeds in a matter of seconds?

Back to the water she goes, though the lifeguards have left their posts, taken down the red flags warning of the tide, and left for the day. There's a slight chill to the air now, at least with the

Pacific on her skin and the breeze coming through. She watches people gather their things and go. They retreat from the tide like the hermit crabs withdrawing to the bushes for food, or to hide from predators.

Isabel is so enamored with the day, with the world right now, that she does not notice the pull at first. The way the ocean tugs, like it wants us to come deeper, to join it.

Funny, isn't it? How we spend so much of our lives looking at death, thinking about it, searching for bodies, wondering how human beings are capable of killing each other, wondering what happens after, if anything. How it's there as we're living, the whole time. Biding its time, sure. But touching everything around us. Taking someone, but leaving behind their things. Their clothes, their money, their shampoo bottles sitting in the shower, half-used. They leave behind their stories of a family in the Czech Republic sent to a concentration camp, the tragedies that happened long ago and that refused to be forgotten. Death, making us think that life is too short and so leading us to spend our money. To hug our loved ones close. To take that trip, because why not, death is coming. See as much as you can, while you can. How it keeps us up at night, its inevitability. We put on noise to quiet the knowledge. Movies watched on little screens, most of them about exactly what we're avoiding, at least in one way or another. Books: same. Meditation apps that tell us to accept a thought and then let it go, let it live then die.

And then we're floating in the Pacific, letting the waves lift us off the sand because it feels like flying. Our shoulders are burnt from too much time in the sun, the salt water both cooling our skin and making it sting, come alive. We are focused fully on life, on all it entails. And here comes death. A riptide, sucking things out to sea.

Isabel has the thought that she should know what to do. That she's sure she's come across the information, somewhere. How to escape this. She swims and swims and tries to cry out, but the water splashes into her open mouth and she's already so far from shore. Below, seaweed waits to wrap itself around her ankles. Little organisms that will feed on her while they can, swim, unaware for now that a meal is coming.

Well, she thinks as her arms tire out, as her lungs take in another gasp of water, *at least I'm going to find out.*

29

Dearborn, Michigan

Chío doesn't know what she expects to find at Roys's. She knows that she's going down a dangerous path, one not too different from what led Isabel to chase superheroes around the world. Faith in that which lacks evidence, the conviction despite all reason that she can find Isabel. That Izzy even wants to be found. That she *can* be found.

"We here for a special reason?" Sam asks as they're standing in line.

"The ice cream," she deadpans. He bumps her with his shoulder, a move that would have felt completely innocent a year earlier, weeks ago, even. Chío has the sense that she's being watched, or maybe that's just wishful thinking. Still, she doesn't reciprocate the bump, doesn't slip her fingers into Sam's. She's not particularly in the mood for a lot of ice cream, but she wants the excuse to linger, so she gets a large chocolate concrete with M&M's and cherries mixed in, and they go out to snag their usual picnic table.

They sit in silence, knees touching under the table, Sam clearly aware that Chío's looking for something, Chío not even knowing what she's looking for. She's studying the people around them, the fellow suburbanites enjoying the changed climate of an early spring, the sun on their skin. Does she expect Isabel to be hiding among them? Is this what she thinks Isabel meant when she said all those months ago that she would try to let them know while being invisible? Chío's heart thinks so, even though all the while her brain is calling her an idiot for interpreting such a loose statement as *I will be at Roys's.*

"C'mon," Sam says. "Enough of this. Tell me what you're thinking. Why are we here?"

Chío scoops out some concrete, the flavor taking her back to a year ago. She can't believe time has passed in that way. It doesn't feel slow, necessarily, and definitely not fast. It just seems like she's stepped through a wormhole from one dimension to another. Izzy was there having ice cream with them, they were talking about stupid, normal things like grades and crushes and the plans for Friday night, and now they're here. Izzy is gone and superhumans are in the mix and Sam is looking at her like he wants to kiss her. Like he has. She imagines this is what grief feels like. Not like a loss, but like a sudden and incongruous shift in the universe. Like it can't possibly be.

"I don't know," Chío says. He gives her a look and she shrugs. "Izzy mentioned once, that first day, I think, that if she were ever to become a Super, she would hide, but that she would find a way to let us know. She clearly isn't going to let us know electronically or she would have sent an email already. Other than Roys's, I have no other guesses." They both look around now, as if she might be hiding in plain sight, wearing glasses with a big nose and a mustache.

They eat quietly, watching others line up, take their cones or milkshakes to the tables, or back to their cars. Isabel always complained about those who took their ice cream to go, especially if they were carrying items for people not with them. "It's a crime," she would say. "Roys's is meant to be enjoyed at these beautiful picnic tables right here."

Chío laughs quietly at the memory, even though it's not particularly funny, and she looks down at the table, wanting to just have one more afternoon with Izzy right here, not talking about anything but the bullshit of the everyday. She's spilled some of her concrete on it, and she uses her napkin to wipe it away. In the act, something catches her eye. Among all the old stains on the wood, the cracks from the winter, the caked-in ice cream, and the many names etched in over the years, Chío sees something both new and familiar.

It's Isabel's handwriting, she's almost sure of it. It's just some numbers, but Chío used to do math homework with Izzy all the time, they were lab partners in AP chem their junior year; she's seen Izzy's numbers many times before. "Sam," she says, wiping over the spot again, as if it'll make it more clear. "Was this always here?"

Sam leans over to take a look. "Hmm. I don't know. Wait, is that her handwriting?"

"It's hard to tell, but I think so. Right? I'm not just grasping here?"

After a few seconds he says, "No, I think you're right. That's hers. Is it a phone number?"

"I don't think so. But how long has it been here?"

Sam is already pulling out his phone. He tries dialing it first, using a plus sign in case a portion of the number is a country code. It's got too many digits, though, so he tries it out as two different numbers, neither of which works.

"Wait," Chío says after staring at them for a little while. "I think these are coordinates. Remember how Izzy and I went geocaching that one time?"

"You're such dorks," Sam says, smiling. He's already copying the numbers over into his phone, though.

"I don't remember her doing this." She looks up dramatically at him, a realization sinking in. "Do you think this is recent?"

Sam shrugs. "I haven't been here in a while. But I don't remember it either." Now he slides the phone over so she can see the screen. She stares at it for a while, her mind racing, trying to make sense of everything.

"I don't understand," she says, but she does. Maybe not the why or the how or a lot of the details that she wants to understand. But she knows what she's looking at, and she knows exactly what she has to do.

It takes a while to figure out all the specifics.

At first, Chío feels obligated to offer Isabel's parents the chance to go. Isabel's dad is dubious about the plan, and though her mom wants to believe that Isabel will be waiting at the coordinates in the mountains of Peru, she feels she can't handle the journey herself. They still haven't received their passports, so if it is to happen soon, it has to be Chío. She was actually hoping to be the one to go. She speaks Spanish, her parents are well enough off that they can bankroll the trip, and as soon as finals are over, her summer is wide open until her college move-in date.

Her parents have already used up their vacation days, so they're out. And while Sam desperately wants to go, the money's just not there, what with tuition due and his parents already strained, always strained.

So all he can do is provide a ride to the airport, watch her get in line for security just like Isabel did. "You're not gonna stay gone for a year and then become a Super and die and then come back to life and then disappear too, are you?"

Chío smacks him lightly across the chest, then gets on her tiptoes to kiss him on the cheek. "No promises."

"What are you gonna do if she's not there?"

"I don't expect her to be there." She steps forward in line, and he follows along on the other side of the rope. "At least, that's what I'm telling myself," Chío admits. "I kinda do think she'll be there, but I'm trying not to hold on to that thought too tightly. Trying not to hope too deeply, because chances are it's a random spot in the world. A place she wanted to check out before she left and etched onto the table because she was waiting for us one day. Some kid's geography quiz answer that he couldn't write down anywhere else and just happens to look like her handwriting."

Another step forward. In a few more, Sam will have to stand back. How come he's always in this position? Saying bye, watching others go? He thinks, briefly, of the past eight months before Mexico. How Isabel was gone and somehow took Chío with her. And even though Chío's just going for ten days, they're attending different schools in the fall, in different cities.

"I'm gonna miss you," he says, instead of asking if she knows a word for feeling loneliness in anticipation of a future time.

"Yeah," she says simply, squeezing his hand.

"Now go find our friend."

Since Chío is limited on time and less limited with her budget, she flies into Huaraz via Lima, and stays not at a dingy hostel but at a nice lodge with a view of the mountains. She arrives at night, feeling out of her element and wholly intimidated by the city, impressed that Isabel has been doing this for eight months straight.

Chío feels out of place at the lodge's restaurant, so she eats quickly, texting with Sam throughout the meal until she can go back to her room and read until she falls asleep. She has restless dreams about Izzy drowning, Izzy lost in the woods somewhere.

When she wakes up, the sun's barely rising. There are people decked out in hiking gear in the dining room, sleepy-eyed and chatting quietly among themselves. Mostly white couples in their thirties. When Chío checked in, she showed the front-desk employees the spot where she needed to get to on the map, right near a tiny town. They offered a bunch of different hike excursions but none of them would bring her directly there, and there was no car leaving from the hotel in that direction. Channeling her dad's schmoozing skills, she persuaded the concierge to make some phone calls to people he knew around Huaraz, and they figured out a way to get her there.

After breakfast she gets into the van, avoiding conversation with the hikers inside because she'd like to explain as little as possible. A couple of hours in, they stop at some seemingly random intersection in the mountains, idling for about ten minutes. Right as the other passengers are starting to notice that they're just sitting there, another van shows up. The driver tells Chío that she's going in that one. Chío smiles awkwardly at the hikers as she gets out, the confusion clear on their faces. *You have no idea,* she thinks.

Four more hours on the road, a twenty-minute walk, and another car switch later, Chío is dropped off in the tiny village of Huayllapa. As soon as she lays eyes on it, she thinks it's a mistake. That there's no way Izzy would retreat to a place this small, this far removed. It's beautiful, yes. A smattering of concrete and adobe buildings that are not without their charms, set against the backdrop of the dramatic peaks. What could Isabel possibly find here, though?

Chío catches herself. She's thinking with the kind of logic that made sense a year ago. The variables have changed, so she should not be surprised by wildly different outcomes, no matter what she may have previously thought was possible. She checks the GPS on her phone and finds she is very close to the coordinates etched onto the picnic table. Three children in school uniforms pass by, not trying at all to hide their staring. She smiles at them and says "Hola," which causes them to shriek with laughter and wave excitedly.

Not long after that, Chío finds herself staring at the screen while standing in a modest plaza that feels like the center of town. The numbers match the ones at Roys's. She looks up, hoping that she'll find Izzy sitting at a bench, waiting for her with a big smirk. Instead, she sees two old ladies in traditional dresses, chatting. There's a stray dog sniffing happily at a trash can. Across the plaza, a woman in jeans and a cardigan talks on her phone, looking generally in Chío's direction.

She sits with the disappointment for a second, then shuffles over to the nearest blue bench. It's one o'clock. The concierge at the hotel, Claudio, had insisted on organizing a trip back for Chío the same day. "Maybe there's no hotel rooms there," he had said. He was probably worried about Chío being like the other hotel guests and having certain luxury standards that a town this small would have trouble meeting. Which might be well and true under normal circumstances, but at the moment is meaningless to her. She would knock on doors asking for any bed to sleep on if it meant finding Isabel.

In the end, the concierge won out, and Chío has until five o'clock, when someone will come pick her up. They'd insisted on packing her a sandwich, which she now pulls from her bag and lays on her lap. Instead of unwrapping it, though, she just stares out at the plaza, the town, the mountains beyond. An old man walking a horse down the road asks her if she's okay, and she says yes, thanks. Eventually she'll start asking people if they've seen a curly-haired American girl around. For now, though, she sits and waits, hoping it's enough.

Although hoping has become exhausting. She's not sure how Isabel did it: searching for Supers, wanting so desperately for them to exist, believing that they could despite all available evidence. How could she hang on to hope for so long, for something so unlikely to happen? Was she this exhausted the whole year? Years before? Is she still, or has she found an answer to her question and that's why she's fine resting here?

Chío stops herself from the thought, though she doesn't know why she's still so resistant. It's a theory. Just that, she tells herself.

Except Chío herself is here. She's in the middle of nowhere, Peru, chasing after the theory that her friend is for some reason silently hiding out in the mountains after maybe being dead in a morgue in Mexico. Hope is like that. Like life, like death. It clings to what it can.

An hour goes by. She eats her sandwich, getting up to toss the foil in a bin. She takes a lap around the plaza, smiling at the people who are probably wondering what the hell she's doing there. One person finally asks her, a woman in her forties or fifties, wearing a puffy jacket over a wool dress.

"Waiting for a friend," Chío says, in Spanish.

"¿Quién, la gringuita?"

Chío perks up. "There's a white girl? Here?"

As soon as the woman nods, Chío is asking for directions, and then she's speed-walking down the dirt road. Hope, again, despite everything. Would she really rather be without it?

She arrives at a building being painted a pretty burnt orange, black lettering curving around the doorway, though Chío doesn't stop to read the words. Her fist pounds the door, hard enough that she wants to apologize for it, which she can after. After they, whoever they are, open the door, and after she can glimpse her best friend sitting inside like nothing happened.

Which is exactly what happens.

A baby-faced man in his thirties wearing a jean jacket opens the door, looking a little startled but still welcoming. "Sí?" he says.

And there, sitting in a chair by an open window, her socked feet up on the sill, is Izzy. She's holding a book in one hand; the other is petting a cat on her lap that seems to have just woken up. Isabel's angled so that she can look at the window and at the door, which she's doing now.

Chío has tried all her conscious life to not be rude to others. But now she stares past the man at the door, not saying anything, neither to him nor to Izzy. Tears come to her eyes, but at the exact same time laughter does too. The urge to run at her friend and hug her is equally as strong as the urge to throw something at her. All Chío can do at first is stare, until Izzy closes her book and a smile spreads across her face.

"You got my message. You chased me."

30

Huayllapa, Peru

Curled up on Jaime and Rosa's couch in front of the fire, Isabel tells Chío everything. Everything she hadn't been able to let herself say over the phone, everything that she was too scared to share before leaving Dearborn.

She tells Chío about her grandmother's mutterings, how Grandma's views penetrated Isabel's bones. She tells her about her dad's secret brain ("That was a secret?" Chío asks), about the pandemic sending her so deep into the news cycle that it felt inescapable. Except for the forum.

"That's why you slept in all the time?" Chío asks, confirming.

"Don't get me wrong, my bed was comfy. But it wasn't magical or anything."

Isabel stirs her tea with her finger, since it's lukewarm. She goes on to talk about Gareth, Rick, those guys in Argentina and the dog. How she started seeing glimpses of Supers everywhere after that and found herself running away from them. And then the hike. Ezequiel, the fall, the quick recovery, feeling better than she should have. After a couple of hours of talking, they finally arrive at Mexico, and Isabel's cheeks burn with shame. Not at missing the meeting itself, because she was dead. Or not exactly dead, but gone, at least. Still, she's ashamed that she didn't reach out.

Chío's spilling over with questions, but she lets Izzy tell it at her own pace. "I came to, not knowing where the hell I was, feeling exhausted, my body sore all over, like I'd been put in a washing machine or something. I burst out of what I found out later was a morgue, wrapped in a sheet, just wanting a glass of water and a comfortable bed."

She had somehow managed to remember where she'd booked a room and stumbled to it, sleeping for days. If only it had been a shared room in the hostel, or if she had told Chío and Sam where she was staying. If only the hostel owners had been in tune with the search for the girl. They'd come to check on her once, and when she opened the door and said she was okay, just sick, they'd reported that all their guests were fine and accounted for.

By the time Isabel was fully resurrected, or whatever, Chío and Sam were gone. The internet had generally forgotten, the journalists had chalked it up to incompetence, though they didn't know whose. But Actually Super was still abuzz, certain that it was one of their own who'd escaped from a morgue, certain that she was a Super. Some people speculated about whether she'd been a Super the whole time, keeping tabs on them, but Izzy hadn't been able to spend much time on the computer without her head spinning.

"Why couldn't you reach out, though? Just to let us know you were alive?"

"I wrote emails so many times. At least, I started to. I didn't know what to say. I didn't even know if I was human anymore. There was a lot to wrap my head around." She takes a sip of tea, curling her legs under the blanket. Her feet touch Chío's leg, and what a joy it is to feel her friend this close again.

Chío wants to keep questioning her. But she understands. There's a lot for her to wrap her mind around too, and it didn't even happen to her. What matters is that Isabel is here, in front of her. She's alive. Whether Chío has to redefine what "alive" means is another question altogether. Her friend is here, and she's so thankful for that, she won't even ask everything she wants to know. There are some things that will forever be unknown. But today, there isn't a body, there's just Izzy, and that's all that matters.

"What happens next?" Chío says.

"Next, we finish this tea. And we go to bed. And in the morning, I take you on a nice hike."

"That sounds lovely. But after that? Capital-*N* 'next'?"

Isabel takes a moment.

"You know that quote about looking for the helpers after something terrible happens?"

Chío nods. "Mister Rogers, I think."

"I think I'm going to try to be one. A helper. Do what I can. Be a body where one is useful. Help. That's the best thing I can do for myself."

"That and therapy."

"Yes," Izzy laughs. "I promise. As soon as I have the money, therapy." The fire lets out a pop, the flames licking at the last log in the fireplace.

"The world is too big for me," Isabel goes on. "Living a normal life, it's too easy to get sucked into that bigness. I'd rather see it a few pieces at a time, a few people at a time. If I zoom out too much, it's overwhelming. The terrible things are too big, the horrible people too loud. Traveling, as strange as it may sound, it makes me feel appropriately small. It makes the world feel tiny in a way that can be helped."

"What about Supers?"

"If there are people out there helping others, that's great. I'm not even sure what I thought of as a Super exists, you know? I'd linked abilities that go beyond our current understanding of the human body with ethical righteousness, and there's no reason to think those two things are related.

"I don't *know* what I am," Isabel continues. "I don't know if I even understand what happened to me. Twice now something unlikely has happened, sure. But I know from you that two inexplicable things do not make a miracle, do not cause the fabric of the world as we understand it to unwind. Maybe death chases after me the rest of my life. Who knows.

"So, for now, I'm going to stay small. I'm going to try to help people, and I'm going to try to not keep score of the world's pluses and minuses. Just do my little bit, in whatever little corner of the world I happen to be in, around whoever happens to be near me."

There's so much more they could say to each other. So many

stories from her travels that Isabel never told her, especially when she started pulling herself away from the internet. Chío hasn't had a chance to tell Izzy about Sam. But they quietly rise and rinse their teacups. They hug for five full seconds, during which Isabel apologizes over and over again and Chío absolves her by holding on. Then they go to the room where they'll spend the next few nights, and they each pull out a book to read under the glow of Isabel's headlamp.

In the morning, Izzy will take Chío on a hike. They will meet Ezequiel on the trail with a new group, and when he's out of earshot, Chío will raise her eyebrows at Izzy and mouth *He's cute!* at her. They will laugh the way they used to, and spend a few more days together in the mountains, Chío alternating between commenting on the beauty of the surroundings and complaining about the altitude and the hiking. They will help Jaime and Rosa paint their house and cook dinner, and then talk late into the night, when the dying fire lets the cold in and sends them to bed.

Then Chío will go back home. Isabel will accompany her to Huaraz, all the way to the airport, but no farther. Chío will board her return flight, only then realizing that she forgot to ask Izzy about how the hell she got the coordinates etched onto the table at Roys's. She will reach for her phone to text her, the habit not dead yet.

Back in Michigan, Chío will deliver a letter to each of Isabel's parents. They will say very different things, both necessary, and maybe someday in the future, she will come home. Perhaps when she feels like she can be helpful. Perhaps when she feels she can survive them. Until then, she promises to be in touch, albeit on her terms.

Chío will sit with Sam at Roys's, and share one last concrete before they go off to college. They will talk about Isabel without an ounce of sadness in their voices, because now they know they have not lost her.

And in Peru, Isabel will sit by the window with that cat on her lap, reading, resting from another day walking the mountains, enjoying the beauty of the world, and her place within it. Death is such a silly trap to fall for when life is right there beside it.

ACKNOWLEDGMENTS

I keep being lucky enough to write acknowledgments. And every time I do find myself here, it's a good reminder that gratitude helps you reach this point.

Every book is a collaborative effort among many, many people, and I wish I knew everyone who helped put this book out into the world. Thank you to all those working behind the scenes to make publishing a possibility.

Thanks to Pete Knapp and Stuti Telidevara for all they do. To Marisa DiNovis and the entire Knopf team.

Thank you to the many booksellers, librarians, teachers, readers, and book champions who have sustained my career.

To Laura, for everything. But also for taking me around the world, for providing inspiration, talking out ideas, going on food adventures. Yeah, everything.

Remy, you weren't here when I wrote this, but I'm really glad you're here now.

To my family, as always.